The stranger's hulking body loomed, and the sharp tip of his scimitar hovered a mere breath from my throat....

"You will leave Egypt, witch," he dictated. "Today."

With a rush, air filled my lungs.

"You will not interfere in matters that do not concern you."

Even as he said it, my fingers clenched around my sword. "Well, they sure as hell concern me now." And I swung.

* * *

Dear Reader,

We invite you to sit back and enjoy the ride as you experience the powerful suspense, intense action and tingling emotion in Silhouette Bombshell's November lineup. Strong, sexy, savvy heroines have never been so popular, and we're putting the best right into your hands. Get ready to meet four extraordinary women who will speak to the Bombshell in you!

Maggie Sanger will need quick wit and fast moves to get out of Egypt alive when her pursuit of a legendary grail puts her on a collision course with a secret society, hostages and her furious ex! Get into *Her Kind of Trouble*, the latest in author Evelyn Vaughn's captivating GRAIL KEEPERS miniseries.

Sabotage, scandal and one sexy inspector breathe down the neck of a determined air force captain as she strives to right an old wrong in the latest adventure in the innovative twelve-book ATHENA FORCE continuity series, *Pursued* by Catherine Mann.

Enter the outrageous underworld of Las Vegas prizefighting as a female boxing trainer goes up against the mob to save her father, her reputation and a child witness in Erica Orloff's pull-no-punches novel, *Knockout*.

And though creating identities for undercover agents is her specialty, Kristie Hennessy finds out that work can be deadly when you've got everyone fooled and no one to trust but a man you know only by his intriguing voice…. Don't miss Kate Donovan's *Identity Crisis*.

It's a month of no-holds-barred excitement! Please send your comments to me, c/o Silhouette Books, 233 Broadway Ste. 1001, New York, NY 10279.

Best wishes,

Natashya Wilson
Associate Senior Editor, Silhouette Bombshell

Please address questions and book requests to:
Silhouette Reader Service
U.S.: 3010 Walden Ave., P.O. Box 1325, Buffalo, NY 14269
Canadian: P.O. Box 609, Fort Erie, Ont. L2A 5X3

EVELYN VAUGHN

HER KIND OF TROUBLE

Silhouette®

BOMBSHELL™

Published by Silhouette Books

America's Publisher of Contemporary Romance

SILHOUETTE BOOKS

ISBN 0-373-51331-3

HER KIND OF TROUBLE

This edition published by arrangement with Harlequin Books S.A.

® and TM are trademarks of Harlequin Books S.A., used under license.
Trademarks indicated with ® are registered in the United States Patent
and Trademark Office, the Canadian Trade Marks Office and in other
countries.

Visit Silhouette Books at www.eHarlequin.com

Printed in U.S.A.

EVELYN VAUGHN

has written stories since she learned to make letters. But during the two years that she lived on a Navajo reservation in Arizona—while in second and third grade—she dreamed of becoming not a writer, but a barrel racer in the rodeo. Before she actually got her own horse, however, her family moved to Louisiana. There, to avoid the humidity, she channeled more of her adventures into stories instead.

Since then, Evelyn has canoed in the east Texas swamps, rafted a white-water river in the Austrian Alps, rappelled barefoot down a three-story building, talked her way onto a ship to Greece without her passport, sailed in the Mediterranean and spent several weeks in Europe with little more than a backpack and a train pass. All at least once. While she enjoys channeling the more powerful "travel Vaughn" on a regular basis, she also loves the fact that she can write about adventures with far less physical discomfort. Since she now lives in Texas, where she teaches English at a local community college, air-conditioning still remains an important factor.

Her Kind of Trouble is Evelyn's eighth full-length book for Silhouette. Feel free to contact her through her Web site, www.evelynvaughn.com, or by writing to: P.O. Box 6, Euless TX, 76039.

To Toni

Chapter 1

One moment I was studying the five-thousand-year-old statue of a husband and wife, one of several in the Metropolitan Museum of Art's sprawling Egyptian wing. What kind of romantic problems had *they* faced, I mused. Deception? Cross-purposes? Old wounds? Had love won out?

The next moment, I sensed someone behind me, all size and impatience and body heat.

And not in a nice way.

"So you decided to be good, huh, Maggi?" The voice was too thick to be pleasant even if its owner tried.

He didn't.

I recognized billionaire slimeball, Phil Stuart, even before I turned. And here I'd thought that this one-thousand-dollar-per-plate event was exclusive.

"I'm always good," I told him, masking my unease

as I turned anyway. Phil was nobody I wanted at my back. "But if you mean well-behaved...maybe not."

"You gave up on those stupid goddess cups, right?"

Gave up? It hadn't been two months since I'd rescued the antique chalice of my ancestors, a holy relic called the Melusine Grail, from thugs sent by this guy. Since then, I'd been preoccupied helping nurse my sometimes-lover Lex back to health after a vicious knife attack.

By more thugs.

Probably sent by this guy.

Supposedly the two incidents were unrelated. I didn't need psychic abilities to doubt that. Either way, I'd had an excellent reason for not seeking out a second chalice.

Really.

I didn't need Phil tossing out double-dog dares.

Phil Stuart always looked a little off to me. Like a poor imitation of something better. Other than to check for the bulge of a gun—or a ceremonial knife—under his tux, I barely glanced at him before noting the two suited gentlemen lurking by the ancient stone archway. Was he kidding?

"Bodyguards, Phil?"

"Right?" He leaned closer, into my personal space. "You've given up on those stupid goddess cups?"

"Not your business." I knew how to stand my ground, even in two-inch, ankle-flattering heels. "Back off."

"Or what?"

He wasn't an *immediate* danger to me. This may sound weird, but...ever since I'd drunk from the Chalice of Melusine—my family goddess, a goddess renowned for her prophetic scream—my intuition had sharpened to the point that my throat tightened whenever something threatened me. And my throat felt fine just now.

Then again, Phil rarely did his own dirty work.

He raised his voice. "Or *what?*"

A smooth voice beyond him said, "Or you'll make your date jealous."

Speaking of deception, cross-purposes, and old wounds...

Lex, my sometimes lover and current escort, had returned from fetching champagne. Beside him stood a small, blond woman in an expensive gown. A *black* gown, naturally—this *was* a New York arts event. But Lex, healthy again and wearing a tuxedo with an ease *GQ* models would envy, was the one on whom my gaze lingered.

Alexander Rothschild Stuart III wasn't so tall he towered, nor so athletic that he bulged. His ginger-brown hair sported an expensive but conservative cut. His face revealed generations of upper-class ancestors, all pulling together in the sweep of his jaw, his cheeks, his nose, understated and yet, well...perfect.

Maybe too perfect. But, good or bad, it was *him*. Lex was what Phil, his cousin, could never copy. When I wanted him, that was great. When I felt unsure of our relationship, it really complicated matters.

Lately, things had been very complicated.

"Maggi," Lex said coolly, passing me a champagne flute, "have you met Phil's new girlfriend, Tammy?"

"Let's go," said Phil—but I was already taking Tammy's manicured hand in my own.

"Pleased to meet you," I said. "I'm Magdalene Sanger. Are you sure you know what you're doing with this guy?"

"Hey!" Phil protested.

Tammy's eyes widened. Her lips parted. "Why do you…?" Then, quickly, she looked down at our hands.

I'm not psychic, sore throats aside. I just knew Phil.

"Now," Phil insisted. But this reception was for patron-circle members, on a Monday night when the museum was normally closed to the public. If he made a scene, he would do so in front of the crème de la crème of city society. I hadn't pushed him that far. Yet.

Then again, this was my first drink of the evening.

Tammy slid an annoyed glance toward Phil, then said, "Pleased to meet you, Magdalene. That's a fascinating necklace you're wearing."

"Thank you. It's called a chalice-well pendant. It—"

"Enough!" At Phil's exclamation, several patrons turned to see who had been so gauche. Even Lex's lips twitched, which is about as close to a guffaw as my ex-lover is capable. "Stop talking to her, damn it!"

Tammy blinked, as if seeing him for the first time, then laughed. "Why in the world should I not talk to her?"

"Probably because his wife left him after talking to me," I guessed. That had been shortly after Lex landed in the hospital. The woman had good reason to be concerned.

Now my throat tightened in warning.

I spun in my heels and nailed Phil with a glare that stopped him cold, before he'd surged forward an inch. Everything about his posture said he'd meant to strike out at me, public place or not. And so it began.

Or continued.

"Here, Phil?" I warned softly. *"Now?"*

And since most bullies are cowards, he said nothing.

This time when someone stepped up behind me, the sense of solidity and body heat belonged to Lex. So was he backing me up, or readying to help his cousin?

Either way, my bare back welcomed his nearness.

"You know," murmured Tammy into the uncomfortable silence that followed, "perhaps I'll catch a cab home. Thank you for the invitation, Phillip, but—"

"You can't leave," protested Phil, and Tammy arched an eyebrow at him in challenge.

"Thank you, Magdalene," she said as she turned away. "It was a real pleasure to meet you."

"For three minutes?" Phil's heavy head swung back to me for one last glare before he trailed his girlfriend from the gallery. "You met her for three freakin' *minutes*. Tammy!"

His bodyguards trailed after them.

"I hope she'll be all right," I murmured in their absence. I'd felt jittery all evening. Not sore-throat jittery, but still…

"Phil's made mistakes." Lex took a sip of his champagne. "But he's a Stuart. There are lines even he won't cross."

I did a double take. Did he honestly believe that? Did he mean it as *assurance?*

Then he distracted me by sliding a hand across the small of my back and murmuring, "Why do you keep doing that?"

So he'd noticed, too. Phil's wife. A nurse who stood up to a condescending doctor. A waitress who suddenly found the strength to take down a rowdy customer.

A little girl, whom I'd helped to her feet when Lex and I were jogging in the park, who finally hit her brother back. *She never does that,* exclaimed her surprised mother….

"And don't say, *doing what*," Lex continued, his voice mild but his hazel, almost golden eyes demanding.

"I'm not doing anything. Not deliberately." That would mean I had some kind of...well...*magic*. I didn't, sore throats aside. I wasn't sure I wanted the responsibility.

He looked particularly inscrutable.

"But maybe," I admitted, mulling it over. "Maybe the Melusine Grail is."

In a nearby display case sat a small, ornate goblet of blue faience. It wasn't a goddess cup, but I turned under Lex's hand and escaped for a closer look anyway.

My name's Magdalene Sanger. I'm a professor of Comparative Mythology at Clemens College outside Stamford, Connecticut. And as it turns out, I'm descended from goddess worshippers. Long ago, when such beliefs became a burn-at-the-stake offense, women across the world hid their most sacred relics and taught their daughters and their daughters' daughters where to find them.

Grailkeepers. Like me.

Until recently, guarding the knowledge of these lost chalices had been enough. But Phil Stuart and a secret society of powerful men had gone after my family's cup. I'd rescued it—and learned the truth, which was this:

After hundreds, maybe thousands of years, mere knowledge was no longer enough.

Lex's reflection appeared in the glass case, over my shoulder. "How's an old cup that's not even here making women more—" he frowned, at a loss "—*more*."

"Legend says the goddess grails will increase the

power of women a hundredfold," I reminded him. "And I do still have the Melusine Grail. Sure, it's hidden away for now…"

He didn't ask where. I definitely didn't tell him.

"But still, I drank from it. I took the essence of *goddessness* into me. Maybe that connection is what's empowering other women…at least when I touch them."

"So you don't need to go looking for more cups?"

"Of course I do."

His ghostly image scowled. In some ways, I thought, he's more dangerous than Phil.

At least I felt certain about where Phil stood.

Even when I turned and looked at Lex straight on, I knew damned well I wasn't seeing all of him.

He breathed out his next question. *"Why?"*

"You know as well as I do. Because a secret society called the Comitatus are after them. They destroyed the Kali Grail in New Delhi—"

"You can't know that was…them."

"You're right, because they work in *secret*." I frowned into my champagne. "But I know some of them went after the Melusine Chalice. I know they came after me. Is there any reason I should give them the benefit of a doubt?"

Lex's mouth flattened as I kept talking.

"That's the problem with secrets," I continued. "I could have been dating a member of the Comitatus for years—hell, I could've dated one of its most powerful members—and never known it. I could have considered *marrying* him, and because of some stupid vow of secrecy, he would never have told me who he really was."

"I can't talk to you when you're like this." Lex's reflection turned away from mine and faded, like a ghost's.

Whether I wanted it to or not, my heart lurched. I turned after him. "That's our problem. *You can't talk to me.*"

Because that whole previous speech had been a big, fat load of sarcasm.

Turns out, Lex *was* one of the most powerful members of the Comitatus. From what I'd pieced together, the only reason he wasn't in charge was that a childhood illness had taken him out of the running as a leader of supposed warriors. More's the pity.

Despite our own problems—previous deceptions, and cross-purposes, and scars that might or might not yet heal—I had to believe things would have been different with him as the leader.

I *had* to.

I caught up to him and put a hand on his arm, hard and fit beneath his tuxedo jacket. "I have no reason to trust them. And since you *can't* talk to me—"

"I can," Lex insisted. "About anything but that."

"It's a hard thing not to talk about. You must know something good about those men, something worth saving, but I haven't seen any proof of it. And now—"

Now Phil Stuart scowled at us from across the room, bodyguards instead of a date at his side. His fear of me, of what he couldn't understand, made him dangerous. I looked from him to Lex again, noting how tight Lex's jawline had gotten with the strain of his own secrets, and I consciously chose *against* fear.

"I trust you," I vowed softly, hopefully. "I trust that you know what you're doing, that it's something honorable and right. I've got to believe that, for both our sakes…."

My voice faded, the closer his face leaned toward

mine, the more intently his golden eyes focused on my lips. The nearer he came, the shorter my breath fell.

But again, not in a good way. I wasn't ready.

The last time we'd been lovers, before his attack, I'd known nothing of his involvement with the Comitatus. Learning the truth had just about broken my heart. I *did* want to trust him…but maybe hearts are slower to heal than knife wounds.

He must have seen something in my eyes, in my posture. We've known each other since childhood, after all. He reads me pretty well.

Abruptly, he turned away. "I'll get us another drink."

And then I was alone in the crowd, feeling cold and foolish and more than a little frustrated…which is when I saw it.

It was another glass case, another small sculpture in blue faience, apparently the Egyptians' earthenware of choice. This one wasn't a cup but a tiny figurine, a woman on a throne with a child in her lap.

I *could* have looked away, if I'd wanted to. But, pulse accelerating, I did not want to.

The size of the figurine, perhaps six inches, in no way matched the scope of its subject. But from the head-dress, I recognized her—or should I say, *Her*—all the same. *Isis.* Goddess of Ten Thousand Names. Oldest of the Old. Sitting there amid relics from her ancient, half-forgotten world, nursing the tiny god Horus on her lap.

This Grailkeeper business would be so much easier if she spoke to me, even in my head—if she flat out said *Maggi, this is your next assignment.* It didn't work that way, of course. So far, a sore throat in the presence of danger was as tangible as the magic of the goddess got. Except…

Something vibrated against my fingertips. I nearly dropped my purse before remembering my cell phone, tucked inside it. I drew it out, saw an international exchange on its display.

I thumbed the On button. "Hello, Rhys," I said softly, and not just out of politeness for the other museum patrons. The moment felt almost...holy. "Tell me you know where the Isis Grail is and I'll believe in magic."

"I do not know for certain," came the lilting Welsh voice of my friend, an archeology student at the Sorbonne who was interning with an expedition to Egypt. "But someone seems to think I do."

My sense of unease returned—and only partly because I'd just seen Lex, across the room, conversing with his cousin Phil.

"Why do you say that?" I deliberately turned my attention back to the statuette. *I trust him, I trust him, I trust him.*

The tiny blue Isis wore a crooked smile, as if to say, "Gotcha."

"I say it," said Rhys, "because somebody tried to kill me today."

Chapter 2

When we reached JFK, Lex turned the car into an open space at the far reaches of the Central Terminal Area lot and shifted into Park. August sunlight bounced off a stretch of windshields and rearview mirrors between us and the terminals. His engine idled almost imperceptibly, to keep the cool air blowing.

He unfastened his seat belt and turned to me.

Here it comes, I thought. Until this moment, Lex's only reaction to my announcement that I was flying to Egypt had been three words: "I'll drive you."

I expected a protest.

I didn't expect him to take my left hand in his.

"Mag," he said. *And he slid a gold band onto my ring finger!* "Wear this?"

Gold band. On the finger reserved for engagement and *wedding rings*.

And I'd thought concern for Rhys and last-minute flight plans had been stressful? This sent the day's pressure into heart-pumping overdrive.

Damn, I thought, staring at the ring. And we were just starting to get along again. Except for the panic attack at the thought of kissing him, that is. Still, I'd already refused to marry Lex Stuart, several times, even *before* this business about chalices and secret societies had come up.

The timing hadn't exactly improved.

"It's company policy," Lex explained with his usual composure, drawing his thumb across the band. "Women wearing wedding rings invite less harassment in Arab countries than women who are recognizably single."

"Policy," I repeated numbly—and the world shifted back into place again. *Policy.* The ring meant nothing. Then the rest of his statement caught up with me, and I regained my full voice to challenge it. "*Invite* harassment?"

"*Attract* less harassment, then. Point being—"

"Point being you think I need the illusion of a man to protect me." I started to tug the ring off.

He closed his hand around mine, stopping me. "I didn't say that. God help any Egyptians who try to harass you."

Appeased, I waited for him to explain himself.

"I just wish you weren't going," he said softly.

Which, as far as ways for him to explain himself went, sucked. "Well that's not your call to make."

"Did you hear me asking?"

Actually, no, I hadn't.

Lex opened his hand enough to look at mine, at the

ring that now loosely circled the top knuckle of my finger. "You're the one who complains that we don't talk enough."

I couldn't help it—I laughed. I had to get rid of nervous energy somehow. "I complain that you've taken a vow of secrecy to an organization that's tried to kill me. And you. More than once. That's not the same as whining that you don't tell me often enough that you love me."

He said, "I love you."

I sank back into the leather seat and closed my eyes, still anchored by his hand holding mine. My reaction to that really shouldn't have been to think, *Crap,* should it?

I mean, this was Lex—my first date, first love, first time. My first, second, and third heartbreak.

But damn it, my plane was leaving soon, and I still had an international security check to get through. "Lex…"

"I love you, and I hate that you're leaving. This is the *Middle East* you're talking about, Mag."

When I opened my eyes, there that ring sat, peeking loosely through our fingers, undecided. "Egypt isn't the same as the Gaza Strip."

"It's not the same as Cleveland, either," insisted Lex. "Less than a decade ago more than *fifty tourists* were massacred in the Valley of the Kings."

"I'm not going to the Valley of the Kings, I'm going to Alexandria. It's the other direction."

Lex stared at me, unswayed.

I fisted my hand in his, ring and all. "I'll be fine."

"Like you were the last time you went after a chalice that certain people didn't want found?"

"Certain people don't know I'm going this time."
Or... Old suspicions settled in my chest. *"Do they?"*

Lex took his hand back and released the parking
brake in an angry movement. "You've really got this not
trusting me business down, haven't you?"

Again—*crap*. I reached awkwardly across my lap to
reengage the brake, since my left hand was still fisted
to keep from losing the ring. "Hey. I wasn't saying you
told them. Did you hear me saying that?"

Then again, if they learned about my quest some
other way, I wasn't sure he could have told *me,* either.

When Lex turned back to me, his expression was im-
passive—and his eyes desperate. "We really don't com-
municate well, do we?"

I might not be able to tell him that it would all work
out, not with any certainty, but I could at least reach for
him, cradle my palm across his clean-shaven cheek. If
words couldn't ease his uncertainty, maybe simple touch
would.

As if I'd drawn him, Lex leaned nearer, braced his
forehead lightly against mine. "I can't lose you
again."

Which on some levels was so tender, so vulnerable,
that I felt half-ready to ditch everything, just to taste his
lips, just to ease some of the uncertainty from this man's
deep, golden eyes. When I looked at him I saw too
much—a boy dying of leukemia, a teenager grieving his
dead mother, a man determined to keep promises he
should never have had to make....

But on some levels, intentional or not, his words
were manipulative as hell.

"You first," I whispered, turning my head to rest it
on his shoulder. Lex really had great shoulders, solid

and strong, even without the crisply tailored suits. He would make a really great leader of warriors.

"Me first, what?"

"You promise to stop doing dangerous things, taking transatlantic flights to unsafe places—"

"Mag." The sardonic note he put into my name told me we were done with the puppy-dog eyes for now.

"…move to the suburbs, ditch the sports car…."

He sighed and leaned his weight into me, hard enough to nudge me fully back into my own seat.

"Then maybe," I finished, silently laughing at his scowl as I straightened, *"maybe* we'll talk a deal."

The scowl didn't falter. "I know you can handle yourself, but I'm just not hardwired to leave it at that. Maybe it goes back to cavemen killing saber-toothed tigers that threatened the camp, but there's something in men that makes us want—need—to protect our women."

Our women? Instead of jumping into that frying pan, I chose the proverbial fire. "A lot has changed since then. For one thing, those cavemen probably worshipped a goddess."

"In the good old days before testosterone screwed up the world, right?" Sarcasm clearly intended.

"I never said testosterone didn't have its uses." And whoa—I sure didn't mean that to sound quite as seductive as it did. I saw it immediately in the way his expression stilled, his eyes darkened to a whiskey color, his breath caught. He glanced quickly toward the tiny clock display over the rearview mirror.

Worse—I did, too.

The heat that washed through me had nothing to do with summer in the city, and everything to do with my body's dissatisfaction at having gone so long without his kisses. Maybe my heart *was* wary. But the rest of me...

"I've gotta go," I murmured, turning the air conditioner dial to full blue.

To his credit, Lex managed in three long, deep breaths to regain his mask of disinterest. He released the parking brake and shifted into Drive. "Yes. Security gets more complicated every day."

"I'll call you when I have a hotel room."

"Please do." But before he pulled out of the space, he turned his head to look at me full-on again. "And wear the ring, Maggi. Let me do that much for you."

And really, what could it hurt? "'Wear the ring,' *please*," I prompted softly.

"Please," he repeated, and the edge of his mouth quirked before he eased onto the gas. "With sugar on top."

So what the hell? I slid the band fully onto my finger, as if it belonged there. "Fine. But it's all about not rocking the Egyptians' boat, right?" I clarified. "It has nothing to do with making Rhys Pritchard uncomfortable?"

"I like Rhys." Lex sounded waaay too innocent for my tastes. "I'm sure neither of us would want to make the other one uncomfortable."

Yeah. Like guys thought that way. The same gender that came up with the concept of a pissing contest. "Uh-huh."

But I was stuck. I'd already agreed to wear the ring.

The other player in this triangle, Rhys Pritchard, was my prize at the end of the long process of my arrival in

Cairo—a metal staircase onto the hot tarmac, a bus to the terminal, customs, a temporary visa, and an increasing awareness of all the head scarves and galabiya and Arabic being spoken around me.

It was great to see a familiar face.

I surged toward him as best I could amid the crowd and saw that he was making the effort to shoulder his way to me, too. The closer he got, the better he looked. Rhys has a coloring I would normally call "black Irish," except that he's Welsh. Dark, unkempt hair. Bright-blue eyes. Lanky—what he has on Lex in height he loses in breadth. But here in Egypt, Rhys had gained a secret weapon—sunshine. His U.K. complexion, though still pale by swarthy Egyptian standards, had been gilded by the Mediterranean sun. A touch of pink on his nose and cheeks made his eyes seem to glow.

Or maybe that was just pleasure at seeing me.

"Maggi!" he exclaimed, his smile wide and welcoming. I reached for him—

But he stopped short. "Let me look at you."

"Only if you return the favor," I warned, eyeing him up and down. He wore his usual faded jeans and a slightly wrinkled, long-sleeved jersey that had been washed too often. "Are you sure you're okay?"

"I told you—I dodged the car that tried to run me down." From the scrapes on his hands, where he'd landed, I judged he'd had only modest success in that. "I wouldn't have mentioned it except for what it might signify."

"That you've found a lead about the…you-know-what."

The Isis Grail.

He nodded, a moment of complete accord—and I

hugged him. After the briefest hesitation, his long arms wrapped around me, no matter where we were. *Mmm.* He felt stronger than he had back in France, where we'd enjoyed a mild flirtation and the start of a powerful friendship. He smelled faintly of the sea.

That was Rhys for you. No nefarious associations. Totally supportive of my grail quest, since his mother had also descended from a line of Grailkeepers. Classic nice guy. Wholly, wonderfully uncomplicated...

Except for his having been a priest, once. Actually, still—as he'd be the first to point out, ordination is even more permanent in the Catholic Church than marriage. But he no longer worked for them. The Catholic Church that is.

Okay, so *that* part was complicated.

He pulled back first, ducking his head only in part to take my suitcase. "Ah. That is...do be careful, Maggi. The Egyptians don't approve of PDAs."

I blinked at him. "Personal digital assistants?"

"They don't approve of public displays." *Of affection.*

Oh.

I looked around us and did, in fact, intercept a few glares aimed our way. I also saw a pair of men beside us, hugging and then kissing each other on each cheek. "Really?"

"Not between the sexes," he chided, grinning. "Not even if it's obvious that the couple's..." His grin faded. "Oh."

He'd just noticed the wedding ring.

"It's fake," I assured him, fast. "I'm supposed to attract less harassment this way."

"Most of the women on the project do the same

thing." Rhys sounded relieved as he supported Lex's story.

Having him there eased the foreignness of this place. Between a few necessary stops—the public bathrooms, and an in-airport bank to change money—we caught up on the basic niceties. How my great-aunt and his recent boss had been when he left Paris—she was well. How my parents had been when I left New York—also good. Everything but the goddess grails, which needed privacy, and the topic of me and Lex, which was just plain awkward.

In the meantime, for a country where we weren't supposed to hold hands or even walk too close, the other travelers sure crowded us against each other.

"Here," said Rhys, as another passenger bumped me in passing. "You'll want to keep this on you."

I took the matchbook he handed me. In swirling Arabic letters it said something I couldn't possibly read. But in smaller text, beneath that, it said *Hotle Athens, Alexandria.*

"It's for if we get separated," Rhys explained over the bustle and push. "This is where most of the people on the project have been staying. Show it to a cabdriver or a policeman, and they can get you safely back."

"Like a kindergartner with a sign pinned to my shirt?"

"Something like that, yes." By now we'd reached the doors out onto the afternoon sidewalk. Despite that the sidewalk was covered, for shade, we stepped into a blast of dusty, nose-searing heat—

And chaos.

Men rushed us from five different directions at once, getting in our faces, shouting at us in Arabic with snippets of English: "Cab?"

"Good ride!"

"Take care of you!"

"La'," said Rhys, speaking more firmly than usual.

And a dark man with a bushy moustache snatched my suitcase right out of his hands! Rhys reached for it, but I got it first, yanking with all my strength. The man let go, shouting his displeasure, and I stumbled backward from the lack of resistance—right into someone else's hand on my butt. When I spun to face that one, he smiled proudly and held out a hand, as if for a tip. That's when I felt someone pull at the laptop case over my shoulder.

"La' la' la'!" said Rhys again, louder, but intimidation isn't his thing.

Me, I spun to face the man who had my laptop and, hands full, I kicked at him. Not an hour in this country and already I was resorting to violence.

"La'!" I said, whatever the hell it meant.

Somehow he jumped clear of my kick, which was maybe for the best. Annoying or not, these men didn't seem to be trying to hurt us, or even rob us. Even the luggage snatching seemed to be a twisted sales technique. The same thing was happening to other travelers up and down the sidewalk.

Most important, my throat wasn't tightening with any kind of warning.

Still, I'd had enough gestures, offers, pleas and definitely enough gropes! We were surrounded, the hot, already suffocating air thick with garlic breath and sweaty bodies and pushing, grabbing men shouting foreign words with only moments of English clarity: "Give ride!" or "Help you."

"I don't want your help," I insisted, first in English

and then in French, and bumped into Rhys. *"La'* isn't working," I complained. "What's Egyptian for *piss off?*"

Two of the men shouted louder and gestured more rudely. Apparently they understood and disapproved, despite that *they* were harassing *us*.

I was about to show them some freakin' disapproval....

That's when a suited, square-shouldered, swarthy man stepped up to the fray. He made a small motion with his right hand, like scooping something away from him, and the others immediately drew back.

Why did I think this couldn't be good?

"Try *imshee*," the gentleman suggested in cultured, British-accented English—to Rhys. "It often works."

I said, "And that really means…?"

Finally he looked at me—and smiled, charming as any sheikh hero in a romance novel. "My dear lady, it means *get lost.*"

Close enough. Although they'd already backed off, I glared at the remaining hawkers and said, *"Imshee!"*

Several turned away from us, gesturing that we weren't worth the trouble. The ones who remained, hands still outstretched for my luggage, weren't getting as close.

But was that because of the word, or the man?

The still-crowded sidewalk by no means became an oasis of calm. But at least I could actually look around us. A handful of mosques and minarets cut the smoggy, uneven skyline of dusty stone skyscrapers. Cement was winning the war against a stretch of grass here and a cluster of palm trees there; the plaster facade above us read Cairo Airport, followed by Arabic lettering. The stench of heat and car exhaust was dizzying. A cacophony of horns mixed with shouts and music from open car windows…but okay, that part just sounded like New York.

This may once have been the land of the goddess Isis, but it sure looked like a land of men now. Men's values. Men's importance. I couldn't help feeling vulnerable.

I turned back to grudgingly thank the man who'd helped us.

He was gone.

Then Rhys caught my elbow and ran with me across a road snarled with traffic, toward an open parking lot, and I let the matter go. Sort of.

By the time we'd let the worst of the heat out of his borrowed car's open doors, I'd made at least one decision. "Can we stop somewhere on the way to Alexandria?"

"Absolutely." Rhys started the car, a battered, dusty, blue Chevy Metro. Something that resembled air-conditioning sputtered from its vents. "Museums? Pyramids?"

Well, of course I wanted to see the pyramids—who wouldn't? But, "I want to go shopping," I told him, and didn't smile at his double take. Damn it, I hadn't yet made it off airport property, and already I was awash in testosterone. Women with veils. Guards with assault weapons. Double standards.

Hopefully I wouldn't run into actual violence this time around, not like my last grail quest. The Comitatus didn't know I was here, after all.

But just in case they found out…

"I want to buy a sword."

Chapter 3

Isis may not have been anywhere near the airport, but she made multiple appearances in Cairo's ancient shopping bazaar, the Khan el-Khalili. The labyrinth of narrow medieval streets and plazas snaking between four- and five-story buildings burst at the seams with goods, wares and of course souvenirs. Here I saw Isis and many of her fellow gods on T-shirts and postcards. I saw her painted on papyrus and ceramics, on figurines of varying sizes, on jewelry.

"Pretty lady try on necklace," shouted one turbaned man from outside a *souk,* or store, that sold jewelry. And sure enough, the handful of necklaces he held up included not only scarabs and sphinxes and Eye-of-Horus design called an *udjat,* but ankhs and pendants with a circle topped by a half circle, like horns. Those last two were major Isis symbols.

"Rings for rings," called the woman behind him. Veiled. In this suffocating heat. "Pretty things."

People shouted. Chickens squawked. Children laughed and dodged past shoppers—or begged. The way both handcrafted and plastic-wrapped merchandise spilled out into the already littered streets, and bright banners draped across the open area above us to provide shade and color, I found myself increasingly glad I didn't suffer claustrophobia. With claustrophobia, this would be hell.

Instead, it was fun, if ovenlike. The smells of spices, incense, perfumes and produce—mountains of oranges and bananas and white garlic bulbs—overwhelmed the lingering scent of diesel like an exotic time travel. Quite a few merchants dressed as their predecessors must have for hundreds of years.

"Welcome to Egypt!"

"Where you from?"

"No charge for looking!"

Leaning close to Rhys, I raised my voice. "Are you sure they sell swords here?"

"I'm told they sell everything here." He readjusted the laptop case, which we'd decided not to risk leaving in the car. "Legend has it some of the most ancient Christian scrolls were recovered at a bazaar like this."

I smiled at his clear envy; he'd become increasingly interested in the early history of the church since he'd gone civilian. "Good luck finding some more of them."

"You want swords?" asked a little boy with huge black eyes, suddenly ahead of us. "Here was once the metalworker's bazaar. I show you swords—come!"

So what the hell, we followed.

The first shop he brought us to had only swords with

animal-horn handles, not exactly what I wanted. The next sported highly decorative weapons that looked fit for Sinbad in the *Thousand and One Nights,* but were actually letter openers made out of tin. And the third one—

Just right. The third *souk* displayed a collection of real blades laid on silk-lined tables and hung from rope outside the shop. The inside walls displayed them one above the next.

Steel blades. Fighting swords.

Rhys slipped our miniature guide some coins—*baksheesh,* don't you know—and I went shopping.

It's not like I'm an expert on swords. Most of my experience before this summer came from practicing tai chi forms with a straight, double-edged saber. It's used not so much for fighting as for an extension of one's self in a fluid, moving meditation. But that practice came in damned useful when the Comitatus attacked Lex and me with ceremonial daggers.

Apparently society members had nothing against guns for your average peons, but knives were used for attacks of any ritual significance. I hoped I'd risen to that much esteem, anyway.

Mainly because I hate guns.

Some of the swords inside this hot little *souk* I could immediately reject. Almost half of them were just too large for me to comfortably wield, much less carry with any discretion. Just as many were curve-bladed scimitars, high on style, low on personal practicality. But some…

Several dozen straight-bladed swords beckoned me to pick them up, test their heft, swing them.

The grizzled shopkeeper stepped back to give me as

much space as he could, which wasn't much. Luckily, tai chi is all about control over oneself and, when swords are involved, one's blade.

I barely heard the merchant's explanation of the benefits of this piece or that—Toledo steel here, Damascus there, replicas of swords belonging to sheikhs and knights. I was too busy listening to the swords themselves.

I tried a sword with too thick of a grip, then one with a basket hilt, like a rapier, which felt awkward to me. I tried one that turned out to be way too long, and another that weighed too much. Rhys said something about being right back, and I nodded, but mostly I was lifting swords, holding them over my head, spinning with them, thrusting them at full arm's length…trying to find my perfect extension.

For the first week or so after Lex's attack I'd avoided practicing, and not just because I'd wrenched my wrist in the fight. Every time I'd picked up my sword, I would remember exactly what it felt like to thrust a blade into another human being. Through skin. Into muscle, ligaments, bone. And yes, it *was* sickening. That's the point. It's not that I regretted doing it—those men had given me no other choice when they tried to kill someone I cared about. But I regretted having been in a situation that demanded it.

Then my *sifu* had suggested that I either choose to swim across the blood or to drown in it. That was when I'd reclaimed my practice, my extension. It didn't happen right away—but by now, I could lose myself in the slow dance of forms that is pure tai chi without the guilt.

Embracing the moon.

Black dragon whipping its tail.
Dusting into the wind.

I was halfway through a routine, stepping slowly from one movement to the next, before I realized this was it. The sword I held had great weight, great balance. It was the one I wanted, the one that wanted me. Lowering it, I saw that it had a slim blade with a stylish brass S hilt and, intriguingly, a pattern within the hand-beaten steel that reminded me of snake scales. Snakes are a universal goddess symbol, not just for Melusine or Eve or the Minoans. This was perfect.

Wiping my face on my sleeve, I turned to ask the shopkeeper the cost—and was surprised to see that sometime during the last couple of swords, he'd vanished.

How odd. Worse, my throat tightened in warning. Because of that, I had my blade up and ready as I turned toward the front of the shop—and stopped short.

The sharp tip of a scimitar hovered, a mere breath from my tardy throat.

The man who held the sword, swarthy and square-shouldered, was the man who'd helped us at the airport. He still wore the suit. But now, weirdly enough, he had a protective, Eye-of-Horus design painted in blue on his cheek.

"Well, witch," he said. "Let us see how good you are."

And he swung.

Had he just called me a *witch?*

Thank heavens for practice. If I'd had to actually think about anything at that moment, I may have ended up as shish kebab.

Instead, my new sword leaped upward almost before I knew I was moving it. The two blades collided with a steel clash that echoed through the *souk*.

One steel clash.

That was all I needed.

Tai chi is all about passive resistance, resolving everything into its opposite. Softness against strength. Yielding and overcoming. To meet this man's force with more force would be foolish, him being so much bigger and clearly more aggressive than me. Instead, I met it with concession, sliding my blade around his.

He did the work of thrusting. His mistake, since my blade remained in the space he was thrusting against. The only reason it merely scratched his arm, instead of stabbing him, was my reluctance to have it yanked from my hand.

I'd drawn first blood, all the same.

He drew breath in a quick hiss. "What kind of fighting is that?"

"Maybe I fight like a girl," I said. *Warned.*

When he drew back to swing again, my blade continued to rest against his. When he sliced the air with his scimitar, my sword coiled around his and struck a second time across the light sleeve on his forearm.

Another stripe of blood.

I was the one who demanded, "Would you *stop* that?"

"I?" The bastard groped outward with his left hand, picked up one of the display swords and, with a sharp jerk, flipped its scabbard to the stone floor. Such a guy. When in doubt, up the weaponry.

Crap.

Now I had two blades to deal with, using only one.

My sword couldn't flow around both of them, and I'm no two-handed fencer, so I had to make myself flow around the man instead. Try to. Wouldn't you know I'd be wearing a skirt for this, gauzy but long—dress is very conservative in Arabic countries. At least I had on boots.

The cluttered walls loomed in, too close.

When the man rushed me, I had no choice but to back up—fast—rather than take the full force of his attack. Even as I pivoted out of his way, letting him push past me, I stumbled against another table of merchandise. When he charged again, I dived under his weapons to avoid them both.

Gauzy skirt material twisted around my legs, and sand from the floor grated across my skin. Luckily, I managed to roll to my feet—barely—before hitting the opposite wall of this small *souk*. My skirt tore under one foot. A dagger fell behind me. "What the hell is your problem?"

He swung with his right-hand sword. With my empty hand, I caught his from behind and encouraged it in the direction it was already going as I dodged, throwing him off balance.

He stumbled.

"Why did you call me a witch?" I demanded.

Catching himself, he now sliced the left-hand blade toward me. I blocked it with my own weapon, one ringing impact and then silent adherence, sinuously winding my blade about his.

That didn't protect me from the first sword, his scimitar. It flashed upward too quickly. To dodge it, I would either have to drop my sword or—

No way was I dropping my sword. Instead, I sank into an almost impossibly low crouch—without having stretched first, which I would regret—and ducked under his elbow. The scimitar whipped through the air above me. But it missed.

I tried to bob quickly back to my feet, behind my attacker and away from the immediate threat and his weapons, but I'd stepped on my damn skirt, which yanked me off balance long enough for the bastard to bodycheck me.

That was unexpected—which was why it worked. He rushed at me, filling my vision with his shoulder, his elbow. I meant to dance backward myself, like riding a wave. Let him do the work. Let him expend the effort.

But *wham!* Too soon, my back met a sword-covered wall. The back of my head slammed against a hard scabbard. And Sinbad's swinging elbow knocked the breath right out of me.

I sank, fingers curling desperately around the grip of my own sword. *Don't drop it, don't drop it.*

As if lifting it were even possible, at that moment.

My damp knees hit the gritty floor, and I folded forward, catching myself with one hand, one fist.

Don't drop it!
Breathe!

My body obeyed the first command, but not the second. I fought the physical panic that comes from having breath knocked away and arched my neck, straining my face upward.

The stranger's hulking body loomed above me.

"You will leave Egypt, witch," he dictated in his impeccable British. "And you will take your friend with you."

My chest tightened, and my view of him began to waver. *Goddess help me....*

Maybe it was Isis, or Melusine, or just that universal, maternal force of goddessness that answered my prayer. Or maybe it was just timing.

Hot, exotic air filled my lungs with a rush. And with it came power.

Even as he said, "You will not interfere in matters that do not concern you."

My fingers clenched around my sword. "Well, it sure as hell concerns me now." And I swung. A quick, angry arc across his ankles. Not enough to cut anything off— I doubted I had that strength, or this new sword had such sharpness.

But definitely enough to bite. And unexpected.

That's why it worked.

With a startled cry, the man jumped back. I surged up onto one knee, capturing my gauzy skirt with my free hand, and swung again while he was still off balance. It forced him back a few inches, which was all I wanted.

Before he could stop me, I ducked under his weapons, right past him and toward the front of the shop, no longer trapped.

He lunged, and I practically floated backward on the surge of energy before him. One step. Two steps. I reached my hand back for the door.

"Do you really plan to take this into the street?" I asked. "With all these nice bystanders and policemen?"

The policemen around here carried automatic weaponry, after all.

He scowled, and the air around him seemed to crackle with a most annoying version of alpha-male condescension. "You have no business here."

But I lived outside the whole male pecking order, thank heavens. I stood my ground and channeled a personal power that was uniquely feminine. "You just made sure I do."

When I heard the door behind me open, I deliberately ignored it. This stranger and I were in a staring contest, with nothing childish about it.

Then I heard Rhys's distinctly Welsh voice. *"Uffach cols!"* he swore. "What's this? Aren't you that fellow—"

"From the airport," I said, not looking back. "Yeah. Now he thinks he's Sinbad."

The door opened again, and Rhys shouted, *"Shorta! Shorta!"*

I hoped that meant *police.*

My opponent and I continued to glare. Then in a single smooth movement, he spun and vanished through the curtained doorway into the back.

I slowly lowered my sword, my breath resuming for real. Now I felt even less guilty about using a weapon.

"What the hell was *that* all about?"

"I only knew I was coming to Egypt last night...I guess that's night before last, now," I said, accepting the bottle of icy cold water Rhys had bought for me. "How the hell is it this guy was waiting for me? *At the airport!"*

"I didn't tell many people." Rhys hadn't lost the crease of concern between his blue eyes. Not while I talked to the police, and not while I bargained the merchant down to a third of his asking price for the sword that had protected me.

Normally I'm a wimpy barterer, but after the merchant's earlier vanishing act, I was in a combative mood.

Now I wore the sword's wooden scabbard slung innocently over my shoulder, a recent tourist's purchase. I hadn't decided on a name for the blade, yet. I would worry about concealing it later.

"It's not your fault," I assured Rhys.

"I told the hotel, to get you a bed. I told my friend Niko, when I asked to borrow the car. A group of people working on the project own it together, so it is possible one of the others know."

"I never said to keep it a secret."

"I told Tala, the woman I wish you to meet—"

"Rhys." I stopped and fixed him with my best scowl, swordfight-proven. "Let's not empower fear. The man didn't even use my name. He may not have even known who I really am."

"Then how is it that, so soon after the airport, he found you here?"

I looked around us, at a rope of guitars hanging outside one *souk* and a rainbow of glittering material draped before another, at the press and flow of people all around us. "Well…we wouldn't have noticed anyone following us around here, that's for sure."

"But how is it the man *could* have followed us in this crowd, and in Cairo traffic? And Maggi, *why* would he?"

Yeah, that one had me stumped, as well.

"Rings for rings," called the veiled woman working at the jewelry counter nearby, which made me look down at my left hand.

My breath caught in my throat, stopping as surely as it had when Sinbad shoved his elbow into me. "Unless…"

I could barely form the words. But the sudden rush of possibility was too horrible to keep to myself. "Unless I'm wearing some kind of tracking device."

"But who could possibly—" Rhys apparently saw how I was staring at the wedding ring.

The one Lex had given me.

Lex, one of the lead members of the Comitatus.

That's the problem with old wounds. They reopen.

"The guy attacked me with a sword," I whispered.

Rhys grabbed my hand, PDA or not. "Now wait a moment, Maggi. You were in a shop chockablock with swords. Just because this stranger used one does not mean he's a member of that secret order."

Yes, Rhys knew. *I* hadn't taken any vows of silence.

"They used ceremonial daggers, didn't they?"

"There is a difference between the two. Even if there were not, even if the man were—" he lowered his voice "—Comitatus, that could mean *Phillip* Stuart sent him, not necessarily Lex."

"But Lex is the only one who could have told Phil, and *how else did that man follow us from the airport?*" I freed my hand from his and waded through the crowd to the jewelry counter, where I could see the female clerk's smile in her eyes, over her veil. "Do you speak English?"

"Yes," she said, nodding. "Yes. Rings for rings."

"I don't want to buy—well, not a ring," I decided, since if I wanted help, I couldn't expect her to give it for free. I glanced impatiently at the cluster of cheap pewter pendants and quickly chose the horned disk that symbolizes Isis. "But I was hoping you could check *this* ring and tell me if there's anything strange about it. Anything like a…a tracking device?"

The clerk stared at me blankly, as if disappointed. Apparently her English wasn't good enough to include *tracking device.*

Great. "Is this a normal ring?" I tried, tugging the wedding band from my finger and sliding it across the counter toward her.

Then I froze, because of what she'd just slid hopefully across the counter toward *me*.

A brass chalice-well pendant—two intersecting circles, also called a *vesica piscis*. Similar to the pendant I already wore, had worn in one version or another since I was fourteen, except for the Arabic flourishes.

Symbol of the Grailkeepers.

Chapter 4

When the hopeful clerk repeated, "Rings for rings," I finally understood her. I'd simply known the childhood rhyme as *Circle to Circle*.

But circles, rings…they were all eternal loops. It lost little in translation. And it was a recognition code.

"Never an end," I greeted softly, purposefully giving the next piece of the Grailkeeper's chant.

She clearly recognized it. She beamed. I even caught a pale hint of white teeth behind her veil as she reached across the counter and grasped my hand. Her grip was firm. Then her eyes closed and she drew in a long, deep breath, as if savoring…

What? Was she sensing the essence of goddessness that seemed to empower women whom I touched, of late?

It wasn't like I expected her to rip off her veil and

head scarf and demand equal pay for equal work. But when she opened her eyes, all she said was, "It is you!"

Uh-huh… "What is me?"

"You have come to reclaim the sultana's magic," she continued. "As in the tales."

For a moment I had the sick feeling that there was an actual sultana out there somewhere. One more responsibility I hadn't meant to take on. Then I realized that my word for the position would be *queen*.

"You mean like the fairy tale, about the queen and her nine daughters?" I asked.

"Seven," corrected the clerk—but as surely as I'd heard different versions of the story, I'd heard different numbers. Sometimes the queen had as many as thirteen daughters, sometimes as few as three. "Seven beautiful daughters."

Rhys, behind me, asked, "Does she mean the story where the queen gives her daughters magical cups?"

The clerk's eyes widened. She backed away two steps, making what I assumed was a protective gesture.

"It's all right," I assured her. "His mother is a Grailkeeper."

She stared at me blankly.

"A…Chalice Keeper," I tried.

She nodded slowly and said, "A Cup Holder."

"Um…yeah. A Cup Holder." Now that one suffered in translation. "He knows the story."

Pour your powers into these cups, the queen instructs. *Hide them so that your energy can live on even though you be forgotten.*

The veiled clerk continued to eye Rhys as if he meant to attack her. Or me. With his big, manly hands and all that…testosterone.

"Perhaps I should go look at…yes, there," said Rhys, choosing the first thing he noticed. "One can't have enough T-shirts, can one?"

Only after he'd backed away did the "Cup Holder's" shoulders sink in relief. Poor, gentle Rhys.

"Let me try again," I said. "Hello. My name is Magdalene Sanger."

"I is Munira," said the clerk, clearly pleased. "It is…*honor*…to meet champion."

"To meet what?"

"Champion of the Holy One." She opened her arms toward me, like a tah-dah move. "It is you, is not?"

"I'm looking for goddess cups, but I wouldn't call myself a champion." Certainly not *the* champion.

Even factoring in the number of women who'd forgotten or dismissed the legends, I suspect the number of hereditary Grailkeepers had to count in the hundreds, if not the thousands. The whole world had once worshipped goddesses, after all. We'd just kept such a low profile for so long, we'd lost track of each other.

There still had to be a handful who understood what the stories meant. Not just me.

"Blessings upon you, Champion," said Munira.

I gave up arguing with her, in favor of better information. "Well…thank you. Would *you* happen to know where a goddess cup is hidden?"

Like the Isis Grail?

She stared, brow furrowed.

"Did your mother teach you a rhyme or song about where the Holy One's cup might be waiting?" That's how most of our knowledge had been kept. Power mongers rarely think to dissect fairy tales or nursery rhymes.

"Ah!" She nodded—and recited something sing-song in Arabic.

I smiled a stupid half grin of ignorance, and Munira took pity on me, but her attempt at translating was clearly an effort.

"She…she sleeps, yes?" She mimed closing her eyes, head tipping sideways in illustration. "With no light. She is."

"She is what?"

Munira shook her head. "She *is*. And much…al-ways…will she be such."

Then she nodded at her completely unhelpful at-tempt, proud of herself. To be fair, her English so far outshone my Arabic that I couldn't do anything but thank her.

That, and make a mental note to come back with someone—a woman—who was fluent in *both* lan-guages.

"May she smile upon you," said Munira—then looked down at the wedding ring I'd set on the counter. "What is you wish for this ring, Champion? You say…*trapping?*"

No reason to confuse matters with the concept of a tracking device. "Is there anything unusual about this ring? Something that does not belong, embedded in it?"

I felt sick, just having to ask. Lex and I were work-ing on trusting each other, damn it. If it turned out he'd bugged me *again*, the man would need more than a sword to defend himself.

Munira raised a jeweler's loupe to her eye, a strange contrast to the veiling, and professionally examined the ring. If there was anything artificial there, she would surely see it.

"It is written," she said. "Graven?"

"Engraved?"

Nodding, she found a pencil to trace the unfamiliar letters, right to left. They came out sloppy, like a child's—but again, any attempt I made to write the beautiful flourishes of Arabic would have looked worse. All I needed was legibility.

That's what I got. *Virescit vulnere virtus.*

Latin. Something about vulnerability and strength. I'd seen the words before—over Lex's father's fireplace.

It was the Stuart clan motto.

"Does this…understand…to you?" she asked, and I nodded tightly. "Is all I see. Is fine ring. Very old. Very expensive."

So, just for giggles… "*How* expensive?"

She named a price—in American dollars, not Egyptian pounds—which staggered me. For just gold? No diamonds or anything?

"You have generous husband, no?" she asked.

No. What I had was a contradiction to Lex's oh-so-casual, standard-for-women-overseas story. Was it also company policy for businesswomen to wear expensive, been-in-the-family-for-generations, complete-with-motto rings?

"We sell much fine jewelry," offered Munira. "Very low price." And like that the strange Grailkeeper interlude turned back to the assumed normalcy of souvenir shopping at the Khan el-Khalili.

I'd seen the Pyramids of Giza as we flew in, and caught glimpses while we were in the city, they were so close to urban Cairo. But they were the opposite direction from Alexandria.

The drive had its points of interest, for sure, like the occasional sight of *fellahin,* or peasant farmers, riding overpacked bicycles, donkeys or even camels down the road. Rhys pointed out the road we would take if I wanted to check out the oldest Christian monastery in existence. But contrasted against pyramids almost anything would seem anticlimactic.

Even speculating about who had attacked me with a scimitar—and what Munira had meant about me being "Champion."

"Perhaps you're special," offered Rhys.

"I'm not special."

He glanced toward me as if he wanted to contradict that but hesitated from propriety's sake.

"I mean, I'm no more special than the next person. Certainly no more than the next Grailkeeper."

"Perhaps you are. That is to say…perhaps you *have* been somehow chosen. You did find the Melusine Grail. And you did drink from it."

"My cousin Lil drank from it, too," I reminded him. "And my friend Sophie, and Aunt Brigitte."

"That happened some days later, did it not?"

It did, but… "One thing I've liked about being a Grailkeeper, ever since I realized the concept was bigger than my grandmother's old stories, is that there's no hierarchy. No inner circles. No one woman—one person, I mean—is more important than another."

"Unlike the Comitatus?" Damn, but Rhys could be insightful when he wanted.

"As far as I can see, the only difference between a secret warrior society and a pyramid scheme—the financial kind—is that nobody tries to sell you anything."

"Instead, they try to kill you." Rhys shared my grin,

then asked, "Do you still believe that Lex was denied leadership simply because he had leukemia as a child?"

"It makes a weird sort of sense, especially if the order was established during pagan times. An ancient belief equates the health, even the virility, of the land with that of its king. Who knows? That could explain how my country has managed to prosper under presidents who were real hound dogs."

"But surely if Lex has fully recovered…"

"Oh, he recovered all right." But thinking about Lex and virility at the same time wasn't going to uncomplicate anything. Besides, I was still annoyed that he'd tricked me into wearing a family heirloom—so annoyed that I'd taken it off. "I used to wonder why he was so driven to stay in shape. Now I guess I know. But no way would Phil relinquish control that easily. My best guess is that Lex will try for a peaceful coup."

"That would be the path of a true leader, would it not?"

Depends on how you defined *leadership.* "He said something strange to me, Rhys. He said he needed me, needed *balance,* in order to do something important."

"He needs you, and you flew to Egypt?"

"He said it a few months ago. Hasn't mentioned it since. Besides, you needed me, too, right?"

Rhys slanted a skeptical look my direction. "I didn't invite you here to be my bodyguard, Maggi. I do care for your safety rather more than that."

"But if someone thinks you're close enough to finding the Isis Grail to try killing you…"

"Then you deserve to be here for the actual discovery," he finished. "I've gotten permission for you to participate. As an academic observer, that is."

"To participate in…" Belatedly, I realized exactly what he meant. "The project? Cleopatra's sunken palace? *Really?*"

He grinned. "You and she have a great deal in common, after all."

Noting how his eyes shone at the gift he'd given me, I thought, Attracted to two men?

Or, worse, was he going to say something gushy about immortal beauty? I didn't want Rhys admiring me that way, at least not saying so.

I was officially dating Lex, trust or no trust.

"You are both strong women," Rhys clarified, to my relief.

That seemed the safer analogy.

Speedboats bounce. At least, they do around other boats, as in the partially enclosed harbor of Alexandria. Salt spray flew into my face, sunlight glared across the water, and I loved it. This no longer felt as foreign as Egypt. It felt more familiarly like the Mediterranean—which, just beyond the crescent of land enclosing the harbor from either side, it was.

You may have read about the discovery of Cleopatra's Palace in *Newsweek* or *National Geographic,* or seen a special about it on cable television. I had, even before I'd started my search for the goddess grails…or learned that Cleopatra herself had claimed to be the reincarnation of the goddess Isis.

"That's common knowledge to Egyptologists," Rhys assured me, shouting over the engine of the motorboat we rode toward the anchored cabin cruiser where the main archeological team worked. "Pharaohs were gods on earth, or so they and their followers believed—hence that little tiff between Moses and his foster brother, before the exodus? Cleopatra VII was simply maintaining an important tradition passed down from millennia of rulers."

"Cleopatra *VII?*" Had there been that many?

"She's the one you're thinking of," Rhys assured me.

"Seduced Julius Caesar, then Mark Antony, heavy-on-the-eye-shadow, death-by-asp Cleopatra."

"The very same. It's well-known that, amid her palace complex, she had a temple to Isis. But we now assume that the same earthquake which destroyed the Pharos Lighthouse submerged the palace complex as well. It was long after that nasty death-by-asp business, though."

I looked from the approaching cabin cruiser back toward the coastal city of Alexandria, which, from the water, vaguely resembled an especially dusty, disorganized Venice off the Grand Canal...except for the chunks of cement blocks at the water's edge, to fight erosion. Then I turned to the medieval fortress that guarded the harbor entrance from the sea, and tried to imagine how this ancient city would have looked a thousand years before even that had been built. "And where there is a temple to Isis..."

"It stands to reason there may be a reliquary," agreed Rhys. "And where there is a reliquary..."

"There could be relics like a goddess grail." I shivered happily at the thought. Another font of female power, just waiting for us under the salty water. If only I could collect enough—however many that might be—then they could finally be revealed to a world in need of their balance and power.

The man we'd hired to ferry us out to the cabin cruiser

steered well around what I recognized as a diver-down buoy. He cut his engine and levered the motor up out of the water for safety. Momentum carried us the rest of the way to the ship. When I saw the name of this floating headquarters—*Soeur d'Aphrodite,* or *Aphrodite's Sister*—I felt all the more certain of the rightness of this visit.

Aphrodite, whom the Romans called Venus, isn't just a goddess. She may well be another face of Isis.

"Several significant archeologists have been leading the effort to explore these sites since their discovery," explained Rhys, grabbing hold of the ladder on the side of the ship as we coasted in beside it. "Whenever they can get permission. This is one of the few places in Alexandria where the scholars aren't having to fight developers for rights to the land. There is even some talk about creating an underwater tunnel system specifically so that tourists can view the finds—once the government manages to lessen the toxicity in the local seawater. After you."

He had my laptop case again, so all I had to do was gather up the excess of my torn cotton skirt, twist it, and tuck it into the waistband before I climbed up. If anyone had a problem with seeing my knees, they'd just have to get over it. I wasn't about to risk falling into water Rhys had just announced was toxic. Once I swung onto the lower deck I freed my skirts, while Rhys followed me.

What came after was a pleasant jumble of introductions and welcomes from an international assortment of divers and archeologists. The director of this particular branch of the project, Pierre d'Alencon, shook my hand but seemed busy with other matters, so I backed to the

edge of the deck, out of the way, to simply observe.
Rhys got permission to show me the computer pro-
grams being used to map the underwater finds, so I
turned in that direction—

And faced blazing green eyes.

"You," snarled a sickeningly familiar female voice,
in French.

Right before its owner pushed me over the railing.

Chapter 5

I made a desperate scramble at the metal railing as I fell over it. But I was too surprised, and it wasn't enough. The impact against the back of my legs, against my grasping hands, gave way to weightlessness.

Then, with a splash, I vanished beneath the surface of the toxic harbor—and quickly closed my eyes. Sinking downward, before my frantic strokes and kicks stopped my descent, I wouldn't have seen any goddess relics even if they waited right there in front of me.

Some champion!

Only after I managed to struggle upward, boots and soggy skirt and all, and my face broke the waves into the air, did I open my eyes to the sunshine—

And behold, far above, the bitch who'd pushed me.

Catrina Dauvergne of the Musée de Cluny, Paris.

The woman who'd once stolen the Melusine Grail from me.

The willowy, tawny-haired Frenchwoman was not
smiling.

That made two of us.

Once I managed to drag myself up the chrome ladder and back onto the deck, I took two dripping steps
in my attacker's direction, my hand fisting. Maybe
women don't normally default to violence as quickly as
men, but this was by no means quick. This had been
simmering for weeks.

Rhys shouldered himself between us. "I forgot to
mention her being here, Maggi. I'm so sorry."

He would be. "Move."

"I will not." Protecting people brings out the tough-
guy in Rhys, even when they didn't deserve protection.

"Yes, Pritchard," agreed Catrina in smooth French.
"This is not for you to interfere."

"But it is for me to interfere," insisted a new voice,
that of Monsier d'Alencon—also in French. The French
seemed to be running this particular show, after all.
"Explain yourselves."

I wrung out my skirt into a splattering puddle; it
clung like wet tissue. "You want *me* to explain?"

My French, unlike my Arabic, is fluent.

"I wish *someone* to explain so that I know which of
you two—or three—" his gaze included Rhys "—to
dismiss."

Catrina and I glared at each other. But this was a
choice expedition, remember? *Newsweek. National
Geographic.* Cable. The threat of expulsion carried
weight. I could read her hatred in her narrowed gaze.
She'd once accused me of playing archeologist, raiding
medieval sanctuaries and stealing the Melusine Chalice instead of leaving it in situ—not that I'd had any

choice! She, on the other hand, had pretended that she would put the chalice on display in the Cluny, where it might empower countless visitors with its proof of goddess worship, only to then sell it onto the black market.

Either way, Catrina and I each had enough on the other to permanently ruin both our chances of involvement with either Cleopatra's Palace or the Temple of Isis everyone hoped to find there—and, worse, to end Rhys's internship, which he'd gotten through the Sorbonne. I was comfortably employed, waiting only for the fall semester to start. Catrina, I assumed, still had a job with the Cluny, unless she'd quit to live off her ill-gotten gains. But after he'd left the priesthood, archeology was the only profession Rhys had found that spoke to him.

No way would I ruin this opportunity.

No way would I allow Catrina to do so.

"I apologize," I said slowly—to the project director. "Catrina and I are old friends. Sometimes our little jokes get out of hand, don't they, Cat?"

Catrina Dauvergne might be disloyal, dishonest and vindictive—but she was not stupid. "But of course, Magdalene," she said tightly. "Now we are even for the little *joke* you played in Paris."

Bitch.

D'Alencon glared from one of us to the other while I stood there dripping—so much for making a professional first impression. "There will be no more *jokes* on my time, yes? It is how injuries happen." And, blessedly, he turned back to other demands.

"This is not over," Catrina whispered menacingly.

"Not even close," I answered—and deliberately turned to Rhys, who had some explaining to do about forgetting to mention this woman's presence.

But first I needed to know... "Just how toxic *is* this water?"

Catrina laughed, disgustingly pleased—but turned back to her other duties.

As it turned out, the East Harbor of Alexandria was so polluted from raw sewage that the divers who went in regularly were supposed to wear cautionary headgear and dry suits, though not all of them took that mandate to heart. Locals still swam in the stuff. Brief exposure was unlikely to infest me with parasites or turn me radioactive. And in the meantime...

In the meantime, my introduction to the scope of the project quickly distracted me from any inauspicious beginning.

I'd arrived too late in the day to make suiting up for a dive practical. But more than in the relatively shallow waters of the harbor—which is maybe twenty-five feet at its deepest—most of the work was being done by computer, and much of that was on shipboard. The following few hours became an enjoyable blur of information about latex molding techniques, aquameters, nuclear resonance magnetometers and sonar scanning. The archeologists really *weren't* collecting artifacts from the sea and transferring them to some museum. They were mapping them, photographing them, sometimes raising them long enough to make molds, and then leaving them exactly where the assumed earthquake and/or tidal wave had once left them.

In situ.

I was so enthralled by the catalog of watery finds—sphinxes, statues, algae-covered pillars—that I almost forgot why I was there. *Almost.* Then Rhys reminded me that we had a dinner engagement for which I should probably clean up, and I remembered my real goal.

Isis.

Goddess grails.

And a supposed Grailkeeper whom he'd met, who'd said she would share the rhyme she'd learned about the location of the Oldest of the Old's chalice. Hopefully in English.

Considering that someone had tried to run Rhys down a few days ago, not long after he'd spoken to this woman, he wasn't the only person to suspect she might know what she was talking about.

The Hotel Athens, where most of the expedition was staying, had slotted me into a plain but neat third-story room, which I would share with a fortysomething Greek scientist named Eleni. It had two twin beds, one plain wardrobe, and a window overlooking trolley-car tracks with overhead wires that sparked whenever a trolley passed. As with many midrange European hotels, the bathroom and shower were down the hall.

I dressed as conservatively as before with the exception of sandals—my boots would take a while to dry. Since this was a social call, I decided to wait on rigging up a harness for my still nameless sword and instead left the weapon under my pillow. But I put my essential belongings—cell phone, money, matchbook—in a modest leather fanny pack, to keep my hands free. My passport had its own special pouch under my long-sleeved shirt. I pulled my hair back in a long brown braid.

And, after some deliberation, I put Lex's damned ring back on. Things can get stolen in hotel rooms.

I hadn't even been in the Arab Republic of Egypt for a day, but already I assumed that Mrs. Tala Rachid would be wearing a head scarf at least, maybe even a veil.

I assumed wrongly.

The vibrant, sixtysomething woman who greeted us when we arrived at her beautiful villa looked more Greek than Egyptian. She had beautiful black hair slashed with gray at her temples, which she'd drawn off her swanlike neck into a modest bun. Her knee-length blue dress would have been appropriate for the museum soiree I'd attended a few nights back. And, sure enough, she wore the sign of the *vesica piscis* on a beaded chain around her neck.

"Circle to circle," I said softly, upon our meeting.

"Never an end," she greeted—the correct response—and extended her hand to shake mine. A small blue cross, tattooed inside her wrist, peeked out from beneath the sleeve of her dress. "I'm pleased to meet you, Professor Sanger," she said warmly, her accent exotic but her English impeccable. "Or should I call you Doctor?"

"Neither, please," I insisted, trying to hide my surprise at her appearance and poise. She was, after all, a Grailkeeper. "I'm only a postdoc, it takes a while to earn tenure. And *doctor* still makes me think of medical professionals."

"As a medical professional, I appreciate your modesty."

Now I stared. "You're…?"

"Dr. Rachid," she confirmed, gesturing us into a luxurious parlor. "As was my mother before me—and *her* mother was a midwife. There are still some of us on this side of the world, Mrs. Sanger."

Missus? Oh…the ring.

"Maggi is fine. I didn't mean offense."

"Of course not." Gracefully, she managed to seat us before settling onto a sofa herself. She kept her knees together, her ankles crossed. Her posture was excellent. "My career is admittedly less common here than in the West. But even the Muslim women can practice as doctors."

The…? "You're not Muslim?"

"I'm a Copt," she clarified, extending her wrist again so that I need not sneak a peek at the tattoo I'd only glimpsed before. Definitely a cross. "Coptic Christian."

Hello. While Christianity in Rome wasn't sanctioned until the fourth century, it had flourished in Egypt from its very beginning—yet another reason that we'd passed the first monastery. Early writings such as the Gnostic Gospels had also been recovered here.

Rhys said, "The Copts, though a minority now, are the Egyptians who can most directly trace their lineage back to the Pharaohs." Like Cleopatra?

"And to priestesses of Isis?" I guessed, with a shiver of comprehension. "That's how you can help us find her chalice."

Most of the Grailkeepers I'd met, myself included, had learned special nursery rhymes as children. Those rhymes held within them the riddle to where their mothers' mothers' mothers had hidden their ancestral grails. Maybe it was the dry heat, or the faint scent of tropical flowers in the air, but I could easily imagine this woman's ancestors protecting holy relics in the court of Pharaohs.

"Precisely," said Dr. Rachid. "The truth of the cup's location has been in my family for centuries."

"Then the divers are looking in the right place?"

She nodded, but her smile was mysterious. "One could say that. But before I share what I know...I'm afraid I must ask you for some assistance."

I looked at Rhys, whose brows furrowed. "You said you wanted to meet her," he protested. "You didn't say anything about favors."

"I apologize, but I had to make certain she is as competent as you told me." Dr. Rachid nodded, seemingly to herself. "And clearly she is."

My throat didn't tighten with any premonition of danger, but my bullshit meter was sure in the red. "How could you possibly tell my level of competence just by shaking...my...?"

Oh. *My hand.* Whatever force the Melusine Grail had imbued me with, Dr. Rachid seemed to have sensed it.

I probably should have asked if she, like Munira at the bazaar, thought I was some kind of champion—but damned if I could force the question out. It was too overwhelming an idea, way too big a responsibility to handle while jet-lagged. Instead, if only to avoid that particular elephant in the corner, I asked, "What kind of assistance?"

"Ah." She ignored me to stand as her maid showed another woman, holding a notebook, into the room. "Jane. I'm so pleased you're here."

"Tala." If the woman's red hair, spattering of freckles, and blue jeans hadn't given her away as a Westerner, the blunt edge of her East-London accent would have. I guessed her to be about my age, maybe a little older. "Father Pritchard, it's good to see you again."

I arched a look at Rhys. *Father* Pritchard? And here I thought he'd stopped practicing.

"I've been volunteering as a counselor when I have

time off," he explained, low. "I do have training, because of my previous work, and…"

And old habits were hard to break—especially habits one should keep, like helping others. I could get that, and tried to tell him with my smile that I understood.

In the meantime, Jane was asking, "Tala, where's Kara?"

"She will be down shortly," insisted our hostess. "Jane, this is Father Pritchard's friend, Magdalene Sanger. The one I told you about? Mrs. Sanger, this is my daughter-in-law, Jane Fletcher."

"It really is *Ms.* Sanger." I offered my hand. "Or just Maggie. The ring is a bluff."

"And I'm an *ex*-daughter-in-law," Jane corrected, though her grip on my hand was friendly enough.

"My ex-*step*daughter-in-law," clarified Dr. Rachid, just to confuse matters more. "It is on her behalf that I request your assistance."

Rhys frowned. "Dr. Rachid, Jane, I understand how desperate you are, but this is hardly fair to Maggi. This is a…a…"

"A bait and switch?" I suggested. "You get me here by promising the secret of the Isis Grail, then demand that I earn it first?"

"Please, call me Tala." Our hostess's dark eyes showed no contrition at all. "And is not the secret of the Isis Grail worth earning?"

Intellectually, I knew the drill—how many of the heroes in myths and fairy tales first have to prove themselves in a series of trials before they get rewarded with the golden apple, the kingdom or true love? But in reality…

In reality, my head was swimming. I'd never set out

to be a hero. I just wanted to collect the goddess chalices before the Comitatus could destroy them.

And yet…. Damn it. From either curiosity or kindness—or both—I couldn't ignore the pain in Jane Fletcher's eyes, either.

"It couldn't hurt to tell me what's going on," I said, slowly. Reluctantly, even.

Dr. Rachid—*Tala's*—smile was, as ever, gracious. Jane raised a fist to her mouth in a failed attempt to smother a hopeful, desperate laugh of relief. But it was Rhys, blue eyes more solemn than usual, who worried me.

And I'd thought I was in over my head when I fell into the Alexandrian harbor!

"Have you ever fallen in love with the wrong man?" asked Jane.

The only man I'd ever loved, besides my father, had been living a secret life the whole time. The only man who'd come close to distracting me from him was sitting right here—and he was a priest. I chose to say nothing and just looked interested.

"I did," she assured me, opening her notebook. The first page showed a color copy of a wedding photo. "Him."

I looked. *"Sinbad!"*

"What?" Rhys looked, as well. "You are right, Maggi. It's the man from the airport."

Airport, hell. "And the bazaar!"

He looked at the other ladies. "This is Hani Rachid?"

Tala and Jane exchanged worried looks. Then Jane proceeded with her tale, flipping to more photocopied pictures and then newspaper clippings as if to prove her truthfulness.

She'd been working as a flight attendant. Hani Rachid had attended college at Oxford, the epitome of tall, dark and exotically handsome. Even now, Jane's gaze softened as she described their courtship. "He was wealthy, and protective. He showered me with gifts and compliments. And he was such the gentleman. He waited until we were married before he would... well..." A small frown marred the bridge of her nose. "I think my virginity meant more to him than ever it had to me. He later told me that if I hadn't been pure on our wedding night, he would have killed me. I laughed at the time, but..."

He wasn't the man she'd thought she'd married, at all.

Relieved of the need to win her, Hani had become dominating and chauvinistic. His disdain for the law became increasingly apparent. Not long after the birth of their daughter, Kara—that picture, of course, was adorable—their marriage imploded. Jane divorced him and, because he threw such a public fit of temper over that, she got custody. Infuriated that he could only have supervised visits, Hani moved back to Egypt.

"He visited Kara twice a year, and he did quite the job at controlling his resentment, but I could tell he hated being monitored with her. And then—" Here Jane hesitated, desperation darkening her eyes. "Then, a year ago, I got called onto a flight while he was visiting. My father thought there would be nothing wrong with letting Hani take Kara out for ice cream...but they never came back. Of course my parents were frantic. The first thing I did, when I found out, was call the airlines..."

I had the strangest feeling I'd heard this story before—probably because she wasn't the first person it had ever happened to.

"He'd taken her home with him," Jane said, voice breaking. "She was only eleven years old, and he stole her away to Egypt—and nobody in this godforsaken country will give her back!"

A human interest article, including pictures of a too young looking Kara, and copies of letters to and from different officials confirmed this.

"Egypt's laws do not allow a child to leave the country without her father's permission," Tala explained simply, when Jane's voice deserted her. "Unless my stepson signs papers—but of course, he will not sign. He has become increasingly angry, increasingly rebellious. His business activities..." But she shook her head.

Unsure what else to do, I took one of Jane's trembling hands in mine.

She inhaled deeply, strengthened either by the goddess energy or just the caring, then raised her face and continued. "At least tradition frowns upon Kara living with Hani, as long as he remains unmarried that is. She lives with Tala, and I spend as much time here as I can afford, more than he does! But it's not the same as having her home, and I'm afraid..."

Whatever she was afraid of, she couldn't make herself put it in words.

"After the divorce," Tala said, "my stepson became involved with other men urging the return of old-world values. Particularly the domination of women. He is not," she clarified, "a Copt."

As if any particular religion wholly prevented male domination.

Jane turned to a newspaper article in Arabic—I recognized only her picture. "I tried to smuggle her onto a ship, to get her out of the country, but I suppose he'd been watching for me to do it. He has contacts everywhere. Suddenly the police were there, and they dragged Kara out of my arms and arrested me, and she was screaming…" Jane shuddered and squeezed my hand, as if for strength. "Egyptian jail was horrible! I'm still surprised Hani dropped the charges. I could be in prison right now."

"It would have been even more of a scandal," Tala explained, "for a man to need the law to control his wife."

Jane's chin came up. "*Ex*—wife."

"Especially a man who has so little respect for the law, unless he is using it to his own ends," Tala continued, which wasn't encouraging.

"Anyway," said Jane, "that's how I met Father Pritchard. I needed someone to talk to, someone who bloody well spoke English, and he was volunteering as a counselor at a clinic here, on his off time."

"When she learned I was working with the divers, looking for the Temple of Isis, she mentioned the possibility of finding a goddess cup," explained Rhys. "Of course I was interested, so on her next visit she brought Dr. Rachid—"

"Tala," insisted our hostess. "And I must take full responsibility for bringing you into this, Maggi. When I hesitated to tell Father Pritchard my ancestral secrets, he suggested that I might be more comfortable confiding in another woman. He spoke so highly of you that… Well…there had been rumors."

Okay, coward or not, I couldn't ignore that. "Rumors of what? About *me?*"

Rhys looked as honestly confused as I felt.

Tala motioned to a maid, who'd waited quietly in the corner, and the young woman immediately left. "Rumors that the time has come, my dear. That the goddess chalices are calling out to be found—and that a champion has been chosen to do just that."

There was that word again! "Chosen by whom? Assuming there were such a rumor—and I never heard anything about it until I got to Egypt—why would you think I'm that champion?"

I couldn't keep the incredulity out of my voice. Wouldn't I have been notified about something this important?

Tala's composure did not waver. "Because, Magdalene Sanger, you are the one who answered the call."

Before, that had only been because armed men had broken into mine and my aunt's offices! Only because it was our own family's grail they'd been after. And now, only because Rhys had a lead—and because someone had gone after him. Nobody goes after my friends. Unless...

What if that had been someone's ploy to get me here?

"Look," I said, perhaps more abruptly than was polite. "I'm very sorry for your troubles, Jane, and I hope that you and your...your former stepmother-in-law are able to resolve them. But the fact that I've found one single, solitary grail hardly makes me someone who can help you. I'm neither British nor Egyptian. I don't have an ounce of legal or diplomatic experience. I'm a professor of comparative mythology, not a soldier of fortune!"

"Yes, but—" In the midst of her protest, Jane stopped and brightened. "Kara!"

"Mama!" exclaimed a high voice—and a little girl in a white dress launched herself across the room and into her mother's waiting arms. Kara Rachid was small for a twelve-year-old, even smaller than she'd looked in her pictures. She had olive skin, curling black hair, and huge dark eyes that reminded me of a puppy's. Her skinny arms held her mother tightly. "When did you get to Alexandria? How long can you stay, this time?"

In the meantime, the maid had reappeared with a tray of ornate cups that reminded me of Greek kylix, though they were of course smaller than those standard offering vessels. They had wide, shallow bowls with a handle on either side, set on a narrow base. They fit this fine house, I thought, as much as I was willing to notice. They fit this woman.

The maid lay the tray on a cocktail table, and Tala brought the drinks to us. "Touching, is it not?"

I scowled. "This is manipulation."

"I loved my husband dearly," she said, her voice low beneath Kara and Jane's happy reunion. "And I love my granddaughter. But I do not trust my bully of a stepson. Rescue Kara, Magdalene Sanger, and I will help you find the chalice of Isis. Refuse…"

She left the rest of the threat unspoken—but pointedly clear.

"I don't appreciate ultimatums," I warned, taking the cup she offered only to soften what I meant to say next.

She raised her eyebrows, unperturbed. "Who among us does?"

Annoyed, I took a sip of the wine—delicious.

But the next thing I knew, I was lying on some kind of rough wooden flooring, surrounded by absolute, echoing darkness.

Chapter 6

Had Tala drugged *me?*

Not just me.

"Rhys!" I shouted—or tried. Turns out there was cloth tied across my mouth. I inhaled deeply through my nose, smelling damp, musty air. It proved that I was at least alive. I also wore a blindfold. My hands were tied behind my back.

And somebody nearby was arguing. In Arabic.

Lie still, I thought, carefully testing my wrists against the strength of the fabric that bound them. Let them think you're still out.

But footsteps sounded, hollow on some kind of wooden planking. My aborted shout must have gotten their attention.

"Tsk tsk, Mrs. Sanger." I thought I knew that voice— deep and cultured and tinged with a British accent. "Have you been feigning all this time?"

Mrs. Sanger?

Then I remembered the damned ring I got from Lex. I should have left it at the hotel…or at least in my passport case.

Hands sat me up—my feet, at least, weren't tied—and tugged at the gag, pulling my hair. From his voice, at least four feet away and above me, I knew the hands didn't belong to the speaker. "My men assure me they did nothing to render you unconscious."

They didn't have to, if Tala had. "Where's Rhys?"

"His safety depends on your cooperation."

Instead of taking my cue—*cooperation with what?*—I took a fairly large chance. I had to find Rhys. "We might as well ditch the blindfold, too. I already know your face, don't I?"

He laughed and said something else in Arabic. Hands pulled at the second knot behind my head—wrenching my neck slightly and taking more hair—and cloth fell away from my eyes.

Where the hell were we? It was almost as dark as when I'd worn the blindfold. Underground dark. Hugely dark. For a crazy moment I thought—*a pyramid?*

But I'd never heard of a pyramid in Alexandria…and I doubted one could be this roomy. Two swarthy men beamed flashlights into my face. But even squinting against yellow light, I recognized the man in the business suit, standing before me. It was Sinbad. From the airport. From the bazaar.

Hani Rachid.

He still had an Eye-of-Horus design painted on his cheek.

And he had at least four people with him I could only

call henchmen. The implications didn't escape me. It looked like Hani Rachid was some sort of crime lord.

"Imshee," I told him, using his own word for *piss off.*

Again, I tugged at the bindings on my wrists. I thought I felt them give, just a little.

He laughed. "Your husband may be a weakling and a fool, allowing such disrespect. I am neither. You will stay away from my family or suffer the consequences, you and this false priest."

Only when he pivoted and kicked did I see Rhys lying, blindfolded and bound, in the shadows near Rachid's feet. My friend's gag didn't fully muffle his cry at the kick.

I feared it wasn't the first. "Leave him alone!"

"Do not presume to order me about."

"And you wonder why your marriage crashed and burned? If I were Jane, I would have left you, too."

His eyes narrowed, and he took a furious step forward. Good—closer to me was farther from Rhys. But when I merely glared upward, refusing to flinch, he stopped himself—then turned and swung a vicious foot into Rhys's ribs.

Rhys rolled back with a grunt. Another of Rachid's men darted quickly behind him and kicked him from that direction.

Somewhere far below and beyond Rhys, I heard pebbles plop into water, as if the wooden plank we gathered on was some kind of platform. The echo was incredible. Even more incredible was a glimpse I got, when one of the henchmen briefly flashed his light across shadowy pillars and arches.

Colonnades. Definitely too roomy to be a pyramid. *So where the hell were we?*

Wherever we were, it was time to leave.

With a tiny lurch, I wriggled my hands free of their ties. Now all I needed was to watch for my chance.

Five men, total. Not good odds. But if they kicked Rhys again…

"This is your only warning, witch," insisted Rachid. Again with the *witch!* "You and Tala may think you are powerful, but I know ancient secrets, as well. Leave Egypt while you can, or suffer the consequences. As an example—"

To my horror, he turned back to Rhys. "This man pretends to be a priest, in order to insinuate himself with my wife. That was a deadly mistake."

"He *is* a priest," I protested, before Hani could kick him again. My words echoed back at me from who-knew-where. I usually didn't think of Rhys that way— it sure made me feel guiltier about how attractive I found him—but it was the truth. He'd petitioned to leave his clerical duties in order to marry, a petition that was tragically granted a few days after his fiancée died. But technically… "I swear he is."

"This does not excuse his familiarity with my wife."

"Your *ex*-wife. He *counseled* her." But I might as well have been arguing in a cone of silence, for all that Hani listened to me. He drew back his foot to kick my helpless friend—and I had to risk it.

I surged to my feet, stumbling slightly as circulation returned to my blood-deprived legs. Plank flooring bowed under my shifting weight—if this was a plat-form, it was a cheap one. I showed my freed hands. "I said, leave him alone."

Then I bent my knees slightly, centering my balance the way I would at the start of any tai chi exercise. Tonight, however, I meant to incorporate less well-known, combative aspects of the normally gentle art.

Several of Hani's helpers backed away, saying something in Arabic. Hani snapped back at them in the same language, then said to me, "They think this is part of your magic. I think they simply did not tie you well."

At least he wasn't hurting Rhys. "Who says I *need* magic?"

He swung—and I easily dodged the blow. When he stepped forward, I stepped back, leading him even farther from my friend. Scowling, in the darkness, Hani swung again.

Again I ducked. Once I got him far enough from Rhys, I would use the force he was putting into his punches against him, perhaps throw him across this plywood flooring, hopefully frighten the others into running. But for now...

Suddenly, unnervingly, Hani grinned—and surged forward with another punch. Again I ducked and backed from it—and stumbled off the edge of the plywood, onto crumbling rock.

And nothingness.

I went completely still, balanced on the one foot that still had purchase.

The platform seemed to stretch between rock braces, over who-knew-what kind of drop. The space beyond Rhys wasn't the only edge.

Only my tai chi stance, honed after years of practice, kept me from falling into the surprise abyss. More pebbles plopped into water, far below.

Where the hell were we?

Even now, with at least three flashlight beams in my face, my perch was precarious at best. All my weight and balance rested, for a moment, on the ball of one sandaled foot, braced on old, crumbling stone.

Hani's smile widened. "You will need all your magic," he warned. "If you defy *me*. Now fly."

There was too much of him and nowhere to duck, nowhere to leap. Like a schoolyard bully, he simply pushed me.

And for the second time that day, I found myself plummeting backward in freefall, skirts wrapping my legs. But this time, I didn't even know what I was falling to.

It was a void.

For a moment, I felt sheer terror.

When the black surface met me, I hit in a splashing backflop. Darkness and water swallowed me. Not a second later, I impacted a stone bottom that may well have killed me if not for that few feet cushion of water. As it was, I couldn't hold back a grunt of pain and, worse, the inhale that had to follow it.

I surged up, clawing, panicked—and stood in waist-deep water and blind nothingness. I thought I saw the yellow of flashlight beams to one side, but then even they were gone, and I was too overwhelmed to look closer.

I was choking so hard that my back and neck hurt, so hard that I was almost doubled over. Air dragged into my lungs and I gagged out more water, spitting, gasping. Eventually I could breathe again. Eventually I could hear above my own coughing, rasping inhalations.

That's when I heard Rhys's muffled shouts, far above me. I couldn't understand any of it at first, except that he was still gagged and apparently desperate.

"Rhys!" I called back.

My voice echoed in the sudden silence with that unique, brittle texture that bounces off underground water. Great. Like I hadn't had enough submerged caves in my life—and the absolute, pressing thickness of the black that surrounded me was *definitely* like being in a cave. Except…

I remembered colonnades. The water that I'd choked on wasn't salty or, thank heavens, sewage. In fact, it tasted remarkably benign. So where the hell—

"Rhys?"

His muffled return had two syllables with a *g* in the center…even a gag lets you make *g*'s. I realized it was my name. Then more garbled syllables, ending with "kuh?"

As in, *okay?*

"I'm fine," I called. "There's water down here. It broke my fall."

I thought I heard a rush of relieved breath, though I may have imagined that part.

"How are you?" I asked. My concern echoed hauntingly back at me. *Ooo? Ooo?*

I didn't like that he said nothing. They'd kicked him pretty hard and, considering that Hani seemed to have been jealous, they hadn't been playing nice. Rhys could have broken ribs, internal injuries. "Rhys?"

No way could I understand his muffled response, but at least he was conscious.

"I'm going to try to call for help," I announced, hoping the leather of my fanny pack had protected my phone enough that it would work. Wet. Underground. Okay, so it was a long shot but, if nothing else, I wanted the comfort of the lit display in this thick, suffocating blackness.

I still cursed, loudly, when I realized the phone was gone. So was my change purse. "Son of a bitch!"

Rhys's next muffled noise was inquiring.

"That son of a bitch Hani stole my cell phone. *And* the cash I had on me." I patted my chest and sighed in relief. "At least he didn't take my passport, but still..."

Oh, no! In the darkness, I clapped my right hand over my left—and sagged in relief to sense the ring still there. I might well resent it...but that didn't mean I wanted to lose the damned thing.

Rhys's response was a single grunt, like *Oh*.

"I'm going to try to find a side to this...this wherever I am. Maybe I can climb back up to where you are."

Being blind sucks. Heaven only knew what I was wading through as I headed in the general direction that I'd heard Rhys, but when I called again, his return noise sounded farther away. I realized by my own echo that I was apparently under something and had to backtrack. Through an extended call-and-response exercise, like a deadly serious game of Marco Polo, I finally bumped into what felt like a column. It seemed to have enough pits and cracks in its stone face for me to tentatively climb.

I tied my wet skirt up around my waist and started up, scrubbing my open hand across a curve of unseen rock for every grip, not allowing myself to imagine what kind of dirt I felt, gritty, under my palm. I was about ten feet up when one sandaled foot slipped off its supposed toehold, and I plummeted backward. *Stupid stupid stupid.*

Again I splashed, submerged—and had to, with Rhys's help, start over. This time I took off my sandals, too, stowing them in my open fanny pack. I concentrated on Rhys as I climbed, groping blindly for each finger hold, sliding the sole of each foot across curved, unseen rock for each toehold. He was still tied, and probably injured. He needed me to do this, damn it.

My legs and arms trembled from the strain. At times like this, I wished I *were* magic.

Higher…had I gone fifteen feet? Twenty? Higher… "Rhys?"

His response sounded comfortingly nearby, just over my head…and sure enough, my reaching hand slid over the edge of the drop-off from which I'd fallen.

I grasped crumbling rock and then the edge of thick plywood. I said a little prayer to Isis and whoever else could help me past this last precarious maneuver, and used the leverage of my feet to drag myself over the edge.

I only allowed myself a moment to flop wetly onto the planking that had welcomed me back to consciousness, panting. Then I pushed up onto my knees. "Rhys!"

He responded with three weary syllables. Probably, "Over here."

I crawled in that direction and—blessedly—my hand reached warm, dry flesh. Yes!

Except that he couldn't swallow back his groan from my touch. He *was* hurt! I tried to be as gentle as possible as I felt down the length of one long, corded arm to where his wrists were bound. The knots fought me; I finally had to lean across him, trying not to put too much weight on him, and bite the damned material to start it ripping. He felt so solid under me, and I felt so wet. And then—

Free. He accidentally hit me on the head as he raised his hands to his blindfold and gag. I felt my way down his legs to untie his ankles.

"Oh, thank heavens," gasped Rhys on stuttering breaths as I struggled with that knot. "Oh, Maggi."

"I'm here." I reached my hands in his direction, and they collided with his, and then he was pulling me down on top of him, despite his own gasp of pain.

His pain was the only thing that could possibly have kept me from throwing myself wholeheartedly into that embrace. Instead I said, "You're hurt!"

"You aren't." The words squeezed out of him like a prayer of gratitude.

"*How* hurt?"

"I am not sure…." He had to stop to catch his breath, which was in itself telling. "I doubt I can walk."

Crap, crap, crap. This could mean trying to find my way out of wherever this was in the pitch dark, alone, to get help. Which would mean leaving him behind. Which I didn't want to do.

Just because Hani Rachid and his men seemed to have left didn't mean they wouldn't come back at any time.

"Where are you hurt?" I asked.

"Ribs." The Welsh rarely speak in fragments, which also worried me. "Mostly."

"Hold still." And I began to unbutton his shirt. Thank goodness he'd changed for dinner, or I might be trying to pull a T-shirt off over his head without hurting him, which I suspect is almost impossible in these situations.

Instead, I tried not to think of how intimate an act it was, unbuttoning a man's shirt, my knuckles sliding lightly along the material of it, my fingers fumbling from more than having scraped them in the climb.

I told myself that Rhys was breathing heavily from pain, nothing else.

Once I drew his shirt open, by feel alone, I ran my hands over his bare, furry chest. His breathing deepened further. So did mine. It was hard not to remember what an attractive man Rhys is.

Then my hands felt across a lump that made him gulp. I have no more medical training than standard first-aid courses, but I was pretty certain this was a broken rib…and likely not the only one.

Crap!

"What we need is a light," I muttered, tugging my wet sandals out of my fanny pack to hunt for the matchbook. It, too, was soaked. "Damn. My matches aren't any good."

"Try…" Rhys struggled for a deep breath "…my pocket. Right. Rear."

Well that was closer than we'd meant to get…. I'd kind of hoped that if our relationship ever progressed to my groping his butt, it would be for better reasons. But I managed to slide a dry matchbook out of his back pocket, all the same. Then I began to feel across the pebbles around my knees, hunting for the bindings we'd discarded. If only I had something to—

"Handkerchief," Rhys suggested. "Front left."

It wouldn't burn for long, but for now it was all we had. By feel, I tied his handkerchief into several knots, to slow down the burning. Then I lit a match, compliments of the "Hotle Athens," and examined his chest and ribs.

Holy…

If it weren't for the already darkening bruises, Rhys would have one hell of a fine chest, lean, partially covered with black hair. But it was horribly bruised, and unnaturally lumpy in a couple of places, and I wouldn't have light for long.

"Maybe we can turn your shirt into bandages," I murmured, sliding my hand back over the bump I'd found before…but to my relief, now that light was on it, the injury didn't seem quite so severe. Perhaps it was just swollen?

Rhys caught his breath, eyes bright in the light of our makeshift torch—bright, and focused on me. But he said nothing.

Now, the burning light hanging from my left hand, I ran my right hand over his other ribs, ascertaining that each was where it should be. I slid my palm around behind him; several times fear made me think I'd found something worse, but each time the warmth of my seeking hand reconciled his health with my hopes.

I drew my hand across his warm, dry skin beneath the ribs now, down over his tight abdomen, down to the waistband of his trousers.

His breathing deepened.

I tried to ask a question—but it only croaked out of me. I had to swallow before asking, "Any other…injuries?"

"They did not Abelard me, if that's what you mean. Though God knows what would have happened if you'd not been here." Abelard was a medieval churchman, one of a famous pair of lovers, who'd been castrated by his beloved's uncle.

I smiled, pleased by both the joke and the way Rhys's voice was gaining strength. In fact—

To my surprise, he sat up.

"Careful!" I insisted.

"I shall be. But, Maggi, I do feel somewhat better than I'd feared." He ran his own hands over his ribs—gingerly, since *better* by no means meant *well*. "You've a healing touch."

Or maybe he'd just been suckering me into feeling him up…but with Rhys, I sincerely doubted it. "Or maybe with that gag off, you've been able to catch your breath?"

"Or that. Maggi—"

He spoke with a sudden intensity that matched his expression. Maybe he would kiss me. Maybe I wouldn't protest, even though I should, since I was officially dating Lex, especially since Rhys knew it. And yet—

A pain in my fingertips distracted me—and Rhys, eyes widening, knocked the remains of our makeshift torch out of my hand. It went out on the board, leaving us in darkness again.

"We, er, still have my shirt," Rhys suggested, moment gone. "But ought we not have a plan first, before we use up that resource?"

"Good point." My words were muffled around my slightly burnt fingers. "It would help if we knew how we got here in the first place."

"They carried us," said Rhys, matter-of-fact. "But being blindfolded, that's no great help."

"What?"

"They burst into Tala's house and dragged us away, right in front of the little girl. But you know that."

"I don't know that. I thought Tala had drugged both of us."

"Drugged? Neither of us was drugged."

"Of course we were drugged. The last thing I did before I lost consciousness was take a sip of the wine Tala offered us."

Silence and darkness pushed in around us.

Then Rhys said, "Maggi, you were conscious until after Mr. Rachid and his men attacked us."

So why didn't I remember?

Chapter 7

According to Rhys, I'd gotten quiet after my first or second sip of Tala's wine. At the time, he'd chalked that up to my annoyance with the Coptic Grailkeeper.

Then I'd touched my throat and said, "Someone's here."

Just before Hani and his men burst in.

"I don't remember that," I insisted—if this hadn't been Rhys, I might have suspected him of lying. "I don't remember any of it."

"Perhaps you hit your head while they carried us here. That would explain a great deal." Rhys found my shoulder in the dark, and squeezed it gently. "Let's focus for now on finding our way out."

"It would help if we knew where *here* was."

"Actually, I suspect I know. These seem to be the cisterns of ancient Alexandria. *A* cistern, in any case."

He told me more as we put together a makeshift torch, harvesting his socks to burn first. Apparently, Alexandria was honeycombed with a series of fresh-water cisterns, created at the time of the city's foundation by its namesake, Alexander the Great, in 300 B.C.

"This cistern is clearly more recent," Rhys mused, holding up the sputtering torch we'd MacGyvered together from one of his socks wrapped around the top of one of my sandals. The uneven glimpses of columns and vaults that arched into the pressing darkness around us, at least two levels above and one level below to the reflective water, were hauntingly beautiful…and damned eerie. "Ninth century, I'd imagine."

"A thousand years and change," I murmured—then deliberately forced my attention back to the precarious issue of our footing. Even barefooted, I wasn't wholly sure of my balance, much less his. Despite that we were heading where I'd thought the lights had vanished, most of the stone braces we had to traverse, barely two feet wide, didn't have wood over them—and they were crumbling remains of their former glory. "Is that all?"

"They are positively modern, by Egyptian standards," agreed Rhys. "Look—you can tell they used ancient capitals for their pillars. Some of them are upside-down."

I reached back and caught his long hand, only partly to make sure that, in his inspection of this incredible structure, he didn't plummet off an archway. The water below us was way too shallow to risk falling into it from this height. I'd been lucky. If I had landed feet first, I'd probably have broken my ankles. And if I'd landed *head*first…

But I hadn't.

Rhys squeezed my hand. But all he said was, "I know some archeologists who have been trying to map the cisterns for some time, now. We must take note of where we emerge, so we can direct them back to this one."

If we emerged. But I wasn't about to give up. And okay, Hani Rachid wouldn't have bothered with his warnings, if he'd expected us to die down here.

I still felt sharp relief when we found a broken-down stone staircase pretty much where Rhys had hoped we would. Our torch had burned through the rest of our socks and started on a sleeve, torn from his shirt, by the time we reached a more modern passageway of cement, lined with concrete benches.

"It's a bomb shelter," Rhys explained. "From World War II. We must be getting close. Look—there's a ladder."

Our emergence out of a manhole cover into a dusty alley, near an outdoor café where men were smoking hookah pipes, would have garnered us stares even if Rhys *wasn't* missing one sleeve of his shirt. As it was, we smiled, waved and hailed a cab as quickly as possible.

We both exhaled twin sighs of relief as the taxi pulled back onto the street, toward the Hotel Athens.

Then Rhys surprised me. "I am sorry."

"You? What for?"

"Hani seems to believe I've behaved inappropriately with his wife—yes, his ex-wife, I know," he clarified, when I opened my mouth to argue. "I haven't, of course, not by Western standards. But here, the mere fact that I dined with them may be thorough enough insult."

"It wasn't just jealousy," I assured him. "I'm the one he challenged to a duel in the Khan el-Khalili, remember? I'm the one who he keeps calling a witch."

"I'm the one who brought you here in the first place."

I looked at him beside me, on the duct-taped, vinyl bench seat of the cab. He appeared downright tormented, his blue eyes shiny in the shadows, his jaw tight, his sleeve missing.

I grinned and kissed his cheek. "And thank you for that."

The driver, scowling at us in his rearview mirror, scolded us loudly—all I understood of it was *"La'!"*

We ignored him. "For what?" asked Rhys. "For getting you attacked and abducted?"

"For bringing me back to my quest." I found his hand, squeezed it. "For giving me the chance to find the Isis Grail. *If* Tala can be trusted."

Tala was waiting for us in the lobby of our unassuming hotel. When she saw us, her eyes closed in her pale face, and her lips moved in what seemed to be a prayer of gratitude. Several policemen awaited us, as well, and my first assumption was that she'd called them to report our kidnapping.

I'd assumed wrong, which I discovered when the hotel manager and the white-haired director of the project swooped down on us, as did my roommate, Eleni.

My *former* roommate, as it turned out. The fact that our room had been ransacked during my absence had persuaded her that I was too high-maintenance. Either I changed rooms, she insisted in accented French, or she did.

The turmoil following that announcement was too much for me to track, much less describe. Bypassing the antique cage elevator as too unreliable, I rushed up all three flights to my room, leaving Rhys to debrief Tala. There I did a thorough accounting of my belongings.

The manager stood over me, alternating between apology and suspicion, while I unpacked everything onto my bed's worn chenille spread to do inventory. Extra traveler's checks, still there. Clothes, still there. Toiletries, still there. Sword under pillow—I checked that one surreptitiously—there.

Then I moved on to the next piece of luggage.

Laptop—gone. The case we'd been so careful not to leave in the car now held little more than a guide to Egypt and a scattering of pens, pencils, highlighters....

And a strange little metal thing I'd never seen before.

With a shout, one of the police officers scooped up the tracking device and began asking questions I couldn't begin to translate, much less answer.

Still kneeling on the scuffed linoleum beside the bed, stomach sinking, I thought: *Lex.*

It hadn't been in the ring, after all.

Damn!

The last time my belongings were bugged, it had been Lex's doing. I still hadn't fully recovered from that particular betrayal—which is probably why I jumped to that conclusion now. Even when the hotel manager repeated the authorities' questions to me in halting English, I said only, "I don't know. I don't know where it came from."

Now I was lying to the police for him, the bastard.

My eyes burned with an unwelcome threat of tears. I hadn't slept since arriving in Egypt, and I wasn't sure I'd eaten anything, either. My clothes felt sticky and dirty, except the parts that had dried stiff. My bare feet were sore and filthy. My laptop and mobile phone were gone. And now...

Behind me, Eleni's shrill insistence that she be found

a different roommate escalated. When d'Alencon reminded her that there were few empty beds left, she stalked off to find somebody, anybody, willing to switch. That was all in French. The police and the manager discussed the tracking device in rapid Arabic—I couldn't understand their words, but the intensity with which they bent over the gadget was unmistakable.

When Rhys arrived in the doorway, without Tala, he swore in Welsh at the sight in front of him. *"Uffach cols."*

"It's a tracking device," I told him, not bothering to stand. Champion schmampion—I was exhausted. Good thing Eleni was willing to switch rooms, because it would take dynamite to blast me out of this one. *"Someone* put it in my laptop case."

I assumed he would understand whom I meant by *someone*—someone rich, powerful, handsome, involved with a goddess-hating secret society, and determined to protect me against my will. Someone with the initials Alexander freaking Stuart. Rhys had been involved in my last grail quest, after all. He knew the story.

But instead of leaping to the same conclusion I had, he said, "The airport."

I blinked up at him not, well, *tracking.*

"When those men surrounded us at the airport," he reminded me—and of course he was right. We'd been pushed, pulled and prodded. Any one of them could have slipped a tracking device into my case, far more easily than I could have gotten that same case through airport security if I'd had the device in New York.

More to the point, Hani had shown up at both the airport and at the bazaar.

I'd been wrong. It wasn't Lex?

Now I wanted to cry for a different reason.

"You explain to them?" I asked, and rested my face in the bedspread, emotionally drained. *It hadn't been Lex.*

But I'd sure been quick to assume it was.

To my undying gratitude, Rhys did as I asked. The police officers seemed more comfortable speaking to a man, anyway. I only looked wearily up after I heard Rhys name Hani Rachid, at which point I saw the two officers exchange knowing looks.

"How do you know Hani Rachid?" I demanded.

But they said things in Arabic in tones suspiciously like *Don't worry your pretty little head.* I could pursue that at another time. A person could only take so much.

Then Catrina Dauvergne appeared in my doorway, suitcase in hand. "*Bonjour,* roommate," she said, with an evil smile.

I turned my face back into the bedspread.

I've stayed in more comfortable hotel rooms. The linoleum floor of this one was cracked, the mattress was lumpy and the occasional burst of light from outside the window whenever a trolley passed, accompanied by the sizzle of electrical sparks, was hardly soothing.

But I've slept in worse, too.

What kept me awake that night wasn't my room, but my roommate. I've never shared a space with someone I trusted less.

Not even Lex, at our worst.

After everyone else had gone, even Rhys, I made an effort at closing my eyes and getting some of that sleep I so desperately needed. To say this had been a full day was an understatement. But my awareness of Catrina moving around the room, rubbing lotion onto her arms and hands, combing out her hair, kept me awake. When I heard her bedsprings squeak as she climbed in, and then heard the spurt of a match and smelled cigarette smoke, I'd had it.

I opened my eyes to the lamplight. "What the hell are you doing?"

She arched one Gallic brow at me, eyes particularly catty behind a pair of narrow reading glasses, and lifted the paperback novel she held in one hand. The hand not holding the cigarette. Then she went back to reading.

Like I'd leave it at that. "Why did you agree to switch rooms with Eleni?"

She sighed and put the book down. "The poor woman was terrified."

Like she was such a humanitarian.

"But you're not. Why? Is it because you already know who broke into my room?"

She rolled her eyes, which I took as a claim that she did not.

"Then why?"

"I am not afraid," she admitted, on a wisp of smoke, "because I assume that whoever broke in either found what they wished or learned it was not here. This, and I do not frighten easily."

As someone who didn't frighten easily either, I believed that. But— "Then why move in with me?"

Her eyes widened in poorly feigned innocence. *"Pourquoi pas?"* Why not?

"Because we hate each other's guts?" I suggested.

"Mon Dieu, such hyperbole. I do not hate you." Catrina took another long draw on her cigarette, then narrowed her eyes. "I just dislike you very, very much."

"Why is that?" Since I wasn't sleeping anyway, I sat up. "Yes, sure, you think I had something to do with the destruction of the abbey, but even if I did—which I didn't—it wasn't personal. It wasn't *your* abbey."

The image of Cat as a nun, despite the fact that she wore an incongruous Mary medal, was so ridiculous, we both blinked dumbly at one another for a moment. Then the sparks from a trolley outside our window helped me regain my senses.

"On the other hand," I continued, "I brought you the Melusine Chalice in good faith, and you turned around and sold it on the black market. It was *my* chalice, my family's in any case. I'd risked my life to rescue it. *That* was personal. And yet you act as if I...*I*..."

I couldn't think of anything personal to compare it to, but Catrina provided an example on her own.

"As if you stole my tapestry?"

At the time I'd met her, she'd been pretty excited about a unicorn tapestry she hoped to add to the Cluny's already impressive collection.

"Okay," I said. "As if I stole your tapestry."

The bitch threw her cigarette at me!

"Hey!" I dodged it, then picked it up and swung.

I have to give her credit; she didn't flinch as I deliberately missed her and stubbed the damned thing out against the cover of her book. Then I threw the butt into the ashtray on the table between our beds. "Do that again, and I feed it to you."

"You *did* steal my tapestry," she accused, throwing down the book. Whether she reverted to French as a power play, or because she was so emotional, I couldn't tell.

"What? That's ridiculous! I left France two days

after you took the chalice. You're the one with a super-saver card for the black market, not me."

"I do not know how you did it," she insisted, "but I know it was you. I was almost done with my report, advising that we acquire the tapestry, when my supervisor tells me, 'But no. The owner, he has changed his mind. He has already received a more generous offer from the Cloisters.'"

"The Cloisters in New York?"

Her *duh* glare made that clear. And true, the Cloisters' collection of unicorn weavings rivaled the Cluny's. But—

"Sorry to ruin your little fantasy, Cat, but I don't have anywhere near enough pull with the museum community to convince them to buy your tapestry out from under you. Not to mention that it would take a hell of a lot of money to fund a buyout that quick…ly…."

Her eyebrows arched as I remembered that, in fact, I *had* told someone about that particular tapestry.

Someone who could afford to purchase it for the museum.

Someone I'd wrongly suspected of planting a tracking device in my luggage…or my faux wedding ring.

Someone I'd promised to call when I got to the hotel!

"Damn it." If I had my cell phone, I could've called him from the room, but Hani Rachid had taken care of that. There was nothing for it but to put my clothes back on and head downstairs to use the phone in the lobby.

Either that, or wait until morning. And I was already feeling guilty about Lex, after the tracking device.

"You do know something," guessed Cat, as I swung my legs over the edge of the bed and stood to dress.

"Water under the bridge, Catrina." I doubted it really was, but my words seemed to annoy her, which made them worthwhile anyway. "I just remembered I need to make a phone call. Delightful though this little bit of bonding has been…"

She made a rude sound and scooped up her singed book, and I pulled on a skirt and blouse over my PJ's, grabbed my key and some change for the pay phone, and headed down the stairs. By now it was well after midnight, Egypt time, which made it early the previous evening in the city.

The way the desk clerk ogled me as I struggled with the operator on the pay phone made me glad I hadn't just grabbed a robe, even if most of the clientele at this particular hotel were European.

Placing long-distance calls from a foreign country is a challenge under the best of circumstances, much less when dizzy with exhaustion. After finding an operator who spoke English, I finally had to place the call collect. I hated to do it, but my change purse had been stolen. No way did I have enough twenty-five- or even fifty-piastre coins for long distance.

Of course Lex agreed to accept the charges. I hadn't realized how hungry I was to hear his voice until I relaxed at that little reassurance. When the operator went away, the first thing I said was, "Thanks. I'll pay you back."

His response was, "So who's Hani Rachid, and what's he doing with your phone?"

Chapter 8

Compared to the previous day, scuba diving in suspicious seawater thicker than a London fog seemed downright relaxing.

Really. All sarcasm aside.

At least *this* had something to do with Isis and my initial quest. Not to mention, I love diving. I love swimming in general…even when I'm completely protected from the aforementioned iffy water. The dry suit I wore was bulkier than a standard wet suit, with attached booties under my fins and a monster of a zipper up the back which had required a friend's help to zip.

Needless to say, that friend was not Catrina Dauvergne.

The suit also came with gloves and a hood, to complete my protection against the water. It was inflated slightly with a buoyancy compensator, requiring the use of weights on my ankles and waist. I really was dry—and yet I was *swimming,* submerged in almost thirty feet of murky water, trying to stay out of the way of the other divers as they clustered like hungry fish around a stone the size of a minivan which they meant to move.

With any luck, this block would turn out to be a pylon from the entrance to the Temple of Isis. The archeologists needed only to confirm it. That would take hieroglyphs they suspected were carved into the front of it, which, Murphy's Law being what it was, lay facedown in the sand.

If this stone had guarded the Temple of Isis…

Since it looked like the harnessing procedure would take a while yet, and they'd done this sort of thing more than I, I remained in my role as observer. Against the echoing sound of my own breath, I turned my attention to the otherwise silent murkiness around me, the ruined remnants of palace and temple. Everything had a dim green light about it. Visibility was limited to maybe fifteen feet because of the bits of sand and algae floating in the water. But even so…

It was amazing. Like a fantasy world. Like…magic.

Not far from me lay a sphinx, submerged for almost two thousand years. She was pitted and encrusted and yet as enigmatic as when she'd first been carved. A flick of my fins sent me skimming past her to more treasures in the sand—a hawk sculpture that I assumed represented the god Horus, and a headless body in that stiff posture of so many Egyptian statues. And blocks—dozens of stone blocks, some with faint hieroglyphs still visible even after millennia of erosion.

Apparently that's what you end up with if you sink part of an ancient city with first an earthquake and then a tidal wave—the same thing you'd get if you knocked over a child's building blocks, but much bigger and much more historically important.

Cleopatra may have once walked here, I thought, awed, as I drifted through the wreckage. A cluster of ever present little fish, silver flashes of darting movement, flitted by me to add to the surrealism of the moment. *She may have invoked the goddess Isis,* right here, *and now...*

I turned to check on the salvage operation. When I saw that the cluster of divers had all but vanished in the hazy water, I guiltily swam back.

My partner, Rhys, waved with what looked like relief and mimed, *Stay there.* Aware that I'd broken a cardinal rule of diving—never leave your buddy—I nodded. He rejoined the others in fastening the harness that would lift the twelve-ton pylon to the surface. Some of them wore full dry suits like Rhys and I. More of them had grown nonchalant about the risk, after so much exposure, and left off the gloves, or the hood. Cat's honey hair writhed loose, Medusa-like, in the tide.

Catrina...

Remembering my conversation with Lex, the previous night, I smiled around my regulator. He'd taken so long to get over my edited story about our brush with Hani Rachid that I'd just about decided *not* to pay him back for the collect call. By the time he wound down, I'd almost forgotten to ask him about the tapestry.

Almost.

"Did you help the Cloisters purchase a tapestry that the Cluny was acquiring?" I then asked from my crouch, where I'd slid down the wall for heightened comfort during his tirade.

He said nothing, which worried me. *Don't lie, Lex. Please don't—*

"You said it was the pet project of the woman who stole the Melusine Chalice from you."

"So you did what—bought it to avenge me?"

"That's…an extreme way of phrasing it."

"Damn it, Lex! Just because you have more money than should be legal…" But I was having an embarrassingly hard time with my moral outrage. I left it at a decidedly halfhearted, "Shame on you."

I heard the smile in his voice when he murmured, in a particularly sexy way, "Are you saying that I've been *bad,* Maggi?"

And I laughed.

Hell, as much as anyone could deserve that sort of setback, Catrina had. And it's not as if the tapestry had been destroyed. The Cloisters is an incredible museum.

"I'm not having phone sex with you in the lobby of an Arabic hotel," I whispered, after glancing both ways to make sure the desk clerk wasn't close enough to hear. "So don't even start."

"Which leads us back to why you don't have your own phone."

"Not your problem, Lex."

"It is if we can't have phone sex."

"Goodbye, Lex."

"Be safe," he'd pleaded. "Please? Surprises like speed-dialing you and getting someone named Hani have me thinking I'll jump a plane to the Land of the Pharaohs."

"Don't even think about it."

But once we hung up, I'd been glad I hadn't mentioned the sword fight.

Even if I'd forgotten, also, to complain about the ring.

Activity around the submerged pylon drew me from my reverie and back to the present. It looked like they were ready to raise it. They were using a procedure that involved connecting the harness, which had taken all morning to attach, to some underwater balloons which would then be inflated. The buoyancy of them would draw all twelve tons of the fallen stone upward, where they could then tow it to shore and examine it more closely.

D'Alencon, whom I recognized from his white hair, waved everyone back, then signaled upward. Rhys floated to my side as we watched, hovering there in the unnatural silence of submersion. Our first sign that it was working was a stiffening of the slinglike harness straps around the stone, then a billowing wisp of sand from beneath it, and then—

Then whole clouds of sand obscured the pylon as it lifted from its watery grave toward a sun it hadn't seen in millennia. If it told us the secret we hoped for, then the Temple of Isis—and presumably her grail—weren't far behind.

As I craned my neck upward, watching the pylon's ascent, my throat tightened with awe.

Then I realized it wasn't just awe.

Danger!

Heeding the instinct that had sharpened ever since my discovery of the Melusine Chalice, I kicked my swim fins and shot forward, only recognizing my goal as it—she—loomed ahead of me. Everyone else seemed to be watching the pylon. I not only saw what they saw—the rock starting to list sideways—I also saw one of the cables, which had been attached to the harness, whip through the water, scattering sand and fish in its wake....

Before impacting with Catrina's unprotected head.

Her mask veered away from her, and she rolled backward with a limpness that could only indicate lost consciousness.

And over her, the tilting pylon slipped out of its remaining sling and plummeted downward, all twelve tons.

Straight at her.

Kicking harder, I reached her first, catching her slack body and pushing her with all the strength I could manage in near-weightlessness. The sandy floor beneath me darkened in the shadow of the descending stone. I kicked again—

And something hard and heavy bumped past my swim fin as I swept Catrina clear of the worst danger.

Holy crap.

Remembering to breathe—an easy thing to forget while on a regulator, but dangerous—I kicked for the surface with my load. Other divers clustered around me, hands reaching, pulling, and in a moment we broke into the sunlight, into the harbor waves.

The real world. But considering the danger we'd just faced, Cleopatra's Palace and the Temple of Isis were also real, no matter how magical they'd momentarily seemed. Real—and dangerous.

"We need a neck brace," I shouted, as soon as I lost the regulator. "She hit her head, hurry. *Vite!*"

We bobbed in the water, Rhys and I trying to support her head, until a second speedboat could rush some first-aid supplies from the cabin cruiser. Catrina looked so…unlike herself. Helpless. Pale. I held a hand under her nose, then felt her wrist. She was breathing, anyway. She had a pulse. She also had a huge, bleeding lump on her head. Only once the curved plastic brace was fastened with Velcro did the team risk hoisting her limp form into the first Zodiac, the one from which we'd dived.

The first-aid box had smelling salts. I dug out a packet while we sped toward shore where, according to d'Alencon on the two-way, an ambulance would meet us. When I waved the packet under Catrina's nose, she startled, then coughed—then scowled at me, the first face she saw.

"Is this your fault?" she demanded blearily, and I knew she would be all right. I was even foolishly glad for it.

The bitch.

D'Alencon arrived on shore in time to join Catrina in the ambulance. Before they left, he canceled all diving for the rest of the afternoon, until he better understood what happened.

Isis would have to wait—and I had to find some other way to occupy the rest of my day.

Luckily, I had a few ideas.

"You do not have to do this," insisted Rhys an hour later, riding the old yellow trolley car with me as far as the train station. The tram rocked slightly on its tracks and, not surprisingly, shot out sparks from the overhead wires at intersections—but the roof protected us. "She has no right to blackmail you."

She meant Tala Rachid.

"You said that she was at the hotel to make sure we

were okay," I reminded him. "That she meant to call the police if we didn't show up."

"But she did not call the police."

"From what she told us last night, I get the feeling they would dismiss any complaints from her as same song, new verse. You may not have noticed, but the police didn't even act that concerned when *we* filed a complaint, and Egypt has supposedly taken a hard line about protecting tourists."

Ever since that tourist massacre in the Valley of the Kings, which Lex had mentioned in his cheerful, "Visit Egypt, Land of Danger and Death" speech before I left.

"I did notice it," admitted Rhys, trying not to pay attention to some of the people on the trolley who took exception to our standing so near each other. Apparently my wearing a wedding ring didn't mean as much when he did not. "And you are right. It is strange."

"Not if they've already dismissed Tala and Jane as emotional, malcontent females who think they're above the law, and Hani as a rightfully indignant patriarch. Trying to smuggle Kara to safety didn't exactly help their reputation among the local authorities."

"Can you blame the women for it?" challenged Rhys.

I imagined what it would be like to have a child— and what it would be like if someone, even her father, stole her from me. What it would be like if even the law was against me.

Laws be damned. I'd defy death to get her back.

"No," I said tightly. "No, I don't blame them in the least. But I'm really *not* an expert on international custody. If I'm going to help them—"

"This is it," said Rhys, of the stop. It was easy to recognize because the modern train depot stood across the street from an ancient Roman amphitheater that shone white in the sun, anachronistic amid the dusty cityscape. We got off the trolley and dodged traffic to the depot, despite the longing look Rhys cast toward the amphitheater. Only when we entered did he ask, "So you've decided to help them after all, have you?"

"I didn't decide." Since he had to stay and work—there was more to the reclamation project than diving—I gave him a quick farewell hug, whether or not people approved. "Hani Rachid decided for me."

If that man thought he could bully me into submission, he clearly did not know Grailkeepers.

Since I'd missed the most recent Turbotrain's departure, I had to take an express to Cairo. It felt good to be out and unchaperoned, reading up on Isis. After almost three hours, it deposited me back into the chaos of the afternoon city, just in time to hear the haunting, citywide call to prayer, chanted by muezzins from minarets and broadcast from loudspeakers. Almost half the people around me immediately stopped, unrolled prayer rugs to face east, and began to pray, right there in the Ramses Station.

And to think they did this five times a day!

Somewhat chagrined by their devotion, I felt guilty for heading out—but I had my own strange brand of religion to pursue.

Helping Tala with Kara, so that she would help me find the Isis Grail.

I visited not just the British but the American Embassies, trying to find even a hint of hopeful news for Jane. It wasn't to be had. Overseas custody disputes were apparently a larger problem than I'd known—and it wasn't just in the Middle East but Mexico, Austria, Germany, even Sweden. Jane wasn't the first person to find herself in this situation, I was told, and she would not be the last.

"That's just how it goes," said one clerk, supremely unhelpful. "Shouldn't the family resolve this?"

But how was a family supposed to resolve anything, when only half had all the power?

Was this why I'd avoided marriage for so long? I got back to the Ramses Railway Station in time to catch one of the sleek, red-and-black striped Turbotrains, which cut my ride by almost an hour. That was still plenty of time to slide Lex's wedding ring off my finger and squint wearily at the inscription.

Virescit vulnere virtus

I should ask Rhys. He obviously knew Latin. But in the meantime, I put the ring back on.

By the time I arrived back in Alexandria—or Alex, as I was already learning to call the city—the evening sun had begun to sink toward the West.

And I was frustrated.

I might be a Grailkeeper. I might even be some kind of champion, though I very much doubted that. But as much as I wanted to help Tala, Jane and Kara, I just didn't have that kind of power.

And I *did* want to help them, more deeply than I'd allowed myself to recognize until Hani's treachery gave me moral permission. It was true that this was a whole different culture with different values. But damn it, the country from which Hani had kidnapped Kara was not.

This, I decided as I dragged up the stairs to the room I shared with Catrina, was the reason the world needed more goddess grails. Not to conquer men. Just to help restore balance.

Then I noticed that the door to my room hung open. All philosophical musing stopped.

But my step only slowed.

They'd come *back?*

This time, I had my unnamed sword with me, hanging from one hip under my skirts. Luckily there was nobody in the hallway, not that it would have stopped me. I gathered my skirts up far enough to slide the weapon slowly, silently out of its scabbard.

Sure, I could have gone for help. But for one thing, I didn't know for certain that there was anything wrong. Why risk crying wolf?

For another—what was the fun in that?

If Hani Rachid wanted trouble, I was in the mood to give it to him.

Stepping with the silent stealth garnered from years of tai chi practice, I made my way to the door and listened.

Nothing.

I drew a slow, deep breath. One.

Two.

Three! I rolled around the doorjamb and into the room in a move similar to that of a friend of mine, a cop in Connecticut. But I had no intention of pointing the sword and shouting, *"Freeze!"*

Just as well.

I felt silly enough when Lex Stuart looked up from where he was lounging comfortably on my bed, reading Catrina's paperback, and said, "I hear there's a good restaurant for fish on the Corniche."

Chapter 9

Some piece of my heart brightened at the sight of him, the reality of him right here. That piece of my heart wouldn't have objected if I'd done a swan dive on top of both him and the rickety bed. Hell, we had a past with rickety beds. *Lex!*

He was sexy familiarity amid a day of frustrating foreignness. And yet, despite that sense of homecoming...

Another part of me clearly remembered telling him not to come. "What are you doing here?"

"Reading a racy French novel," he admitted, closing the book and sitting up to lay it onto the stand beside him. I recognized Cat's book from the cigarette burn. "That, and worrying about you."

"Well, you shouldn't."

"It wasn't your novel? Damn."

"Shouldn't *worry*."

"Oh. Well, that makes everything easier," said Lex, sarcasm clearly intended. Worry makes him cranky. "I'll stop, then. Just like that. So when did you become a witch, and why are you trying to steal Hani Rachid's daughter?"

"You called him again?" My voice actually cracked.

"He called me this time. He wanted to tell me to do a better job at 'controlling my woman.'" Lex lifted a hand to ward off my reaction. "His words, Mag, not mine."

"And how did he get the impression that I was your woman?" And why was I still standing in the doorway? I came into the room—but I sat on Catrina's bed, facing him. Like he was dangerous or something.

Hadn't we gotten past that notion? Then again, I'd seen this man in action. He *was* dangerous. He just wasn't supposed to be dangerous to me.

"It might've had something to do with my reaction when he answered your phone that first time," Lex confessed, eyeing the sword I laid beside me on the chenille bedspread. He'd had bad luck with bladed weapons lately.

"I can't believe you even spoke to him!"

"I had to know how he got your mobile—"

"The second time," I interrupted. "When he called you back to complain. Why didn't you just hang up?"

"Would you?"

He had me there. "Did you at least tell him that I *wasn't* your woman and *nobody* could control me?"

"And ruin the hail-fellow-well-met mood that kept him talking? Not likely." Lex studied my expression, his own guarded. "Not to mention, I like him underestimating me. Just think of me as a double agent."

Unfortunately, I'd already been thinking of him that

way for a couple of months now. It wasn't the most stable ground on which to build our relationship.

He leaned forward. "Maggi, I had business in the city—important business like you can't imagine—but I dropped it. *For you.* I got here in under twenty-four hours, which wasn't easy, all because I was worried about you, and you're sitting over there looking at me as if *I'm* still the bad guy. Can't we put a moratorium on arguing at least until after dinner?"

Over there was all of three feet away. In fact, our feet were framing each other's on the floor between us.

"You did it for you," I insisted, fully aware of how childish I sounded and resenting being made to feel that way. "I asked you not to come, and you came anyway."

"Maybe nobody can control me, either." His words came out a lot more seriously than I thought he meant them to. But he had a point there, as well. Which was no reason I should drop my own plans—

Except that I didn't have plans, at least not for dinner. And I *was* hungry. When he silently extended a hand, his golden eyes pleading, I abandoned my righteous indignation for the time being and reached for it.

His strong fingers closing around mine felt so necessary, on so many levels, that I experienced a chill of foreboding.

Not danger. My throat didn't hurt.

But I couldn't help wondering how much more than three feet still lay between us, after all.

And how bad a thing that was.

Dinner was…wow.

The Corniche, where Lex had found this restaurant, is the main seafront boulevard in Alexandria, a long crescent following the harbor. We were led onto a tiled balcony that held only four tables, draped in intricately embroidered cloths, diners given privacy by potted palm trees. Discreet fans assisted the sea breeze in cutting the oppressive heat. The pierced stone railing, all arabesques and Persian arches, was the only thing that separated us from a breathtaking view of the harbor, the medieval fort beyond it, and the Mediterranean Sea beyond that. Lights glanced off black waves. Stars glinted in the night sky. Exotic music on lutes and drums drifted over us from a higher balcony.

This place had to cost a fortune, even considering the exchange rate.

"Let me guess," I said, as Lex held my chair for me. "You're buying, right?"

"It's the least I can do after barging out here against your express wishes." He expertly pushed my chair back under me as I sat, then seated himself across the table with equal grace.

I knew full well that I was being manipulated—but that was the problem with dating someone as wealthy as Lex. Sometimes, when you've had a day or two as frustrating as mine had been, the temptation was just too great.

I capitulated with a condition. "As long as you know you aren't staying. Here in Egypt, I mean."

"You can't think I'm going home without—" Lex stopped when our waiter, turbaned and obsequious, handed us ornate menus. The man also placed on the table tall glasses of water and bowls of some kind of delicacies—I recognized olives and figs. Not together, of course.

"Sure you are," I insisted. "You have business in

New York, right? Important business like I can't imagine, you said. Speaking of which…" I took a sip of water, in which floated a slice of lime, to hide my lingering sense of foreboding. Or maybe it was merely good, old-fashioned suspicion. "Just what kind of business was that, again?"

"Nothing you'd be interested in."

"Which means, nothing you're able to tell me." And the only thing he'd taken a vow of secrecy about was his involvement with the Comitatus. That and a nondisclosure agreement he'd signed for work about a year back, but chances leaned toward the former. "Fair enough. But don't let me keep you from it."

"Luckily, we live in a world with telephones and the Internet and I have, er, *associates* worldwide. I can accomplish a great deal while I'm here in Egypt."

"But I can't," I confessed.

Lex tipped the menu down far enough to frown over it.

"Accomplish a lot with you in Egypt," I clarified. "I'm working with Rhys Pritchard, which could be awkward with you lurking around and thinking you're going to take me out to dinner every night." In fact, I'd insisted we invite Rhys along, which Lex had accepted with only a modicum of resistance. But when I checked at the front desk, my friend wasn't in. I'd left a note for him, so at least he'd know I made it back safely from Cairo.

"Why should it be uncomfortable?" Lex asked now, either disingenuous or uncharacteristically naive. I couldn't tell, since he'd raised the menu again. "I have nothing against Rhys."

"And I certainly don't need you questioning my

every move while I decide what to do about you-know-who's daughter." I'd given him the Cliffs Notes version on the way over, and he'd all but begged me not to get involved. I couldn't argue with his logic—but this was about a truth that went beyond logic.

"And," I reminded him, "I'm here to find a certain cup that your cousin and at least half of your, er, *associates* would gladly destroy."

"Phil said he was past that," said Lex. "And my associates may yet be persuaded to reexamine the issue."

"Hope all you want, Mr. Optimism. I'd rather not take the chance of your cousin keeping tabs on me through you. Not that you would—"

The waiter picked that unfortunate moment to ask if we'd made a decision. We both went with the house specials, Lex positively glowering, and resumed our discussion as soon as the man left.

"I'm not my cousin," Lex insisted, low and intense. "Nor am I his spy."

"I didn't say you were. But you work together, so he can find you. From there it's not that hard to find me. If he learns I'm in Alexandria, he's sure to guess why."

Lex said nothing.

"I wouldn't walk into the middle of a business deal of yours and think I wouldn't be in the way. Why are you?"

He didn't like it, that was obvious. But there was a reason I'd fallen in love with him, the last few times that had happened, back before things got this complicated.

Surprisingly, it had less to do with how incredibly sexy he looked on this candlelit balcony than it did with him not being a fool. Or an asshole.

"I'll fall back to Cairo," he offered finally.

Oh, for mercy's sake. "Why not just go home?"

"Because it took me too long to get here. What if you get hurt, or in trouble? I'll hang back as long as you don't need me, Mag, but I won't go so far that I can't get back if you do. You can't make me. I've talked to this—this person who has your phone," he edited, following my example of avoiding Hani's name in public. "He's dangerous, and he's angry at you. Justifiably, in his mind. The only thing protecting you so far is his crazy idea that you've got magical powers."

Here we were, back to witchcraft and magic.

The waiter brought a strange but not unpleasant soup.

"What kind of powers?" I asked, frustrated. "Did he mention any of them to you, while you were chatting him up?"

"Flying," offered Lex. "Disappearing. Breathing underwater. You're a busy lady."

My stomach twisted, and not from the smell of the soup. "Oh, no. Crap, Lex. He's Comitatus."

Lex's eyes widened when I said the word out loud. "Of course he isn't. I'd know if he is."

"Would you?"

He took another sip of soup, rather than commit himself to even that much information. At least he didn't look happy about it. Secret societies suck.

"Either he's an *associate* of yours," I edited, "or he's spoken to one. That's exactly what I told those men in the airport, the associates who tried to take the Melusine Grail. I told them I could fly out windows, vanish from in front of trains, and go down wells unscathed."

A smile flirted at his mouth. "And they believed you?"

Okay, so *sometimes* he could be an asshole.

"It was all in the delivery." And I'd managed more than one surprising feat in the service of the goddess—probably due to luck and good timing, though, more than any magic. "The point is, he must have heard about me from *associates* of yours."

Lex scowled. "I'll look into that."

"Will you tell me what you find out?"

"Probably not, no." Damned vow of secrecy.

We ate in silence for a few minutes, at a mutually annoyed impasse. Now that I'd made my knee-jerk protest, I considered his offer of a compromise. I was supposed to be an advocate for balance, here. Wouldn't the world be a better place if more people met each other halfway?

"Cairo, huh?" I asked.

Lex looked up. Only because I knew him so well could I see the eagerness in his eyes. "I'll stay out of your way, Maggi, I promise. Cairo could turn out to be perfect. I've been looking for a place with...for a place."

I could only wonder what he'd stopped himself from saying—a place with pyramids? Probably not. A place with camels?

A place with historical or ritual significance?

Even working without full disclosure, I could completely buy that Lex was the product of generations of important men, of a royal bloodline that traced back through the family of Jesus and King David to the rulers of ancient Sumeria. The irony that some conspiracy theorists think that bloodline is itself the Holy Grail—or *sang réal*—just added to the number of coincidences that had begun to infiltrate my life since I accepted the reality of Grailkeepers. I'd known Lex had an air of importance about him long before I knew why.

But I still had trouble imagining him in some kind of ceremonial order. He was too down-to-earth, too dignified, too...

Lex.

"This could be just what I need," he stated, more carefully. "And I'm here because of you. That feels...right."

He held my gaze, looking for something, and asked, "Doesn't it?"

"Sure," I said...but I wasn't sure at all.

Some weeks ago, right before he was attacked, Lex had said something cryptic about needing me. Something about feminine power, about balance. Something important.

I can't do it alone. No man can. No woman can.

I need you.

It was one reason we'd started dating again, to present a united front—apparently to other Comitatus members. I'd given him six months to prove it worthwhile. But since then, his plans became just one more of the gazillion things he couldn't talk to me about. Now I had to wonder if his "important business" was somehow involved in his trip to Egypt. Was *that* the only reason he wanted me nearby? To do *him* a favor?

For someone who didn't want him trying to take care of me, I sure didn't like the thought that he wasn't.

Then again, it's not like I told him all my Grail-keeper business.

"I can live with you in Cairo," I conceded, and was rewarded with an actual smile.

He looked even more attractive, smiling.

Then he had to go and say, "So, tell me about Isis."

I stiffened. If he was here to spy on—

"Not about the cup," he insisted, reading me as easily as I can usually read him. "Just…the goddess. Maybe she's something we won't argue about."

So, since it was nothing he couldn't find out on the Internet, why *not* give him the 411 on the Goddess of a Thousand Names?

"Isis was a powerful being in her own right," I started. "A goddess of magic and healing. But her most famous legend has to do with her marriage to the god Osiris."

"So a lot of these goddesses are part of a…a sacred couple, are they?"

"I'm not sure how you'd define a lot—" I felt something brush my foot, and stiffened. Then I realized it was Lex's foot. Sans shoe. Hidden by the fullness of the embroidered tablecloth.

When I caught his gaze, his brows lifted in polite inquiry. The brightness in his eyes contradicted his air of casual nonchalance.

Instead of protesting, I continued, "Remember that the French goddess, Melusine, was married to a mere mortal."

But at the moment, I could see the attraction of mortals. Especially mortals whose very presence seemed right. *Necessary.*

"But she was married," he insisted, massaging my foot with his. "Are most—"

He hesitated when I pulled my foot away, tried not to look hurt, then finished, "Most goddesses married?"

But the only reason I'd pulled away was to use the toe of one foot to slide a sandal strap off the other heel. Then, foot bare and all the more sensitive, I touched the ridge of his toes with mine, then ventured up his sock to his instep.

His eyes closed for a moment.

"Athena never marries," I told him, clinging to the sanity of what could have been a class presentation. "Or Artemis. Or…"

His toes caressed under the arch of my bare foot, which arched farther in welcome. The rest of my body was taking notice as well now, a satisfied warmth like from a good glass of wine. But we weren't drinking wine with our dinner, not in a Muslim country.

"Or a lot of them," I finished lamely, grasping at conversation.

"But a lot of them *are married,* r—?"

He broke off as I drew my foot up the crease of his trousers, toward his knee, then back down, then back up.

"Right," I agreed, smiling evilly. "Isis. Hera. Persephone. Even Aphrodite…wait." My foot paused, resting on his knee. "Why are you asking this? You aren't leading up to another marriage proposal, are you?"

"A little higher, and I am."

He sighed as I deliberately slid my foot away. It would be much easier to insist on celibacy if I didn't continue this. More fair, too.

"According to the legend," I said, resuming the lecture, "their brother Set invited Osiris to a banquet where enemies ambushed him. Set cut him into pieces and scattered those pieces across Egypt. It's only because of her powerful magic that the grieving Isis was able to collect all but one of the pieces."

"Do I want to know what that missing piece was?" From his wince, he seemed to have already guessed that they had, as Rhys would put it, Abelarded Osiris.

"No." I considered it. "But she made him a new

one—Goddess of Healing, remember? She wrapped him in bandages—the first mummy—and breathed life back into him."

"The king who dies and is reborn." Clearly Lex recognized the familiar motif. "Like Arthur."

"Like a lot of gods. Not only did Osiris revive, but he was able to impregnate Isis with the god Horus. Then Osiris became Lord of the Underworld."

"Having been dead and all," mused Lex. "So…he and Isis weren't together after that?"

"One of her ten thousand names is Queen of the Underworld. She was able to move in both worlds, which may explain why her worship continued until the sixth…century…."

But while I spoke, Lex's foot quested up under my skirt. His sock, and the warmth and strength beneath it, grazed the inside of my bare thigh. The rest of my body was definitely paying attention….

Which is when the waiter appeared with our next course.

I watched Lex interact with the man with his usual coolness, there in the starlight, against the sound of waves and sitar music. Damn, but I wished I had a better idea of what I wanted from this man. I wished—

As the waiter turned away, Lex's toes slid back under my skirt and higher, flirting toward the juncture of my thighs, and pleasure skittered through me. My breath stuttered in my throat. Okay, yes, so I wanted that much. But even more, I wanted to understand the consequences. Consequences to the Grailkeepers. Consequences to the Comitatus.

Consequences to us.

"Don't start something you can't finish," I warned

him, my voice thick with pleasure and frustration, my eyes half-mast.

"I can finish it anytime," Lex promised.

I forced my eyes open. "No," I warned him. We were about more than a single night in an Egyptian hotel room, whatever that *more* might be. "You can't."

To my relief and despair, he took his foot back, resuming his cool, protective mask. "That's your call, Maggi."

"It is," I agreed.

And we finished our dinner in relative silence.

Chapter 10

"So tell me what you *do* want," asked Lex, as we stepped into the ironwork elevator in the lobby of the Hotel Athens. He shut the external and internal door grills behind us as I pressed the number three.

The elevator rose very, very slowly, alternating views of the floors we passed with views of the painted concrete shaft. The stairs would've been quicker...but this way, we got to stand together, in each other's warmth and scent, for a little longer.

Dinner had offered ultimate romance. Returning to my room with Lex Stuart, even without holding hands or committing any other culturally verboten public displays of affection, seemed so...right. And yet...

"I wish I knew," I mourned, as the elevator trundled past the first floor. As in Europe, the lobby was on the ground floor, not the first.

"I deserve more than that," he said quietly. "So do you."

And he was right. I turned toward him and said what I'd been avoiding—avoiding because it wouldn't do any good. "I want to know what's going on with you. I want to know what we're getting into. I want to know your secrets."

His mouth twisted before he could stop it; then his usual composure returned. "Maggi—"

"I *get it*." I framed that handsome, aristocratic face between my palms, regretting his composure. I didn't like this wall between us; it felt better to see proof that he didn't like it, either. "I get why you can't tell me, and I understand. I'm not asking you to reveal secrets. But fair or not, that's what I want. If I were to leap into more of a relationship with you, without knowing everything that entailed…"

We slid past an extended glimpse of the second floor hallway. I let my hands fall from his face.

"It would be like diving into a void, Lex. Jumping out into nothingness. And I can't make myself do that."

He took a deep breath. "Not even with me beside you?"

With a grinding of brakes, the elevator slowed as it reached my floor. His hazel eyes were so needful, so desperate, I wished I could say what he wanted to hear. But I'd be lying.

I cared about him too much to lie.

"You know what's waiting at the bottom," I challenged. "I don't."

"I don't know as much as you think I do."

"And that's supposed to make me more willing to jump?"

Lex sighed, and in that sigh I saw the weight of so many of the frustrations and responsibilities he carried. The poor guy couldn't unburden onto me, maybe not onto anybody.

I still wasn't going to sleep with him. I wasn't going to jump.

But I could reaffirm that I cared.

So at long last, I kissed him.

His arms encircled me, cautiously at first but then, as I leaned up into him and slid my hands over his shoulders, his hold tightened. His lips softened to me, opened for me.

It had been so long. Too long.

I loved kissing Lex. He tasted like coming home. Like my first dance, and like the prom. Like my first love.

Maybe I *did* refuse to be controlled by anyone, or even by fate. But I wasn't writing him off because of it, either.

The way he tipped his head. The way he tasted my lower lip. The little catch in his breath…

"Hey, Pritchard," called an obnoxiously familiar, French-accented voice from just outside the elevator. "You may wish to see this."

Still in Lex's arms, I turned my head far enough to glare at Catrina Dauvergne, standing in the hallway, watching us through the grill with an evil grin.

A bandage wrapped her head, the only indication of her earlier close call.

From down the hall, Rhys's voice approached. "What do you—ah." That last as he, too, spotted us. He stopped, then took an awkward step back. "I can return later," he offered, flushing.

"Coward," challenged Catrina.

Rhys actually glared at her. I'd never seen him look so annoyed. He was usually too…priestly.

"Rhys, no," I protested, as Lex's arms dropped away from me. "Don't go. We—"

Okay, so I wasn't sure what to say. I didn't like that I felt guilty. I didn't like not being sure which made me feel worse—Rhys seeing me in Lex's arms, or Lex's embrace falling away as I asked Rhys not to leave.

It was Lex who recovered first, sliding open first the inside grill, then the outside grill of the elevator's cage. "I'm heading out, Pritchard. And Maggi probably needs to catch you up on her day."

Rhys hesitated. "Heading out where?"

Lex's gaze barely grazed me. *A promise made…* "Cairo."

It was Catrina who said, "The last train to Cairo has left for the evening. *Quel dommage.* I imagine you are stuck here."

"Have we met?" When he wants to, Lex can do upper-class snobbery with the best of them. The faint curl of his lip was priceless.

"Catrina," I said, as Lex followed me out of the elevator, "this is my friend, Alexander Stuart. Lex, this is my roommate, Catrina Dauvergne. Cat works at the Cluny. Her specialty is tapestries."

Amusement lit Lex's cool, golden eyes as he recognized the description, but all he said was, "I think I can find a hotel room, Ms. Dauvergne, and catch a morning train."

"But you needn't leave right away." That was Rhys— could this get more complicated? "That is to say…as long as you're here, don't you want to see the project?"

Lex looked to me, reluctantly parted his lips—

Before he could decline, I said, "Do you think it would be all right with Director d'Alencon, Rhys? I haven't even been here two days myself. If I suddenly show up with a guest…"

"He'll be my guest," insisted Rhys.

So I nodded, barely, and Lex said, "Thank you for the invitation, Pritchard. Really. When should I be here tomorrow?"

Before he left with the necessary instructions, he and Rhys shook hands like ancient warriors—clasping each other's elbows—and I wondered what that was all about. Lex kissed me on the cheek this time, a glint of mischief in his eyes at what he seemed to see as a stay of execution.

"I never said you had to leave right away," I chided in a whisper, which, since my lips were so near his ear, made him shiver. His sigh, warming my neck, returned the favor.

As he stepped into the elevator, Catrina hopped in after him. "Do you think I stand by lifts for no reason?" she challenged, when I stared.

Then Lex had the grillwork closed, and the pair of them rumbled out of sight. Lex's head tipped back as they sank, watching me for as long as possible, as if taking some kind of strength from the sight of me.

Catrina, on the other hand, stared at *him*—with blatant hunger.

I reminded myself that Lex had handled worse than her in his time.

Me, I closed the distance to a seemingly disturbed Rhys and unlocked my hotel room. Lex was right. I had to fill Rhys in on what had happened—or more to the point, *not* happened—in Cairo.

* * *

Lex enjoyed himself the next morning, and I enjoyed watching it. Dressed casually in khakis and a polo shirt, he seemed completely at home on the cabin cruiser that served as a floating headquarters. He was genuinely friendly with the archeologists and impressed by their expedition. When I overheard him asking d'Alencon what kind of funding the project had, I sneaked a glance at Rhys, who tried—and failed—to look innocent.

The mystery of yesterday's equipment failure still hadn't been solved, but the rumor being murmured between interns and archeologists was sabotage. I couldn't help suspecting Comitatus…but after the way Lex had kissed me last night, I couldn't believe that he knew anything about it. Since I had no proof about his cousin's involvement—only educated guesses—I kept my mouth shut on that subject.

The plan for now was to delay moving the pylon until we knew more. We had plenty of other artifacts to measure and catalog. More exciting, there was the chance that the pylon had rotated as it fell. The hieroglyphs everyone hoped for might now be on a visible side of the stone block.

Since Lex hadn't packed his diver certification card, he volunteered to help up top while others of us suited up. It's a testament to Lex's air of confidence—either that, or a donation I hadn't heard about—that d'Alencon agreed to let him drive one of the two Zodiacs as we boated out to the dive zone. A salty breeze ruffled Lex's ginger-brown hair, and bursts of reflected sunlight off the water's surface gave him an almost angelic look. Whatever responsibilities or concerns had been weighing him down the previous day, he seemed to have momentarily shaken them off.

I was surprised by how deeply this pleased me.

"Good luck," he said, after we'd cut the engine, dropped anchor, and set out the diver-down buoys.

Rhys nodded, gave us a thumbs-up, and rolled backward off the boat into the water in traditional diver style. I pulled up the hood of my dry suit, and Lex tucked a stray strand of my hair into it.

"Be safe," he added, more intensely. Rather than resenting his concern—he was here helping me do what scared him, after all—I kissed him. His lips tasted salty as he happily returned the favor. When we pulled apart, to the sound of encouraging hoots from the other Zodiac, he waved our critics away and handed me my mask.

For a brief moment, I hesitated to take it. I liked this sunshiny, supportive Lex. I wouldn't mind kissing him some more, with the bobbing of the waves and the cry of the gulls. Did I really need to be there if they learned the pylon had framed the entrance to Isis's temple?

I'd find out soon enough anyway, wouldn't I?

A particularly sharp bird cry from above us, more like a hawk than a seagull, drew me out of that momentary madness. Of course I had to be there. I'd come to Alexandria specifically for something like this.

So I took the mask Lex handed me, adjusted my regulator, and dived backward off the boat, arching downward into the bubbly, misty green water with my momentum.

Rhys, who'd been waiting for me like a good buddy, followed.

He's a good kisser, Catrina had said when she got in late the previous night. *This Lex Stuart.*

The wrench of jealousy I felt took me by surprise, even as I insisted, *He wouldn't have kissed you.*

I even believed it. Mostly. But I'd once believed I knew everything about him, too.

And sadly, he did not, she'd admitted, laughing at my expression. *But I could tell by watching him. Ooh la la...*

Now I shook off the memory, the upset, the significance. I had a goddess grail to find.

It felt like a completely different world, down here. I could hear little beyond my own overloud breathing, what with the hood muffling my ears. And of course visibility was limited. But as our downward kicks propelled us toward the lights of several other divers, the debris of Cleopatra's ancient palace faded into view, as if knitting itself back into reality.

Like magic.

Along with the pylon.

It lay in a different position from yesterday, and again I had to make a conscious effort *not* to hold my breath. The thing weighed twelve tons, and it had barely fallen thirty feet. Chances were it hadn't rolled, right?

And yet, as divers clustered around it as surely as did the little silver flashes of fish, I so wanted it to be true. Rhys swam past me, joining his colleagues—two of whom suddenly shot upward, one of them spinning in exultation.

Was it? *Was it?*

Rhys looked closer, borrowing an underwater light from someone else, then gave me a thumbs-up.

I let out my breath in a bubbly rush.

Another diver was rolling with glee. D'Alencon, recognizable by his white hair, was simply reading and re-

reading whatever he'd found. I was already swimming closer when Rhys beckoned me. Silently, he pointed to the smooth-worn carvings that d'Alencon's gloved hands were clearing of algae.

I don't read hieroglyphs. At first, I didn't understand the picture that Rhys insistently indicated; I guess I'd expected the ankh or horned disk of later Isis symbology. Then I recognized the blocky step-shape for what it was—a miniature throne. *Her* throne.

This really was it.

The Temple of Isis may have stood on this very stretch of submerged sand and debris.

And where the Temple of Isis had been…

There, surely, I would find the chalice used in her worship. A chalice of unimaginable importance…and power.

The rest of the morning passed in a blur of excitement, divers leaving our submerged holy ground only to change out oxygen tanks. The project members were already photographing the pylon's message and starting to more closely map out the surrounding terrain. Despite only being there to observe, I did my best to help with the grunt work—holding a yardstick or an extra light—but that still left some time for me to do some searching of my own. The others were excited about all of it, and with good cause, considering the historical significance of their find. But to them, the pylon alone was incredible.

Me, I was looking for particular clues. An altar. Perhaps a statue of the goddess herself. And of course…

A chalice.

I didn't find it—not yet. But every new artifact that took shape under my searching halogen light held the wonder of possibility. The blood of goddess worshippers ran in my veins, after all. Was that what sensed the call of ancient generations, priestesses—or magic women—who may have performed rituals here? The search became so addictive, at one point Rhys had to swim after me to signal that I shouldn't go too far on my own. And of course he was right. He was my dive buddy, and he had to work.

But what relics were waiting out there, beyond the hazy curtain of submerged green distance, that I might yet find? What kind of feminine power might they possess?

I hated having to wait.

When d'Alencon signaled that we should stop for a while, either for lunch or because extended dives could be too exhausting, I was actually surprised to find Lex still there. Then, as I took the warm, dry hand he offered to help me back onto the Zodiac, I felt guilty for having forgotten him.

I might only be here for Isis—but he was only here for me.

Except…

"I need to head out," he said, as soon as I pushed my hood back so that I could hear him. "You shouldn't be distracted at a time like this."

Not that I had been, damn it.

"I'm sorry," I said, shrugging off my tank and turning so that he could unzip my suit. "This can't have been very interesting for you."

"You kidding? It's been great. Really." While I stripped off the suit—which I wore over a bathing suit, of course—he waved to acknowledge that all his divers were up and started the boat. "It's given me a chance to think through some things, make some decisions."

I knew better than to ask what decisions. So did Rhys. And the other diver on our boat, a Greek guy named Niko, was too wrapped up in the day's finds to care.

When we reached the cabin cruiser, Lex declined to come up. He and Rhys shook hands and thumped each other on the back before Rhys climbed out, leaving us to our privacy.

"So," I said, making no move to get out of the Zodiac. I really wanted to go back to diving. And yet, I didn't want him to head out so soon. Just how selfish was I? "What do you suppose Phil would think about you helping me look for the Isis Grail?"

Just imagining his cousin's reaction amused me.

"I wasn't planning on mentioning it to him," Lex admitted.

"Good plan."

"See? Some secrets do have their place."

I groaned. Then I leaned forward, into his arms, and his embrace welcomed me. I rested my head on his shoulder, marveling at how dry and warm and solid he seemed after a morning underwater. How *real*.

"I've made a reservation at the Four Seasons," he told me, laying his cheek on my head. "I'll leave a message with your hotel once I have a suite number."

I wish you weren't going. I had to swallow back those words—even I wasn't that selfish. Or that cruel. I was the one who'd told him to leave in the first place!

For good reason, I reminded myself. This wasn't his quest, it was mine. His quest...

Not for the first time, I wondered exactly how he meant to regain leadership of the Comitatus—assuming that really was his plan—and how dangerous that might be for *him.* "So you think you'll be in Cairo for a few days?"

"At least a week," he said, rather than asking how long I would be in Alexandria. "I've scheduled some meetings."

I leaned out of his embrace. "Already?"

He tapped the mobile phone hanging off his belt. This man could conduct business anywhere, couldn't he?

Then again, I'd been underwater for a long time, leaving him alone and bored.

"Are they meetings I would be interested in?" I asked.

"Probably," said Lex. "Which is exactly why I can't tell you about them."

When I narrowed my eyes at him, he kissed me. It didn't last anywhere near long enough. Then, because I couldn't keep him here forever, I stood to climb the ladder to the cruiser's deck. "Be careful?" I asked.

"Within reason," he assured me.

Catrina was waiting up top. "It is about time," she chided, before stepping over the rail to climb down.

"What?" I looked over the edge at her, and Lex waved, seemingly unperturbed. Then I looked toward the others, where they'd set out a lunch. *"What?"*

Rhys seemed equally surprised. "Where is Catrina going?"

"I told her she must only work a half day as she recovers," explained d'Alencon, distracted by the papers he was reviewing. "She volunteered to drive the boat back."

When I looked back down, the Zodiac was already pulling away, toward the crescent shore of the harbor.

Catrina seemed to be saying something to Lex. Lex did not look back at me.

And overhead, a hawklike bird circled.

Chapter 11

In a perfect world, I would have found the cup that very afternoon.

Instead, two afternoons later found me suiting up in the Zodiac for yet another dive with no more information than before. I'd talked again to Tala, who held firm that unless I helped Jane and Kara, she would not share her ancestral secrets about the Isis Grail. I'd lost track of how many dives I'd made. Even d'Alencon commented on my extraordinary commitment for an observer.

"Remarkable," mused Catrina dryly as she, too, wriggled into a dry suit. "Is it not?"

She'd been her usual annoying self, worse through the close confines of sharing a room, for the previous two nights. She claimed to have discussed my relationship with Rhys on her boat ride to shore with Lex, and although I had nothing to hide, I felt uneasy imagining the lies she could have told. She talked about how sexy she found both Lex and Rhys, in a blatant attempt to make me jealous.

And if she said the words *in situ* one more time, I wasn't sure I could be held responsible for my actions.

"Then again," she continued now, "we archeologists are all, in our own way, observers. Ours is not to collect the artifacts we find but instead, whenever possible, to leave them *in situ*—"

I pulled my hood up so I couldn't hear her anymore, tightened my mask, adjusted my regulator—and slid backward into the Alexandrian harbor. Since Rhys hadn't expected me to accelerate my departure, I had to wait—letting myself sink farther and farther from the light of the surface—before he appeared in a splash of bubbles above me.

As soon as he righted himself, and gave me a thumbs-up, I turned and kicked out in the direction of some algae-encrusted columns we hadn't yet explored. But I may not have been in the right frame of mind to discover a powerful talisman to feminine power. I was too damned frustrated.

In situ, in situ, in situ. The problem was, I agreed with it—as a theory. Too many archeologists and dilettantes have, in the past, stripped sites of anything that might make a buck, ruining the locations' value for serious scholars or future generations. From what I'd heard while taking meals with other project members— and I'd been here half a week, now—this destruction had been especially bad in nineteenth-century Egypt.

Rhys and his colleagues bemoaned the fact that so many of the digs in Alexandria were already emergency salvage operations. In order to build necessary high-rise buildings to keep up with the population explosion, construction companies would dig down to the bedrock and, in so doing, uncover some ancient cemetery or villa or temple. It was all the archeologists could do to convince developers to postpone construction long enough for them to dig out and record the discovery before it vanished forever under an apartment or office building. The land was too valuable to be declared any kind of historical site.

In those cases, they *had* to move the artifacts.

But in other places like the pyramids, the Valley of the Kings, and even Cleopatra's Palace, archeologists had more choice. Some scholars were arguing that even the pyramids and tombs should be closed to the public, since just the moisture from peoples' breath was damaging some of the art. And for Cleopatra's Palace, there really was hope for an underwater system of translucent tunnels, so tourists for generations to come could see these remains just as we'd found them.

In situ.

So why would I resent so noble a goal?

The Isis Grail, that's why. *What the hell was I supposed to do once I found it?*

With the Melusine Chalice, my family grail, the decision had been made for me—I'd had to take it or leave it to its destruction. In fact, it was the subsequent damage of the abbey where I'd found it, by Comitatus members who'd been after me and were angered by my escape, that prompted the worst of Catrina Dauvergne's disdain. It would be great to prove her wrong, once and for all. Except...

If I found the Isis Grail amid this underwater treasure of relics and left it alone, how would that help other women? How would it help *anybody?*

Until now, my plan had been to gather and hide goddess cups until the Grailkeepers had enough to create a powerful display. Hopefully too powerful to be destroyed as other, individual grails had been.

But that would mean taking a relic that these scholars—good people, people who were *doing me a favor*—intended to leave in situ. Damn it.

Rhys and I reached the spot where we'd left off exploring on our last dive, a tumble of fallen columns and ancient building blocks, splotched green and velvety brown with algae and surreal in thick green shadows. I swam a tight circle around them, shining a halogen diving lantern into the crevices, peering after its light in hopes of seeing something curved and, well…chalicelike.

Conflicted.

Maybe I could tell Director d'Alencon about the Grailkeepers and the Comitatus. He might sympathize enough to protect the grail on his own until I'd collected enough cups to practically protect themselves.

Then again, if he was somehow connected to the Comitatus, he might lose or destroy the cup all by himself. I couldn't forget that attempts had been made against Rhys and against the project. It seemed to argue that *someone* around here was Comitatus.

Damn, but I hated paranoia. In fact—

The sensation was subtle at first, but powerful enough that my head came up. It felt like a…a beckoning.

Like magic.

Rhys must have noticed my sudden distraction. His blue eyes concerned in the shadow of his mask, he touched his thumb and forefinger into a circle. His expression was what made it a question instead of an answer. *Okay?*

I nodded, held up one hand for time—and scanned the underwater ruins, trying to recapture the tickle of sensation I'd just felt. Immediately I sensed my own misgivings blocking me. We were already studying the area with sonar and magnetometers—I'd been studying the revised charts almost every evening. What made me think pure instinct would do the trick? And yet...

Feminine instinct—any instinct—couldn't be completely disregarded, either. Logic only worked when everything was logical. The strange world in which I floated invited something different. Ancient. Infinitely powerful.

I turned away from Rhys and shone my light across the green-and-brown mottled columns and I tried to envision them standing again. I tried to envision priestesses in white and gold, perhaps the great Cleopatra herself with her kohl-lined eyes and legendary vitality, wearing the horn-and-disk headdress of Isis. A reincarnation of the goddess....

What would she do, to call Her? Would she spread her arms, like this?

I put down the halogen light, its beam pushing out across unimportant rocks and sand and darting fish, so that I could mimic the position that I imagined. She might spread her arms wide, like a bird's wings—Isis is often shown wearing brightly colored, human-size wings. She's also shown kneeling, one knee up, one knee down. With my ankle weights already at work, it took little effort for me to reproduce that posture, too.

And then the priestess would say something as an invocation, something faintly along the lines of...of...

Isis, Oldest of the Old, Goddess of Ten Thousand Names, Lady of Compassion and Healing and Magic.

Isis, I invite and welcome Thee into the remains of Thy temple, once grand, now hidden as so much of Your light has been hidden.

Isis, though You may find me unworthy, let me prove my worth. Show me where Your servants have hidden Your chalice, the cup into which You once poured Your powers and Your secrets. Reveal unto me, a daughter of goddesses, what it is I seek, so that Your divine strength may help many. Lift the veil of time and—

Only when I was interrupted, startled by the movement of someone coming at me from the murkiness, did I realize just how deeply I'd imagined the invocation. For a moment, it had been as if I really was back in time, back before the natural disasters that had sunken this palace, this temple. For a moment, I could imagine the Pharos Lighthouse—one of the seven wonders of the ancient world—still on its promontory, lighting the way for sailors at sea. For a moment, I could imagine the original Library of Alexandria still stood, not yet destroyed by fear and ignorance.

I don't mean to say that *I was there.* I knew I hadn't left this spot, that I was wearing fins and a mask and an air tank. But the shiver of power that had begun to ripple through me, at merely *thinking* an invocation of the goddess, gave me chills despite the dry suit. Something deep in the water beckoned me, something powerful, as surely as the Pharos Lighthouse had beckoned generations of ships to safety.

But that flash of movement, of another diver swimming out of the murkiness, caught my eye just as I started to turn toward the sensation's source. I tried to turn back—was that mere rubble I saw, or something more promising?

Before I could even check it out, Catrina Dauvergne had swum in front of me, waving with annoyance. I could tell it was her not only from the almond-shaped eyes behind her mask but because, like several of the other divers, she no longer bothered with the hood or gloves when she suited up.

Maybe she figured that as much as she smoked, a little toxicity in the water wouldn't make much difference. Either way, her hair fanned out around her head in weightless buoyancy. Her Virgin Mary medal glittered absurdly around her throat.

She pointed upward, demanding. Her meaning was clear.

In case my meaning wasn't clear enough when I shook my head, I answered her repeated gesture with a ruder one of my own. Then I jabbed a finger at her and pointed insistently upward. If she would just give me a little privacy…

She rolled her eyes and turned to Rhys, my diving buddy, in open-armed entreaty. He'd swum closer, to see what was up, but simply looked confused.

He couldn't know what I'd just sensed.

Catrina made a hand signal that might get her into a fight in some countries. It was the symbol for horns—thumb and pinky raised, other fingers fisted. For a moment I thought she meant some kind of Isis reference—but then she held the hand to her cheek, like a telephone.

Oh.

When her finger jabbed upward again, Rhys nodded. I understood better, too. I had a telephone call on the ship.

Well, it could wait. I retrieved my lantern, wanting nothing more than to aim it toward the end of the columns where I thought I'd glimpsed something promising. I didn't dare do so in front of a certain French grail thief.

Although really, I'd started to forget Cat had stolen the Melusine Grail and put it on sale on the black market. She did still work for the Cluny. She didn't seem rich.

With a kick of her swim fins and a cloud of sand, Catrina dived in front of me again, clearly frustrated now—I could see that even before she released a burst of bubbles with some kind of exclamation. She mimed the phone again. She pointed up top.

Glimpsing something solid between me and the mirrored surface, I recognized another diver, Niko. He made a wide arc with his forearm, a symbol every diver should know.

Emergency!

Had the images of Cleopatra and Isis and ancient times put me into some kind of a trance? If so, Niko's signal broke it. Suddenly, finding the goddess grail *right now* seemed significantly less important. I could locate this spot again—it wasn't as if the harbor floor wasn't being thoroughly mapped. I could repeat the invocation if necessary, since most of it had come from basic common knowledge of goddess cultures and…and instinct.

What if something had happened to my parents? My cousin Lil or her family? More likely, considering the people he ran with—*what if something had happened to Lex?*

I didn't wait. With a sand-billowing kick of my own, I shot upward, closely followed by Rhys and Catrina. I surfaced first, the other four heads bobbing out into the sun-washed waves after me, and made for the Zodiac.

Suddenly my throat clutched, tight. As if I had to scream, like the goddess Melusine.

It was as sure a sign of danger as Niko's hand signal had been.

Considering how my dive hood muffled all noise, it was also the only warning I got. I grabbed Rhys by one wrist and dived, trying to go deep—

But he'd been taken by surprise, and slowed us down.

A push of current spun me. Something dark blocked out the sun. I saw Catrina career off to one side—without a hood, she'd apparently heard the danger. But Rhys—

Even as I recognized the too close, bottom-up view of a speedboat, cutting past our diver-down buoy and right over Rhys and me, I knew Rhys hadn't gone deep enough.

Boat and diver collided.

Rhys's wrist was yanked from my hand.

A rush of bubbles exploded from his ruptured dry suit or, goddess forbid, a tank. As the boat continued away, not even slowing, a smear of blood darkened the white wake behind it.

Rhys's carefully weighted body began to slowly sink.

No!

I reached him first, encircling him with my arms, kicking desperately for the surface. Once there, I lifted his head out of the water, pulling free the regulator that at this point was as likely to suffocate him as help him. In a moment Niko was there, helping support Rhys's shoulders. I couldn't think. I didn't dare feel. For a moment, as I saw Catrina cutting away through the water to the Zodiac, I thought she was just being a coward—and that it figured.

Then she swam back with a life vest, which wasn't half-bad thinking.

Somehow we got Rhys to the boat, first the Zodiac and then the cabin cruiser, where a concerned crowd had already prepared a litter frame and lowered it over the side for him. As they pulled him up, doing their best to minimize bumps against the hull, the rest of us climbed to the deck, leaving our swim fins and tanks in a forgotten pile in the boat.

They'd laid Rhys out on a blanket, and d'Alencon was holding a towel to his heavily bleeding shoulder. Rhys's face looked even more pale than usual, contrasted against the hood that framed it. Eleni had gotten out the big first-aid chest and opened it, but she didn't seem to be sure what to do next.

"I don't think he's breathing," she sobbed. "What if he's dead?"

And since nobody else was moving fast enough, and since I'd taken first-aid courses for student emergencies, I stepped forward and searched for a pulse. He felt so clammy....

"I've called a water ambulance," d'Alencon insisted. Where was his heartbeat? *Where...?*

There. I found one. But it was faint.

Did I imagine his pulse getting fainter, in those few seconds that I held my fingers to my friend's pale throat?

"Do CPR," suggested someone.

"Not if he has a pulse," I argued, trying to think clearly—a few afternoons with representatives of the

Red Cross did not a doctor make. "But—he might have swallowed water, in the impact. He may need air."

"You should not move his neck," warned d'Alencon. Too late, since he didn't say it until I was tipping Rhys's head back. Crap! The other day I'd automatically assumed Catrina needed a neck brace, and yet for some reason, stupidly, with Rhys...

I swallowed back panic at the thought that I might have just complicated a spinal injury. I told myself that if he didn't get some air—*now*—paralysis would be the least of his problems.

Oh, Goddess. *Rhys!*

I checked his airway, to make sure he hadn't swallowed some piece of equipment. Then I bent over him, pinched his nose, pressed my lips to his in one way I'd never fantasized about—and breathed.

Hard.

Did his suited chest lift under my free hand?

I gasped a breath of my own, then breathed it into his mouth again. His chest did move—but only with my air. I did it again. Then again. In the necessity of the moment, I could concentrate only on the repetitive action. Everything else from the past five or ten minutes became a blur of background thought, echoing through my shock-numbed mind.

Rhys silently asking, with gloved fingers, if I was okay. *Inhale.*

Me taking the half-kneeling posture of "seated Isis." *Exhale.*

Isis... Oldest of the Old...though You may find me unworthy... Inhale.

Who the hell had been driving that damned speedboat? *Exhale—*

And on that last exhalation of mine, when Rhys's chest expanded—he coughed against my mouth.

I drew back, eyes widening.

Rhys coughed harder, spitting water—then rolled to his side, to better cough the rest of it up. He wasn't paralyzed. He was alive and breathing!

I looked upward at the sun, idiotic fragments still tumbling through my head. *Thank You,* I thought dumbly, to whatever god or goddess had helped save Rhys's life. Very possibly, the god had been his own. *Thank You for this man, for this life.*

I thought I heard some kind of bird cry as I turned back to Rhys. "Lie still," I insisted, reaching out for a blanket that Catrina, of all people, had fetched from below deck. "You were hit by a speedboat. An ambulance is on its way."

He looked confused, and why not? Whoever had been driving that boat had been deliberately reckless, if not murderous. And this wasn't the first time Rhys had been injured, here in Alexandria.

But this time, Rhys may not have been the target.

The first words Rhys managed to murmur from his cough-roughened throat were, "Did you just give me…mouth-to-mouth…resuscitation?"

"Yeah." I lay a hand on his cheek and marvelled at how precious he was to me. "My pleasure."

He drew a shaky breath, then asked, "Emergency?"

"I think this counts as an emergency, yes—" But I stopped as Rhys shook his head and glanced at Catrina.

Oh. She'd beckoned us up in the first place with the claim of an emergency phone call.

A chill shook me as I realized the significance of

that. She was the one who had drawn us up top, just in time for the boat to veer right at us!

"Yes, Catrina," I said coolly. "What was that about a phone call?"

Ms. Dauvergne said nothing, she just sneered. But Eleni said, "They left a message for you, Ms. Sanger. Someone named Tala?"

I frowned in her direction, more confused than ever, as she handed me a note.

Scribbled in French she'd written, "Emergency. Come at once. Kara to be married."

Chapter 12

It's either a testament to my selfishness, or to how deeply I did care for Rhys, that I ignored Tala's plea for help until my friend was cleared by a doctor.

In the meantime, it was enough to learn that for the second time in a week, Rhys's injuries were not as severe as I'd feared. Maybe I should believe in coincidence after all?

"I never knew being a priest came with those kinds of perks," I teased, my arm around him to help him from the hospital to a cab so that I could take him back to the Hotel Athens. *Not severe* meant only that he was neither dead nor staying in the hospital. He still had a terrible headache and his arm, which had taken fourteen stitches, was in a sling. Both the doctors and d'Alencon ordered a day's bed rest before he even thought about going back to work, much less to diving. "I guess the Big Guy watches out for his own, huh?"

"Don't...blaspheme," warned Rhys through the painkillers, but he also smiled a loopy grin. "What was...the big emergency?"

I got him settled in the cab, even buckled his seat belt, then came around to the other side and told the driver our destination. "Something about Kara getting married."

His eyes widened. *"She's barely twelve!"*

"I'm going over there as soon as I get you settled at the hotel," I assured him.

"Hotel be damned. We have...we have to..."

He was wincing more with each word, and his good hand fisted as if he were trying not to put it to his head.

"*You* have to get better," I warned. "I'll find out everything I can while you're resting, then I'll report back. I promise."

He looked suspicious.

"I *promise*," I repeated. "We'll figure something out."

"Maggi." For a moment I thought he was losing his balance as we turned a corner; then I realized he was trying to lean closer to me. I stretched closer to him instead.

"If we must get her out of the country, I'll do it," he whispered—I guess to keep the cabbie from hearing, which wasn't a bad idea. "Let Tala and Jane know that."

He meant he would risk imprisonment on kidnapping charges if we failed—or would risk doing something martyrlike to make sure we succeeded. I stared at him, overwhelmed by how blatantly, flat-out *good* he could be.

Uncomplicated. Unquestionable. "Rhys—"

"*If* we must. You and Jane have livelihoods to protect. I threw mine away—"

"You did not! If the church allowed priests to marry, you'd be saying mass today!"

"Tell them," he whispered, closing his eyes to rest them.

Luckily, we arrived at the hotel before I had to make yet another promise.

I still wasn't wholly comfortable returning to Tala Rachid's villa, especially not on my own. My memories of what had happened that first time were still a mysterious blank.

Even when I'd visited with Rhys a few days ago to report what little I'd learned in Cairo, I'd declined the offer of a drink. Just in case.

This time, Tala's servant opened the door to me even before I finished paying the taxi.

"Come in, please," the girl said softly, bowing. "The *sitt* is anxious."

Anxious didn't begin to describe the mood in the parlor to which I was led. Jane's eyes were wild and puffy from crying. Even Tala's usual well-groomed composure, as she stood at my appearance, had a brittle edge to it.

Kara, looking particularly frail on the sofa, glanced from one adult to the other with nervous suspicion. The child actually had a doll on her lap!

Not exactly your standard bride-to-be.

"Hello, Kara," I greeted awkwardly, unsure how much the girl knew. "I need to talk to your mother and grandmother for a little while about some grown-up things. Could you—"

"*No,*" protested Jane, but Tala interrupted.

"Perhaps you can listen to your new CD, dear?" Kara's stepgrandmother suggested.

Kara rolled her eyes but obediently drew a Discman from her tote bag and put on earphones. A moment later, we heard rhythmic white noise whispering from her music—and she began to make her doll dance.

"I'm sorry," said Jane softly, as Tala showed me to a seat across the room. "I'm afraid to let her out of my sight, afraid he'll snatch her again. I'll d—" She glanced back at Kara, then to me. "I'll die before I let him do this. I mean it."

Tala said, "Then she would have nobody to go home *to,* Jane. You must stay calm."

"Please," I said. "Tell me exactly what's going on. When does Hani mean to have her marry?"

Jane's tears thickened her words. "Tomorrow night!"

I stared, going cold.

"That's when he means to have her betrothed," corrected Tala. "Of course a marriage will take longer to arrange."

Jane whirled on her. "They're practically the same!"

I stared at Tala, wishing they'd get their stories straight.

"I'm afraid that's true," admitted the older woman. "Betrothing Kara to a local boy—"

"Boy? He's in college!"

"—is the first step toward taking custody from me. Likely Hani will grant it to the boy's mother, who can then refuse Jane visitation."

"And he may actually marry her," insisted Jane. "At twelve. It's been known to happen. It's legalized rape is what it is!"

At least I could understand the extent of her panic. If I were in her situation, I'd probably be panicking, too, no matter how useless that was. Luckily, I *wasn't* in her situation. And I had a clear enough head to notice something.

A shadow, beyond the archway to the foyer.

"I apologize for involving you," said Tala, her humility surprising me. "If you were not the champion—"

Oh for the love of—

"I'm *not* the champion," I insisted, standing. "How often do I have to tell you that?"

"But you must be," whispered Jane. "We *need* you to be."

It was for her sake that I put my finger to my lips before I said, with deliberate clarity, "Well that's too bad."

Even then, she looked crushed.

"I feel sorry for your family," I continued, widening my eyes in hopes they would catch on. "I do, but I've had enough of Egypt. I've had enough of my friends getting hurt. I've had enough of threats and manipulation. And most of all—"

Which is when I dodged around the corner—and caught the eavesdropping maid by one arm.

"I've had enough of secrecy," I said.

The girl—I'd be surprised if she was twenty years old—screeched and tried to pull free, but her struggle was surprisingly ineffective. She would not look at me as she babbled in frightened Arabic.

"She asks," translated Tala coldly, as she and Jane gathered around, "that you not put the evil eye on her."

"Speak English," I ordered. Normally I hate playing the ugly American, but if I didn't want this whole situation to get away from me...

"Please," sobbed the maid obediently, still cowering. "Please, witch. Do not...please..."

What? My first instinct was to assure her either that I wasn't a witch or that, if I was, I was a nice one. Then practicality shouldered kindness out of the way. I said, "I *will* curse you, you little spy—*unless* you answer my questions."

"Please!" She fell to her knees, but still she wasn't struggling. This was not the effect my touch had been having, lately. I realized that she must be afraid to strike out or scratch at me, aka the witch.

I wasn't sure whether to find it funny, annoying…or, worse, empowering as hell.

"You will answer honestly? I'll know if you don't!"

She nodded, tears streaming down her face. Oh…goddess. I looked to Tala for help. She took the girl by the shoulders and steered her to a chair.

My first question was, "Who are you spying for?"

"Isn't it obvious?" demanded Jane. "It's that son-of-a—"

"We have to hear it from her," I interrupted, then tried my best to glare at the maid as I lied, "so I'll know with my magic if she's telling the truth."

The maid, whose name turned out to be Layla, nodded frantically—and spilled. As it turned out, she'd been spying for Hani Rachid for months. That's how Hani knew that Jane had met Rhys. That's how Hani knew about my arrival, and when I would be there for dinner, and that Tala wanted me to help Kara and Jane.

"Please do not curse me," Layla begged. "This is all I know. I swear it is all I know. I…I see now that he was using me." Maybe, with the help of my goddess touch, she really did. "I will tell him no more, not even if he beats me—"

"No," I interrupted, thinking fast. If I simply told her to pass on a message, she—or at least Hani—would be suspicious. But if I phrased it right… "Do you think I care what he knows? I am leaving Egypt tomorrow. After that, his affairs will mean nothing to me."

Everyone stared at me. Even Kara, who seemed to have surreptitiously turned down her Discman when the excitement started. Jane said, "You can't!"

"If I'm a witch," I reminded her, "then I can do anything I want, right? But only when *I* decide. Why should I trouble myself with these...these petty affairs?"

I held Tala's gaze for an extra long moment and, thankfully, she seemed to figure it out. About damned time. If I had to get more melodramatic than that, I wasn't sure I could respect myself.

"Take her away," she commanded Jane, of the servant. "Of course I am terminating her employment as of this instant. See that she actually does leave, while I try to convince our *champion* to take our cause."

"You won't," I warned her loudly. It was all I could do not to fling my hair back and glare down my nose. But it gave the right impression until Jane got Layla out of the way.

Then Tala said, more softly, "You *will* help us, won't you?"

"Yes, but not because I'm any sort of champion or witch. I'll help you because I'm a decent human being who thinks the law is wrong in this case. But it's going to be a long shot."

"It's worth a try," she said. "At worst, if you and Jane are arrested at the border crossing, there will be publicity—"

"We aren't crossing any borders." I hadn't realized I had a plan until those words left my mouth. When they did, and my subconscious let me in on things, I thought—Not half bad.

For a crapshoot.

"We're going by boat, then?" asked Jane, returning. "I tried that already. He was watching for me."

"No." My firmness surprised even me. "We're going inland. And you're not coming with us."

* * *

The next morning, as planned, I packed the largest rolling suitcase I could find—bought off another of Rhys's archeologist friends. I checked out of the Hotel Athens, to Catrina's apparent delight, and headed out for the train station.

With one stop, of course.

Rhys insisted on driving me. He rested in the car while I dragged my suitcase through the walled courtyard at the entrance and into the villa to say goodbye to the Rachid family.

"I have given Jane the rhyme," Tala whispered, holding my hands in hers—that seemed to be her poised version of a hug. We stood in the foyer, just inside her entryway. More important, my suitcase was hidden from view inside, as well. "As soon as she knows that Kara is safe…"

I wished I had her conviction, but I knew better than she that I was neither a witch nor a champion. I was just Maggi…and, okay, a Grailkeeper. That might help.

Instead of jinxing us through overconfidence—or fatalism—I just said, "I hope you know that I'm not doing this for the secret to the Isis Grail."

Her dark eyes softened. "I know this," she said. "It is what I sensed upon our first meeting. And it is why the Oldest of the Old will surely smile upon you."

After we'd waited a suitable amount of time, I grasped the handle of my suitcase and rolled it back across the courtyard, toward the car. The car was the same battered blue Chevy Metro, joint owned by several project members, in which Rhys had originally picked me up.

The suitcase rattled across exotic tiling, under the

striped morning shadows of the pergola's trelliswork.
The car was fifteen feet away. Then ten. The air smelled
of jasmine. Then the car was only five feet away, just
beyond two palm trees and the open iron gate....

Then, just as I was beginning to wonder if so crazy
a plan could actually work, two swarthy men in blue
jeans and polyester shirts stepped out from behind the
palm trees to intercept me.

I stopped, immediately tried to back up, but one of
them reached out and caught the handle of my suitcase.

"No!" I protested, but the other caught me, hard,
with an arm around my waist. He lifted me off my toes,
so that I hung from his grip like one of Kara's dolls.

He hadn't showered in a day or so, either.

I struggled, once, but when he tightened his hold
painfully, I stopped. I needed my breath too badly.

"Maggi!" called Rhys, from the car. He began to
get out, still moving slowly since yesterday's ordeal,
but I shook my head at him. No point in endangering
both of us.

The first man, glaring at me, unzipped the overlarge
suitcase and triumphantly threw it open to reveal—

My clothes.

"Stop it," I protested, again. When he dug out a handful of my underwear, peering deeper into the case, I
added, "You pervert!"

Now Rhys limped closer, leaving the driver's door
open. "Leave her alone!"

And Tala, from the front door of her villa, called
something in Arabic, then translated, "You will stop harassing my guests at once. I have rung the police!"

Confused and embarrassed—and unsure what to do
without their leader—Hani's thugs had to let me go.

"This is why I'm leaving your damned country," I scolded as I threw my clothes back into the suitcase and zipped it shut. "I haven't been here a week and already I've been kidnapped and attacked and almost run over by a speedboat—"

I still hoped the incidents *weren't* related to me. But it made a good rant.

Tala continued to scold the men in Arabic. I, on the other hand, loaded my suitcase full of now messy clothing into the back seat of the Metro and climbed into the passenger seat.

Rhys said nothing as he pulled away. Neither did I.

Not until we were well away, and I could risk peeking over the back of my seat. "Are you okay back there, kiddo?"

"You guessed right," announced Kara proudly, sitting up from under a light blanket. "They were so busy with you, they didn't even notice me sneak into the car."

"You're a suspiciously good sneaker." I pretended to be *particularly* stern as I said that, but Kara just laughed. If she'd had any reservations about this plan, I doubt I could bear forcing her into it. It was going to be far more difficult for her than for me. "So you know what to do, right?"

"Hide the clothes under the blanket and get into the suitcase," she recited. "Sit on the wheel side. Then you'll zip it most of the way up before we get on the train."

"Did you use the bathroom? Er…the loo?"

She nodded. "I'm not a baby!"

But good heavens, she didn't look far from it, even at twelve. Her face shone with the excitement of this adventure. Her dark hair was neatly braided. She had a cartoon kitty on her T-shirt.

"Yeah, but it's a very long train ride. Don't drink too much of your water—"

"And don't play my Discman too loudly, I *know!*"

So instead of continuing to lecture her, which could garner suspicion from anyone who saw us drive by, I settled back into my seat. See what I mean? A crapshoot.

"I did not see the father," I said to Rhys—in French. No reason to worry the girl further.

"Nor did I," he answered in the same language. "You must let me come with you, Maggi."

"You're still recovering. And it will look less like something big's going down if you stay here. Besides, it's relatively safe for me. This isn't kidnapping," I assured him.

The Roman coliseum across from the train station came into view, and I added, "At least, not until we reach the embassy."

Chapter 13

Sometimes, chivalry can be a pain. The hardest part about smuggling Kara onto and then off of the Turbo-train to Cairo was keeping men from wrenching the suitcase away from me. Once we arrived at the Ramses Railway Station, I wheeled Kara down the open platform to the white, brightly lit terminal and its rest rooms. There, using the relative privacy of the oversize, handicapped stall, I could let her climb out and stretch for a few minutes.

"This is exciting," she whispered, her face shining. "Like in a film!"

At least one of us was having fun.

"Glad you're enjoying it," I mused, swallowing back my own uncertainties. I wondered if her Grailkeeper grandmother, or ex-stepgrandmother, would be able to visit her in England and pass on some of the legacy. Now *Kara* might grow up to be a champion.

I politely turned my back for her to make use of the facilities. Then I had to zip the kid back into the suitcase for the last leg of our journey out of Egypt—here, in the very *heart* of Egypt.

So many women wore head scarves around here, I already felt conspicuous. Feeling conspicuous in an area guarded by men in white uniforms, with machine guns, is even less pleasant. But soon enough I made it into the ungodly midday heat and blinding sunlight in front of the station, with its huge statue of Ramses II.

Again, I had to fight the cabby to load my own damned suitcase. When he tried to yank it from my hands, despite my loud protest, two old women swathed in full black burkas ran to my rescue, swatting at him and scolding in Arabic until he let go. When I tried to thank them, they simply nodded and turned away.

There are different kinds of feminine empowerment, I guess.

"American Embassy," I told the driver.

"Ah, Fortress Amerika," he said in good, if singsong English, with a knowing nod.

Once we pulled away from the curb unaccosted, I tried to make myself relax. The embassy district in Cairo, as I had learned on my previous day-trip, was in an area called Garden City, not two miles from the station. We turned off the main road into a lacework of tree-lined, curving streets and stately, colonial buildings.

We were almost there.

But almost isn't always good enough. Cairo traffic was bad enough—and this from someone who grew up just outside New York! Amid the chaos of bumper-to-bumper cars wandered bicycles, pedestrians, donkeys and even camels. As we neared the embassy, the interlacing of one-way streets and private drives only complicated matters further.

Unlike the first-class railcar, the taxi wasn't air-conditioned. I already had my window rolled all the way down, and I leaned across my suitcase to crank down the one on the other side, too. I could imagine how hot it was inside the suitcase, but I only dared leave a few inches unzipped for air.

Come on, I urged silently. *Come on!*

"Ah, me," mused the driver, after we'd been sitting dead still for about five minutes. "This may take time."

I leaned out the window and saw that there was some kind of accident ahead involving a camel—which seemed to be unhurt—and a haystack-size pile of alfalfa fallen across another car. On the one hand, we could wait. This escape would be easier if we were dropped off at the embassy door. On the other hand, it was stifling in here....

And every minute that passed was another minute Hani Rachid might discover Kara gone from Alexandria.

"How far?" I asked, digging out my Egyptian money. "How far to Fortress Amerika?"

"Two blocks," he assured me. "We wait. I give you discount."

But instead of taking his discount I paid him and climbed out of the cab, hauling the suitcase with me. I began wheeling it and Kara in the direction he'd indicated, glad to note that at least the sidewalks around here were well kept. The greenery helped temper the heat a bit. I could catch glimpses of the wide expanse of the Nile to my left, felt its ancient call.

But damn it, I wanted to have this done. I had to know Kara was safe.

And then...

Damn it. I sensed it partly from a prickling along the back of my neck and, more, from a tightening of my throat.

We were being followed.

I picked up my pace, never so glad to see the stately embassy rising ahead of me, beyond a high iron fence that I didn't doubt was wired to the max.

The Stars and Stripes beckoned to me from over the building's entrance.

Armed marines stood outside.

Having already visited once, I fully understood why the cabdriver called the place Fortress Amerika. There was no way I could simply dart into the sanctuary of the building with an oversize suitcase, even carrying my passport and singing "The Star-Spangled Banner." Not with terrorism such a real threat.

But I could get closer. I sped my step, my breath starting to rasp in my lungs from the exertion of pulling the heavy suitcase.

Only when my throat actually clenched did I glance behind me—and start to run.

Crap.

It was Hani.

No way could I pull a suitcase with even a *small* twelve-year-old in it faster than he could chase me. But we had the attention of the guards, anyway.

And I had one last trick up my sleeve.

Just as I heard Hani's footsteps pounding up behind me, I spun and raced across the street, *away* from the American Embassy. I unzipped the suitcase as it fell to the sidewalk, and I yelled, "Head right!"

Then I spun to face the girl's father, deliberately blocking his way.

Hani's eyes burned bright, like a predator's in mid-hunt. He must have guessed who was hidden in the luggage. Even so, I could see him visibly start when Kara scrambled out of the case and scampered not left, toward the American, but toward the British Embassy across the street.

Hello? *I* was the only American here.

I wished I could watch her, wanted to make sure she was waving her passport the way we'd told her to. It's not like the British guards were any less aware of terrorist threats than the Americans. And, terrible or not, we weren't that far from a part of the world where children were sometimes used in suicide bombings.

I could hear her little-girl voice yelling, as instructed, "I'm a citizen, I'm a citizen, God save the Queen!"

And all I could do was keep her father from catching up to her. But that would be more than enough.

Hani tried to dodge around me—I was clearly no longer his target—but I cut him off. When he tried to run right over me, like an American football player, I dropped low—and tripped him.

He was heavy, but I was careful to roll, so as not to take his entire weight. My fighting style is more about using my opponent's force against him—better that Hani take his own damned weight! And he did. Even as I sprang back to my feet, Hani Rachid sprawled heavily onto the pavement.

But not for long.

Scrambling upward, still focused beyond me, he let out a frighteningly bestial bellow of rage. If hatred and violence had a sound, that was it.

Okay, so that scared me. But—

"I've got her, Maggi!" called another familiar

voice—Jane's. She'd come to Cairo the previous night, although, with her wearing her flight attendant uniform and Kara visibly waving goodbye as she'd left, Hani's men had no reason to think Jane was doing more than returning to work. "She's here now. It's safe!"

"You thief!"

This time, as Hani charged past me toward the embassy, I didn't dare get in his way—not if I wasn't needed. Instead, I turned and satisfied myself with the sight of mother and daughter, clinging to one another behind high iron bars.

Oh…goddess.

If I accomplished nothing else in Egypt, this would have been worth it.

Not that I was giving up on the Isis Grail just yet.

Meanwhile, the two armed guards who stepped forward to block Hani's path were more than up to the task.

"She's a thief!" Kara's father insisted, though he quickly backed away from their presence…and from the presence of their automatic weapons. "She has no right to take the girl."

But in Britain, Jane damn well had that right. In Britain, she'd had custody all along. And the embassy grounds were, for all intents and purposes, part of the United Kingdom.

Jane stared at the husband who had made her last year hell. Then she turned and hustled Kara safely through the heavy double doors into the embassy building…and that was that.

There would be no betrothal tonight.

There would be no underage wedding.

Of course, I was still out in the open. Hani spun on me. "You think you have helped her, witch?"

I steeled myself, so as not to flinch from his fury. "Yes, I do."

"She is a prisoner now. She cannot leave. She will rot in that damned building, and I will celebrate it."

I frowned. "Which 'she' are you talking about?"

"My wife!"

"*Ex*-wife. You don't give a damn about Kara, do you? This is all about hurting Jane."

"It is about keeping women in their proper place!"

"And how's that worked for you so far?" We've won, Sinbad. You've lost.

"When the child leaves the embassy, she will rightfully be mine," Hani insisted. "I will arrange her life as I see fit. When my wife leaves, she will be arrested, and she will beg me to help her, and I will only spit upon her as she is dragged to prison. That is all you have done."

I didn't like the suspicion that he was correct—about Kara and Jane being more or less prisoners in the embassy, that is, not about the begging and spitting.

It was still better than a betrothal and possible marriage for a twelve-year-old. "I'll take that."

"Not for long you will not," warned Hani, breathing hard.

"Where's your Eye of Horus?" I asked, and wiggled my fingers at him. "No magical protection today?"

His eyes widened.

Luckily, at that point, Jane hailed me. She did not have Kara with her. "Maggi, come on," she called, from safely within the grounds of the embassy. "I have something for you."

The clue to the Isis Grail?

"See you soon," I told Hani. Not that I *wanted* to see him…but I certainly wanted him to know I expected to.

He spat something at me in Arabic—something that sounded extremely rude—and turned away. As I passed the guards outside the British Embassy, allowed in with my American passport and her request, I gestured toward the sidewalk and the man and the open, empty suitcase. "That's garbage," I said.

Then I muttered, if only to myself: "You might want to send someone after the suitcase, too."

High in the heavens and under the sea
Isis is everywhere, she cannot be contained.
Look for her where she is honored.
There, you shall find her cup.

I guess the words lost their rhyme in translation. But my disappointment, as I read the paper that Jane handed me, was over a hell of a lot more than the poem's free verse.

This had been passed down for generations in Tala's family?

I reread it, hoping to notice something new.

I didn't.

Tala Rachid's "rhyme" didn't tell me squat! At least, no more than I'd already guessed.

Around us, the office was in chaos. An ambassadorial assistant was protesting that they hadn't agreed to Jane and Kara's defection into their embassy—something Jane and I had done deliberately, figuring that it was easier to get forgiveness than permission. Another reminded him that they couldn't exactly evict her now that she was here. Telephones were ringing, and voices had an edge of strain.

And against the cacophony, Kara had her skinny arms around Jane's waist, gazing up at her mother adoringly. *They were safe.*

Even more than me finding the Isis Grail, that was what mattered. Surely England could work *something* out before laws or circumstances forced either mother or daughter back out onto Egyptian soil, unprotected.

"I hope it helps," said Jane honestly, about the poem.

Look for her where she is honored. I supposed that could mean the cup was wherever I would find the altar to Isis, in her submerged temple.

"Yes," I said, with forced enthusiasm. "It's just what I needed. Are you going to be okay?"

"Some of the people here seem to resent the trouble, but that one—Cathy—says they're making up a guest room for Kara and me. She said we can stay until the diplomats come to some kind of agreement."

Surely that agreement wouldn't include Jane giving Kara back. One nice thing about politics being so competitive—England wouldn't want to buckle to Egyptian pressure, any more than Egypt wanted to give in to England.

"I hope it doesn't take too long. You have my number at the Hotel Athens, right? You'll call if you need anything?"

Jane gave me a hug. "I can't thank you enough!"

"Don't bother trying. You've fought the good fight. Just hold out a little bit longer, okay?"

She nodded, too emotional to say more.

I shook hands with Kara.

She said, "I don't care what my papa's lawyers say. If he ever gets me back and tries to make me marry some stupid boy, I'll...I'll *spit* on him!"

If that was the goddess energy speaking, I wished I could channel it more deliberately. "Just be careful you choose your battles, Kara. And take care of your mom, okay?"

The little girl nodded, eyes still glowing from our recent adventure. A Grailkeeper in the making, for sure.

Speaking of choosing battles, it was time to leave them to theirs and return to my own. I had to go diving again, to follow that prescience I'd had about the grail. If I found it, I had to talk to d'Alencon about how to protect the grail. I had to check on Rhys, make sure he hadn't overexerted himself as my wheelman this morning. He might have once been a priest, but he was still a guy, and guys—the good ones, anyway—don't like standing back when women are in danger. Whether or not it went back to cavemen killing saber-toothed tigers that threatened the camp or not. I headed out of the British Embassy full of plans.

Not a one of them included what happened next.

"You are Madeleine Sanger, yes?" demanded a dark-skinned, white-uniformed police officer as I stepped onto the sidewalk.

"Magdalene," I corrected him, immediately wary. "Why?"

"I am afraid that you are under arrest for kidnapping," he said pleasantly, and took my arm. "Come with me, please."

I looked around me—and, sure enough, there stood Hani Rachid in full triumph, across the street.

With an Eye-of-Horus design drawn onto his cheek.

"I didn't kidnap anybody," I protested, not moving even when the officer put pressure on my arm. "I took a little girl to Cairo with the permission of her grandmother."

In fact, I had deliberately not accompanied Kara onto the embassy property that first time. She went of her own accord.

"Perhaps we can resolve this at the police station, miss," said the officer, his grip tightening.

"Or perhaps you can check the laws," I argued back. "I had Tala Rachid's permission—"

"Miss." The officer sounded much less pleasant, now. "A complaint has been filed. You are under arrest. I am being polite, as you are a visitor to our country, but you come with me now, or I will force you to come with me."

And really, what was I going to do—make a break for it? I *could*. I had no doubt that I could twist from the officer's hold on me and outrun him. Especially if he tried to follow me in the police car I now recognized parked against the curb.

Traffic would be on my side.

But I wouldn't do it. The law was also on my side, for now at least. Going fugitive over something this minor would be a mistake.

So I let the policeman lead me to his car—and cuff me.

But the thought of being imprisoned in an Egyptian jail even temporarily sure didn't sit comfortably in my stomach.

Neither did the white grin of Hani Rachid as he watched his vengeance play out.

Chapter 14

The worst part was when the police took my passport. Unlike in the States—or what I'd heard, having never been arrested myself before now—they left me with my jewelry and even, after searching it, the fanny pack with my money. But the passport, they confiscated.

Suddenly, I wasn't just in an Egyptian jail.

I had no proof that I was even an American.

And I sure wasn't being treated like a *guest*.

"I want a lawyer," I stated, more than once, during the booking process. Many of the officers just ignored me; I couldn't tell if they even spoke English, which was an unnervingly helpless feeling. "I have a right to a lawyer."

One officer answered, "You have *no* rights."

Maybe he was joking…but I suspected he wasn't. This wasn't exactly the Land of the Free. So I started asking for a phone call.

"We will do the calling," insisted the officer, filling out paperwork for me since, in a country that used Arabic, I was as good as illiterate. "Who is your husband?"

Lex. That's whose ring I was wearing, wasn't it? If I had them call Lex Stuart at the Four Seasons, I'd be out as soon as humanly possible. Maybe sooner than that! Lex had powerful contacts I could barely imagine.

And yet...

I know what you're thinking. I was thinking it, too. Now was no time to handicap myself with stupid principles!

And yet, if I only had principles when it was easy, how important were they, really?

It wasn't just that I was remembering Hani's recent gloat about Jane—*She will be arrested, she will beg me to help her.* As if it really *was* a woman's place to have freedom only through the intervention of a man.

It's that Lex *wasn't* really my husband. This *wasn't* his fight—in fact, he'd been against this trip, much less my helping Jane, from the start. Surely I could get myself out of this without claiming myself as his property.

Besides, the statement was a legal document. For all I knew, if I announced Lex as my husband on it, we would end up common-law married for real.

"He is not here," I said.

"Yes, but what is his name?"

"You don't need his name. You have mine. That's what counts. The woman whose granddaughter I'm accused of taking from Alexandria will vouch for me—Dr. Tala Rachid. And I have a friend in Connecticut who can help me. Officer Sophie Douglas, of the North Stamford Police Department. That's D-O-U-G..."

The officer scowled, but wrote it down.

The cell they brought me to was straight out of a bad exploitation movie—dirty, cramped and stinking of sweat and human waste. There were no beds; the women who were sitting or lying down did so on the stone floor or on worn blankets. One was coughing heavily. One was moaning.

I didn't realize I'd hesitated, there in the doorway, until the guard shoved me hard enough that only my good sense of balance kept me from sprawling onto the ground.

I spun and glared.

He yelled something that was clearly an insult and turned away. Apparently, just by being accused of a crime, I'd lost that shiny halo of invulnerability that tourists sometimes start to believe they wear.

So here I was. In jail. *In Cairo.*

Crap.

I looked at the other women in our small cell—there were eight of us total, two not much older than Kara. Over half wore the traditional head covering. One woman sat in a corner slowly peeling an orange. Two others stared at her with obvious envy. Wherever she'd gotten it, I had the feeling nobody else had one.

At first I just stood quietly and tried to look inconspicuous—as if, with my skin and hair color, that would ever happen. Finally, as time passed and nobody did anything worse than stare at me and talk among themselves, I ventured, "Does anybody here speak English, please?"

Several of the women stared. Several glanced at me, then looked away in disgust.

"Parlez-vous français, s'il-vous plait?" I tried. I was going to run out of languages pretty soon.

"I speak the English some," offered a soft voice, and a teenage girl with thick black hair stepped tentatively closer to me. Another woman said something rapidly in Arabic—a protest? The teenager waved her away. "I learn in school, yes?"

I cannot describe how wonderful it felt to hear words in my own language. It was as though I'd been deaf, but could suddenly hear again. I wanted to hug the girl. Instead I said, "Hello. I'm Maggi."

"I am Samira," she said. "You be American, yes?"

"Yes."

She said nothing, but her face got so serious as she cocked her head that I guessed what she was thinking.

I said, "Do you want to know why I'm here?"

"Only if you wish to say, miss. I mean not disrespect." Her posture was submissive. Most of the women's were—at least when the guards were watching. When they weren't, a clear pecking order quickly developed.

Nobody had bothered me—probably because they hadn't figured me out yet. Did Samira hope I'd be able to protect her...or was it possible she was trying to protect me?

I kind of hoped I wouldn't be here long enough to find out.

"I am accused of kidnapping a little girl," I explained. "I brought her to Cairo, with her grandmother's permission, and she ran into the British Embassy to see her mother. But it is a mistake."

Samira nodded solemnly.

"Do you know what happens next?" I asked, glancing around us again.

"Next?"

I nodded. "After this. After now."

"The guards maybe take us to clean," she admitted, brow furrowed in thought. "They do not make men clean. Only women. When it is time for the lunch, they bring bread and cheese."

"But when can I get a lawyer? When do I get to make a phone call? How long will I *be* here?"

She nodded, better understanding my question. "You be brought before Public Prosecution Office in only day, maybe two day."

"A day or two?"

She nodded.

The moaning woman ducked behind the privacy screen, where I assumed the toilet was, and threw up. Loudly.

And here I'd thought the hole in my gut couldn't gape any larger. Desperate for distraction, I asked why Samira was there.

"I am…*mu`aridin li inhiraf…*" She frowned, trying to work out the words. "Exposure to bad behavior," she decided.

"Exposed to…? What did you do?"

She looked at me blankly. She'd already answered that.

"What were you doing when you were arrested?" I tried.

She shrugged. "Walking."

By the time I got more of the story from her, we also were sitting on the bare floor. As it turned out, a lot of children who were homeless, or begging, or simply truant—like Samira—were arrested on the mere *risk* of going bad. They were supposed to be taken to a children's facility, rather than housed with adults, but it

Evelyn Vaughn   *169*

didn't always work out that way. Usually they were only held a few days, she assured me, but sometimes it could last longer.

"Do you have parents? Won't they miss you?"

She shook her head sadly. "They do not come for me here. They be much frightened."

The guard—or *mukhbir,* as she called him—said something sharply at us, which made her flush. She protested in Arabic, and he said something else and leered and laughed.

I glared at him.

He shouted at me.

I didn't look away.

He shouted at me more loudly, and waved some kind of weapon at me. A rubber hose.

I angrily moved my glare from his eyes to his crotch—to the limp hose. Then back to his eyes. I curled my lip in disgust. Then I turned away.

He was screaming at me now, but I didn't look, and finally, after spitting in my direction, he turned away.

"Has he bothered you?" I asked Samira, who was staring in outright awe.

She nodded, and I felt fury stiffening my back.

"Has he *touched* you?"

But here, she shook her head. "He say I am arrested for dirty things," she whispered. "I am not arrested for this. It is only that I do not go to school. He say I can have orange, if I do for him, but I do not do for anybody. I am good girl."

I couldn't help it—I looked at the woman who'd had an orange earlier.

Samira shook her head and smiled a shy smile. "She buy it. Her family bring her money."

Lunch really was just bread and some gelatinous cheese spread. We were left to portion it ourselves. I made sure I got a piece on the suspicion—which proved out—that Samira might not, then gave her mine.

It's not like I had an appetite.

Thankfully, not long after that, a man in a suit came for me. He was clean-shaven, with bright black eyes.

"Magdalene Sanger," he called in English, walking down the main corridor of the jail. "Where is Mrs. Magdalene—"

"I'm Maggi Sanger," I called, pulling myself to my feet. My legs had gone to sleep while I talked with Samira. "Are you here to get me out?"

"I believe something can be arranged, if you sign this." Through the bars, he handed me a sheet of paper on a clipboard.

I took it, looked, and felt even more helpless. A lot of good a Ph.D. did me here. "It's written in Arabic."

"It says that you are innocent of all wrongdoing," he assured me breezily, and offered a pen.

I almost took it. I wanted out so badly. I wanted to check on Rhys, to talk with Lex. I wanted to find the Isis Grail and *go the hell home.* Mostly, I wanted to get out of this smell—it felt like things were crawling on me, even if they weren't. The woman with the cough didn't cover her mouth. The one who was moaning had thrown up again. I really didn't want to have to face that toilet, but time was against me.

I wanted out so badly, I could scream. In fact, my throat *ached* with the need to scream…which was my warning.

Heart racing, I held the clipboard out to Samira. "Can you read this and tell me what it says?"

She glanced at the paper, frowned—and the gentleman in the suit reached through the bars and snatched it away from us. "She knows nothing!"

I felt ill, but I wasn't about to show it. "Get me an English translation, then."

He laughed and shook his head, as if I were joking. "This is impossible, Mrs. Sanger."

"French will do," I offered.

"All you need do is sign at the bottom—"

"Not until I can read it."

And in that moment, from the way his eyes flashed at me in furious frustration, I knew I'd made the right choice. Whatever he wanted me to sign, it wasn't for my own good, or he wouldn't resent my refusal so sharply.

"Perhaps in a few more days you will change your mind," he warned, and stalked away. The guard yelled at me—at least, he seemed to be yelling. Arabic can be a pretty intense language.

I turned my back on the bastard and only then closed my eyes and shuddered. I asked Samira, "Did you see anything?"

"At top it say c-on…" She was searching for the correct translation. *"Confession."*

Son of a bitch! The consequences, had I signed that, were dizzying. This was a lot bigger than a mistaken charge, and I was definitely too far in over my head. Maybe my principles could take the hit after all.

"I changed my mind," I said to the *mukhbir.* Damned right I was selling out. I felt relief to be doing it, too. "I want someone to call my…my husband."

Samira translated, though her presentation was more plea than demand. The guard laughed and turned *his* back on *us.*

Guess I'd missed my chance.

Well, I couldn't just sit here and do nothing, despite my limited resources. They wanted me scared and helpless? They had me more than halfway there! But other women manage to make the best of worse situations than this every day; I could hardly allow myself to do less.

Even these women were daughters of the goddess. So after some thought, I tore a strip of cloth off the bottom of my shirt, dampened it from our pail of drinking water, and went to sit beside the sick woman, the one who'd been moaning, to wipe her face.

She soon quieted. *"Shukran,"* she whispered gratefully.

I knew what that meant, even before Samira translated. Her thanks helped put my own problems into partial perspective.

As it turned out, this woman really was a prostitute—a prostitute with morning sickness. I admitted only to being a "teacher"—admitting I was a college professor suddenly seemed unforgivably arrogant. If I'd been born in another country, or to another family, or in another time, who knows what I might have been?

As the afternoon crawled by, I distracted myself further by sharing the "fairy tale" about the Great Queen, her seven powerful daughters, and their magical cups.

"The chalices wait to be found and shared, if ever the world is ready for them," I concluded into the almost silent cell—the only sound other than Samira's quiet translation was that of men, from down the hallway. "They wait to be discovered. They wait to be united. They wait to change the world. And they are waiting still…perhaps—"

The guard barked something at us, but though the others jumped, I deliberately finished—"For you"—and held each woman's gaze for a long moment before I turned to look.

The guard repeated his demand, glaring at me. The other women drew back as if I were suddenly radioactive.

"He say you must go with him," said Samira, worried.

"Why?" I asked.

Her eyes widened. "I cannot ask that!"

"Then why do you think?"

"I do not know! I hope…not…." She flushed.

I met the *mukhbir's* gaze, my suspicions taking on a violent undertone, and asked him. *"Why?"*

He'd had enough of my insolence. Now he was definitely shouting—and unlocking the cell door! I scrambled to my feet, ready to fight back if I had to, but all he did was charge in and grab me roughly by the arm, his words a staccato battering.

"'You will come, you disobedient rubbish, you will come because I say,'" translated Samira from behind me, but when the guard turned on her she stopped with a squeak.

Only as I was yanked from the cell did she whisper, "Goodbye, Maggi."

I reached into my fanny pack and pulled out a fistful of small bills, passing them through the bars into her smaller hand, before I was bodily steered away from her.

Toward where?

As much as I was frightened, maybe more than that, I was angry. *Because I say so?* However, I wasn't stupid—or any more stupid than I'd already been, depending on how you looked at my day. I didn't glare directly at the *mukhbir* again, and I didn't twist my arm from his bullying grip.

Yet.

If I'd interpreted Samira's flush correctly, a bigger fight might be waiting for me. I didn't want to tip this bastard off to what fighting skills I *did* have…even if his vehemence practically invited me to use his own force against him.

But I still damn well kept my head up and my shoulders back, no matter how hard he yanked.

I was all the more glad for that posture when the *mukhbir* shoved me into a large room with overhead lights, desks, phones—I'd been here before. It was the booking room. And standing in the middle of it as if he owned the place, tall and broad-shouldered and exuding control…

My eyes met those of Lex Stuart.

And I can't say I was sorry.

All Lex had to do was stare at the *mukhbir*—rather, at his hand on my arm—and the man released me immediately. I didn't blame the guy. Lex was in full monarch mode, murmuring requests—more likely commands—to the suited Arab beside him and simply assuming they would be carried out…or else.

"Maggi," was all he said, his voice dangerous, and he held out his hand.

In other circumstances, I might have demanded a please.

This one time, in this one place, it took all my self-control to walk quietly, instead of lunging across the room and grabbing him by the lapels and begging him not to leave me here. He looked so familiar and so…so *good!* Clean and competent and…and English speaking.

Still, I managed marginal dignity as I crossed to him. But I did give him my hand…the one with his wedding ring on it. His hand closed tightly around mine and somehow, his pulling me closer to him didn't feel like defeat. His hooded eyes studied me closely, as if looking for damage. Jaw clenched, he murmured, "We're almost ready to go."

Go? "You bailed me out?" I asked.

"I got the charges dropped."

I didn't bother to ask how. "Who told you I was here?"

His eyes narrowed. *"Not you."*

Okay, so the guard wasn't the only person with whom Lex was angry.

"For what it's worth," I murmured, "they didn't let me call anyone."

Lex's golden gaze didn't waver. "Would you have called me if they did?"

Well, he had me there.

His brows lowered. "Did you even give them my *name?*"

Now I felt guilty about it—I was the one who'd been falsely arrested, and I felt bad for slighting *him?*

Lex swore under his breath, language he wouldn't have used when his mother was alive.

"She must sign this," said his suited companion in truly cultured English. I pried my gaze from Lex, and saw that it wasn't the same man who'd tried to make me sign the disguised confession earlier. This man was taller, older, impeccably groomed, with a thick moustache. His suit was almost as expensive as Lex's. Considering where I'd just spent the last few hours, I felt like a trash heap standing between these two. "It says only that she will not lodge an official complaint."

Funny how he talked to Lex while offering the paper to me. "I've heard that before," I said.

"Magdalene," warned Lex, low in his throat, and I turned on him. In part, because he was wonderfully safe to turn on.

"I *have,* Lex. Not two hours ago, someone tried to get me to sign a confession. How do I know—"

"Because I trust him," he said simply.

Now I searched *his* face…and slowly nodded. If Lex trusted him, that had to be enough.

Not to mention, my throat didn't hurt.

I took the pen the gentleman offered.

"Magdalene Sanger, Mr. Ahmed Khalef," said Lex, belatedly. "Ahmed, this is Ms. Sanger. Ahmed is one of the leading corporate attorneys in Cairo, Maggi, and he's worked with my family for years."

"A *corporate* attorney?"

"I was in a hurry," Lex pointed out.

"It really does read as I stated, Miss Sanger," Mr. Khalef assured me with a kindly smile. "You agree to let bygones be bygones, no more. Here—I will translate it for you."

And he actually did, pointing out areas of text as he went, using the kind of legalese that made it sound legitimate. I was glad both for the translation and the chance to get my bearings.

And the chance to stand there with Lex, practically a free woman, feeling…safe. *Safer,* anyway.

As I signed it, I said, "Perhaps, Mr. Khalef, you could do me the favor of recommending a good criminal defense attorney?"

"But the charges have been dropped."

"Not for me. For a girl I met in lockup. Her name is Samira, and from what I can tell she was arrested for no more than being a down-on-her-luck kid, so I'd like to—"

He turned away from me and beckoned a police officer.

"I can…pay…." I protested, completely ignored as the men conferred.

"Is that it?" asked Lex, after the *mukhbir* was sent back. "Shall we bail out the whole cell block?"

"Not bail," corrected Mr. Khalef solemnly as he returned my passport. "The charges of vulnerability to delinquency have also been dropped."

Just because he *asked?*

I took my familiar blue passport gratefully; I wanted to kiss it. But I was also wary of how easy this had been. How powerful was this guy, anyway?

And how powerful was Lex, that Mr. Khalef worked for him?

"What is this costing you?" I whispered to Lex, as soon as our lawyer turned away to sign more paperwork.

"Is that all you care about?" he asked, still taut with anger. At me. True, we were still holding hands. Nobody dared look at us askance for long, not with the glare Lex aimed at them. But we were as much holding each other captive as giving support.

"I'd rather not owe you for something this big."

"I hadn't realized we were keeping score." His attitude was getting old, real fast.

"I apologize for getting falsely arrested and making you come down here and—no, wait," I whispered back. "I didn't make you do a damned thing, did I?"

"No, you didn't."

"Then why are you so angry with me?"

"Why are you so set against asking me for help?"

"Because." Okay, it wasn't the most mature answer, but the real reason tasted bitter in my mouth as I forced it out. "Because I shouldn't need it. I shouldn't need anyone to come to my rescue, not even you."

Especially not him.

"You think accepting help diminishes a person?" He stared at me, incredulous. "Is *that* why you haven't slept with me since the knife attack?"

Ahmed Khalef looked over his shoulder, surprised. I thought I caught the quirk of a smile as he turned discreetly away.

Lex didn't give a damn who stared. He was waiting to hear what I had to say.

Oh, my…goddess. He thought I didn't find him manly enough? He'd fought off as many attackers as I had, that day!

"No!" I protested. "There are plenty of reasons I'm not sleeping with you, Lex Stuart, but not one of them has to do with—"

At which point the guard returned with a pale Samira in tow. So, to use Lex's usual phrase, we *tabled* it.

The sun was still high as we left the station. It felt like I'd been locked up a lot longer. Then again, the sun stayed up pretty late in Egypt during the summer. As soon as we made it to the street, Samira gave me a quick hug—and bolted.

"Samira!" I shouted, turning after her. I immediately

saw the futility of trying to follow, the way she dodged expertly through the crowd. Her only acknowledgement was to pause on the corner for a quick wave.

"Rings for rings!" she shouted, gesturing to her own bare throat—and was gone.

My throat wasn't bare. I still wore my chalice-well pendant. Had she meant...?

She was a *Grailkeeper?*

Mr. Khalef shook his head, seeming amused by the whole thing. "Children."

"But she needs help," I told him, told Lex—was willing to tell anybody who would listen. "She'll just get arrested again."

"What else could you have done?" asked Lex, his tone gentler than before. He still hadn't let go of my hand.

"I could have...I don't know. Gotten her settled at a boarding school, or convinced Tala Rachid to take her in, or...something. She shouldn't have left."

Lex said, "Isn't that Samira's choice?"

At least he didn't sound angry anymore.

I looked back to him. "I didn't even get the chance to leave her with any more money."

"I passed her a twenty," Lex admitted. "Look, Mag, I don't want you to take this the wrong way, but I need to talk with you. Today."

He'd passed her a twenty?

He didn't even know her. But he knew I cared.

"Yes," I said.

"If you don't want to come back to my hotel, then we can find some kind of neutral ground—"

I pressed my fingers to his lips and repeated, "Yes. We'll go to your hotel. We'll talk."

He blinked, only then realizing that I wasn't arguing. His lips softened under my fingers as his golden eyes warmed—and then narrowed in suspicion. But not at me.

I turned, following his gaze.

Right there, across the street, stood Hani Rachid, glaring at us. The only thing more disturbing was how he took one look at Ahmed Khalef and, blanching, sank back into the crowd.

I felt a shiver, despite the nearly unbearable heat.

If Hani Rachid was afraid of someone, that *couldn't* be good.

Chapter 15

"Look at it this way," insisted Lex, using his key card to unlock the door to his suite. "If Ahmed's so dangerous that this Rachid guy is scared of him, aren't you glad Ahmed is on our side?"

"I'm not sure someone who orders the police around and terrifies crime lords can legitimately be on *anybody's* side." I went ahead of him when he held the door open for me…and entered paradise.

Lex's suite was large and lush and tasteful. The floor shone an intricate design of highly polished, inlaid wood. A plush sofa and chair of fine brocade framed a marble cocktail table with a crystal obelisk. The air smelled of fresh flowers from numerous arrangements placed around the room.

"You're out of jail, aren't you?" Lex reminded me, closing the door behind us.

"I'm not saying Mr. Khalef didn't help me. Just…"

"That you're paranoid."

"Don't I have a reason to be?" I reminded him. "Since I got to Egypt I've been kidnapped, arrested and attacked with a sword. I'm being told repeatedly that I'm some kind of champion—a job, by the way, that I never applied for."

He made a noise that sounded suspiciously like, "Hah."

Oh. Whatever was going on with him and the Comitatus, he'd been born into it, hadn't he?

"And don't forget, my boyfriend turned out to be descended from a hallowed bloodline of ancient kings, making him the head of a ruthless and powerful secret society."

"No," he murmured, shrugging off his suit coat. "Not the head."

I went still, surprised to get even that big of an update. But it was clearly further than Lex had intended to go in breaking confidence.

"So," he said, more firmly. "Which do you want to partake of first—shower or food?"

I decided not to pursue it; he'd told me what I needed to know. Phil was still in charge of the Comitatus…and Lex still wasn't happy about it. That was their business, just like the goddess grails were mine.

"Food," I announced. "As long as I don't smell too bad. I didn't have any lunch—which is a good thing, considering. But first, would you mind…?"

"That way." Lex pointed through a latticed archway. "I'll lay out some snacks in the dining room."

The bathroom was resplendent with silver marble, large mirrors, a sunken tub and a separate glass shower.

It had not only a toilet but a bidet, a built-in hair dryer and a telephone. A silver tray held scented oils, real rose water, perfumes. A large arrangement of fresh flowers perched on the granite countertop. The contrast to the hole I'd been in not an hour earlier seemed surreal.

This, I told myself, drying my hands on one-hundred-percent cotton towels, was why I had to be careful of how much I accepted from Lex. It would be too easy to confuse my values in a place like this.

But oh heavens, the towel was soft. And when I went back into the sitting room, Lex had opened the drapes onto the marble-banistered balcony and, beyond it…

Pyramids.

I kid you not. Just beyond the double glass doors stretched a carpet of remarkably green treetops, and beyond *those,* the three Pyramids of Giza.

"There you are," said Lex, from the suite's formal dining room. "I put crackers and cheese out, and I ordered room service. I hope you don't mind, I just chose two dinners I thought you'd like and figured I'd take whichever one you didn't. Oh. Nice view, isn't it?"

Nice view?

It was a freaking *stupendous* view, and he damn well knew it. But when I tore my gaze away from it and back to him—he'd rolled the cuffs of his crisp linen shirt off his wrists—that view wasn't half-bad, either.

There was something golden about Lex. Always had been. Part of it was his warm coloring, the ginger-brown hair and the aged-whiskey eyes and the faint tan from golf and sailing. Part of it was his body, shoulders broad, waist narrow, every bit of him kept in determinedly good shape as if to make up for the sin of having once been a sickly child. Part of it was the way he wore those tailored trousers. But most of it was just…him. His regal posture. His easy confidence. His *presence*.

Lex wasn't movie-star gorgeous; I doubt I could ever have wholly trusted him if he were. Instead, he had the genuine good looks that seem to come more clearly into focus the longer you look at him.

I'd been looking at him for years.

It's the pyramids, I warned myself as I noticed a different, deeper hunger insinuating its way through my limbs. *It's the expensive towels. It's because he came to your rescue—this is why you can't let him* do *that!*

And yet…

"Did you really think I wasn't sleeping with you because I helped you fight off a knife attack?" I asked softly.

His blink was slow as he got his bearings. "No. Maybe. I'm…not sure. Forget I said anything."

"When we started dating again, we had an agreement. It wasn't just about us. I don't know what else it *was* about…."

Feminine power. Balance. I can't do it alone….

"I know," he said, sounding apologetic.

"And things are so complicated now."

"Yes. You can't leap into a void, not even with me. Which…" Lex's hesitation was so uncharacteristic, he might as well be shouting. "It makes what I have to ask you sound particularly ignoble. I'm really just after information."

"This doesn't sound good."

"Maybe you should have some cheese and crackers," he insisted, masking his discomfort behind simple etiquette. And to be honest, it had been a long, long time since I'd had breakfast.

"Maybe I should," I said and passed him into the dining room and sat. The flatware, the crystal, the china plate…all of it bespoke entitlement the likes of which most of us can only dream. How could he need anything from me?

"I have a…a comparative mythology question," Lex admitted, sinking into the chair across from me as I tried some truly delicious cheese. Compared to this, the stuff at the jail didn't bear remembering.

I swallowed, slowly savoring it—and was amused by his serious tone. "Then thank goodness I teach comparative mythology. Ask away."

"But you can't ask questions. That is—" He raised a hand to fend off my silent, wide-eyed challenge of that. "Of course you can ask questions, but you should know ahead of time that I probably won't answer most of them."

Which meant that this was Comitatus business. I could live with that compromise. "So what else is new? Cut to the chase."

"I'm trying to learn more about an ancient ritual, and I don't trust what I've gotten off the Internet. Things on the Net can be so lurid, that it's hard to tell—"

"Lex." I reached across the table, put a hand on his. "If you don't tell me what this is about soon…"

I wasn't used to him looking so helpless. "It's called a…Sacred Marriage?"

If this were a sitcom, I would have choked on Brie. As it was, I just stared.

"Oh," I said, the word like a thud.

"Yeah," he said. "Oh."

Here's the thing. The Sacred Marriage, or *hieros gamos,* is a sex ritual: the divine marriage of god and goddess symbolized through, say, a king or a pagan priest making love with a priestess. As in, intercourse. But for religious purposes. Complete with candles and incense and prayers. Really.

Clearly, as the world turned to monotheism, that particular style of worship fell out of common practice.

No wonder Lex had been asking about married goddesses!

"Okay," I said, taking refuge in a nice, safe, academic facade. "So what do you want to know about Sacred Marriages?"

"Were they real?" When I stared, confused by the question, Lex ducked his head and tried again. "Did people seriously *do that,* as an accepted practice? Or is it just some salacious rumor for neopagans and speculative fiction?"

"Oh, it was accepted all right." Since those first few bites had taken the worst edge off my hunger, I sat back in my chair to better explain. "Sacred Marriage was the prerequisite to kingship all over the Western world. Sumeria, Assyria, Ghana…Ireland, even. Unless the goddess—in the form of her priestess—accepted a king, then he couldn't rule. Simple as that."

"Accepted as in…?"

"The communion of female and male. Yin and yang. Chalice and blade."

"So the priestess sleeps with the king?"

"The prospective king, anyway. The strength and fertility of the kingdom depends on the strength and fertility of its king, which is why…" Okay, so I'm enough of an egghead that I'd gotten caught up in my own lecture, but finally, *finally* the implication of all this dawned on me. "But you know that part already. The whole reason Phil is head of the Comitatus, and not you, is because you had leukemia. If the Comitatus is an ancient warrior society, with ancient values, then the leader has to be healthy."

Lex stared at me for a long, weighty moment before he carefully said, "You know that I can neither confirm nor deny that, Mag."

He didn't ask me to stop speculating.

"But that's it," I insisted, as if he were the one who needed it explained. Hello, he'd been living with the consequences since he was what, thirteen? "Like the Fisher King in the stories of the Holy Grail. The Fisher King is wounded—" in the groin, I might add "—so his land suffers. Or the Irish king, Nuada, who had to give up his throne after losing his hand in battle."

Lex had once used *Nuada* as a password. *He knew.*

"But when Nuada had a new hand made out of silver," I continued slowly, "he was able to take back his throne. The rightful king can return once he's healed, and you're healed, Lex. You're the healthiest man I know."

Lex stared at me, unable to comment—but his gaze was poignant. If I'd ever doubted that he *wanted* to talk about this…

It was as good a time as any for a knock on the door, announcing dinner. Lex used the peephole before letting the white-coated waiter roll in some covered trays that smelled like heaven itself.

It gave me a few minutes to consider the significance of all this. Lex clearly didn't need to hear about the spiritual importance of a leader's health; that wasn't why he'd asked about this. Maybe he just wanted to confirm that I understood, as well.

Then again, what he'd asked about was Sacred Marriage.

I neatly refused to face the most obvious possibility there. Even when I'd thought Lex was the bad guy, I'd believed him smooth enough not to use *that* kind of pickup line on anybody. And where, exactly, would he find a priestess in the first place?

"Something more is going on," I guessed, as soon as Lex had paid the bellman and sent him on his way. "Obviously, Phil doesn't want to give up leadership of this superpowerful secret society of yours, no surprise. Honor was never his strong suit. But his reluctance wouldn't stop you…would it?"

Lex lifted silver lids off the dinners, waiting for me to decide between what neatly printed cards described as seared salmon on polenta, and smoked duck and quail salad with caramelized almonds. I pointed at the salad, then took a fork and tried a bite of quail, and I'd been right. Seventh heaven.

"What do you think?" asked Lex, by way of encouragement. Instead of sitting across from me, he sat to my right. He wasn't asking about the food.

"You owe him for the bone marrow and all, but I doubt you'd let even personal gratitude get in the way of doing what's right."

He kissed me—just like that. Kissed me with wonderful, warm lips, and ran a finger adoringly down my cheek—then went silently back to dinner.

That took a moment to process. Damn. The more I took care of one kind of hunger, the more insistent other primal appetites became.

Towels, I reminded myself. Pyramids. Rescue. You're not thinking clearly.

Focus on comparative mythology.

I had to take a surprisingly deep breath before I continued. "You're a big-picture guy. If Phil's turning this society into a perversion of its original purpose, and if you care anything about it, you'd do what you could to fix that."

"Delicious," said Lex, of his salmon—well, it wasn't like he could say *Yes, Maggi, that's exactly what I mean to do.* "Want to try this?"

I leaned closer and he slid a morsel of seared salmon carefully between my lips. Oh, goddess, yes...

It was several minutes before I could resume talking.

"And to fix things, you'd want to regain leadership, right? I know, I know—you can't answer questions." And I already knew that a secret code of blinking or touching his nose would still count as breaking his word—as far as he was concerned, anyway. "But to avoid infighting, maybe even a schism, you would want to do it honorably, convince the other society members that you, and not Phil, are their rightful leader. Which in a ceremonial order I guess you'd accomplish through some kind of ritual, like..."

Suddenly, no matter how delicious, the salad sat heavily in my stomach. *"You really* do *want to perform a Sacred Marriage in front of the Comitatus?"*

Lex's golden eyes widened. "What?"

I pushed back from the table. "And where *would* you get someone to be your priestess?" Yes, it *was* one of those damning, have-you-stopped-beating-your-wife kind of questions. If he named someone else, that would mean he planned to cheat on me. Sort of. Since we *were* dating, even if it was celibate. And if he named the only person I knew that he knew with ties to ancient goddesses...

It would mean he was not only asking me for sex, he was asking for exhibitionism!

"No," protested Lex. I guess that, at least, didn't count as a secret. "You think I'd ask... *In front of people?* Christ, Mag, I just wanted information, maybe ideas for how to, well, modernize the whole thing. Like how in church we sip wine for communion, when enough millennia ago they probably drank the blood of some sacrificed animal. Or for that matter, how some churches use grape juice instead of wine. If I hope to accomplish...things...I can use all the help I can get, but...God, Maggi, *no!"*

So my first instinct there had been correct. Even Evil Lex would have more class than that.

Oops.

"Well...good," I attempted weakly.

"If that's what you think about me, then no wonder..."

"That's not what I think about you," I insisted, but I couldn't blame him for arching a skeptical eyebrow. "It's what I'm *afraid* to think about you, so I'm...wary."

"Right." He sounded tired. "Enjoy your dinner."

Further protest seemed futile, so I did as he asked—at least, I tried. The food really was good, but I was distracted now. For one thing, I felt guilty for casting him, yet again, as the enemy. For another, it wasn't like I could take back the image of Lex and me role-playing king and goddess, like some kind of kinky sex game. Even if we *weren't* going there, the damage had been done.

My only form of damage control was what had turned me into an academic in the first place—information.

"I've heard witches have a parallel ritual using a cup and a knife," I offered slowly, into the uncomfortable silence. "The symbolism isn't exactly subtle, but that may not be a bad thing."

"Witches?" Now Lex looked wary.

"As in, Wiccans. It's a legitimate religion, if you look behind the negative spin. A lot of Wiccans still see deity as a god-and-goddess pairing, which should help us. Maybe I could find something on one of their Web sites."

"When?" He probably couldn't tell me when he needed this—but clearly he needed it soon.

"I'll just take a quick bath first, so I can stand myself. Then I'll use your computer. I can have something downloaded for you and still catch an express back to Alexandria before the trains stop running."

"What if I need help with it?" he asked, holding my gaze. "What if the ritual's something I can't do alone?"

And he had a point. From what I knew of rituals— far more scholarship than experience, mind you—the main purpose was to sort of reprogram yourself, like a form of self-hypnosis. Meditative elements like candles and incense help with that, but so does being able to focus on someone else.

It was Lex who drew back first. "I'm sorry, Maggi. This is all too crazy. It's too much to ask."

"Hey, I'm the one who keeps getting accused of being a witch," I reminded him, standing. "And some kind of champion. You haven't cornered the market on crazy yet."

"But I'm the one asking for help."

"And so far, you've been the one giving it."

He gazed up at me, not at all uncomfortable with his

head being lower than mine. He knew who he was, no matter the trappings of power. "For what it's worth, Mag, that's all I did at the jail. I didn't rescue you—*rescue* implies that you were weak, and clearly you were never that. I just…helped."

Which implied only that I wasn't alone.

"Thank you." It was something I should have said at the time. Poor Lex had taken the brunt of my uncertainties more than once.

"I was glad to do it."

I backed away. "I'm just going to…quick bath…"

"Don't hurry. You deserve the break. As long as we find something this evening, I'm good. I don't even know if I'll use it, I just…I believe in being prepared."

For what? I didn't ask, because I knew he couldn't answer. My best guess was some kind of ritual to decide who would lead the Comitatus. But whatever it was, for Lex Stuart to ask me for help—no, for the goddess's help—it had to be big.

Not my business, I reminded myself. The Comitatus was *his* business, one which his vows neatly shut me out of. The Isis Grail was my business.

But his request did kind of mix the two.

The marble bath really was incredible—its water warm and deep and pulsing with tiny jets. Deciding that I *could* use the break, whether I deserved it or not, I'd lit a few sandalwood-scented candles and turned down the lights. I'd turned on the upper-end, built-in stereo to play soft music full of drums and sitars. I'd added rosewater to the bath—true rosewater, the kind distilled from steam when rose petals are pressed for oil. The scent drifted intoxicatingly up and around me in the candle glow with the water's mist, almost in time to the music, like little hints of spirit.

Like magic.

Ironic that I'd been swimming all week, but—because of the dry suits and the cramped shower at the Hotel Athens—this was my first full-body immersion into water since leaving the States. I felt like a mermaid—or the fairy goddess, Melusine—who'd been deprived of water too long. As if I were soaking something necessary back into my body, back into my soul.

Like I've said, sensory elements like candles or incense—or drumming—are used in rituals because they encourage relaxation, an almost altered state of mind. Stretched out in the softly purring Jacuzzi, I let random notions roll gently through my mind and vanish indiscriminately into the mist around me.

Lex's request did mix our two goals.

And there really were a lot of married goddesses. In almost every legend, the husband, god or mortal, could not have risen to such power without the abilities of his goddess wife. Of Melusine. Of Isis. My sleepy gaze caught on the sight of my floating left hand—with the wedding ring on it. *It's fake,* I reminded myself—but of course, as I'd found out, the *ring* wasn't fake. Just what it symbolized.

And not through any hesitation on Lex's part.

For just what weakness was I overcompensating, that I hadn't wanted his assistance? He was willing to shelve his pride enough to ask *me* for help. Just as important, I wanted to do it. Whatever was going down with the Comitatus, Lex *had* to be a better leader than Phil. I wanted Lex to have all the advantages he could get, so yes, I would help him with whatever kind of toned-down ritual we found.

Except…

Maybe the scent of roses was fogging my brain—or just lowering my inhibitions. Maybe I was being influenced by the sense of divine connection I'd felt when I drank from the Melusine Grail or, more recently, when I invoked Isis in her underwater temple. But for something this important, was *toned down* really the way to go?

It suddenly seemed so clear, so easy.

Lex and I had found each other as children, unaware that he was the heir to the Comitatus and I would become a freaking champion of the Grailkeepers. We were already lovers—had been before, probably would be again.

If this wasn't fated, what was?

And really—if I was just looking for an excuse to sleep with him, then hadn't I already made my decision?

"Lex," I called, sure that he would hear me. He always heard me.

In a moment, he cracked the door. "Is everything—?"

"Here's what we're doing," I said, stretching luxuriously with a light splash, enjoying the sensation of water and warmth on my naked body. "Turn off your computer—"

"I'm doing an Internet search," he interrupted, which is how I knew he actually wasn't looking.

"We don't need one. Turn off your computer and mobile phone, unplug the phone in the room, and hang out the Do Not Disturb sign. Light any candles you can find, and turn down the lights. Can anyone see in the window from the balcony?"

"No. The Botanical Gardens are out there. But, Mag—"

"Then leave the drapes open so we can see the pyramids. Turn on some quiet music, preferably with drums. Move the furniture back to give us room."

As I'd spoken, the door had gradually eased farther open. Lex was fully visible now, his sleeves still rolled up, his tie off, his shirt collar unbuttoned. He was definitely looking.

His lips parted slightly as he stared at me, naked in the bath. His gaze was like a caress, and my body tightened in nothing short of anticipation.

It wasn't just the soft towels or the expensive room or the delicious meal that attracted me, after all. Nor was it just his need of assistance. I'd been careful for too long.

I wanted *him.* He had to be able to see that.

I sure saw it on him that he wanted me.

"No promises," I warned him, my voice undeniably husky. "But take off your clothes, just in case."

He continued to stare.

"Are we doing this?" I prompted.

He nodded—and backed out to prepare.

If I was going to jump into a void—the unknown world of rituals, of championship, of magic—then so be it.

But I didn't have to always do it alone.

Tonight, I was jumping with him.

Chapter 16

I wiped a film of steam off the candlelit mirror and stared at my reflection. I'd put on one of the deliciously soft hotel robes, but my hair hung wet and natural down my back. I still wore my jewelry, the chalice-well pendant of the Grailkeepers, the horned-disk pendant of Isis which I'd bought at the Khan el-Khalili bazaar and the wedding ring.

An antique Stuart wedding ring.

My reflection and I spread our arms in the candlelit shadows of the luxurious bath suite. The robe fell open, revealing a few inches of my nakedness—the soft valley between my still-hidden breasts, the gentle swell of my belly, the shadowy juncture of my thighs.

"Isis," I whispered fervently—nobody had to hear me but Her. "Oldest of the Old, Goddess of Ten Thousand Names, Lady of Compassion and Healing and Magic.

"Isis, though I have yet to prove myself worthy, know that I seek to continue Your work. Help me, a daughter of goddesses, to know how to best serve this world which we both love. Guide me in granting Your strength, Your blessing, to this leader of men and, through him, perhaps the world.

"Be with me."

And yes, on some levels it did seem a little silly. But what did I have to be embarrassed about? It's not like I hadn't gotten personal proof that there really were goddesses—or different faces of the same goddess—I hadn't completely figured that one out. In any case, I had to make the effort.

Sometimes the effort is everything.

I picked up my makeup case and, deliberately not thinking, went on instinct. I found the eyeliner pencil which I usually apply lightly, but this time I held its tip over a candle, tested it against my finger, and drew a thick, dark tracing—Egyptian-like, Cleopatra-like—around each eye, extended at the outer corners. I lifted the Isis pendant off over my head, then shortened its cord and slid it on like a headband with the medallion on my forehead, where psychics and magic users would say my third eye was. The face staring back at me, exotic and powerful, was not the face I usually wore....

Yet it was still mine.

Cool.

On pure impulse, I shrugged out of the robe completely, letting it pool around my bare feet. Then I lifted the crystal glass in which I'd mixed scented bath oil with pure body oil, which I'd had warming in hot water, and went out to meet Lex.

He'd done as I asked. The suite was full of low-thrumming music, flickering light, scented wax. Standing nude, cut like a stone statue of Achilles or Adonis or a completely different, more famous Alexander, stood Lex.

With the twilit pyramids visible through the doors behind him.

"Holy…" he murmured, unable to finish.

It was a brave thing for him to do, to just wait for me like this. I was aware of that and admired him all the more for it. Pink lines still traced his ribs and forearms from that previous knife attack, but the battle scars only added to his masculinity. Soft, gingery hair dusted his chest before tracing down his hard, flat abdomen to his own sexuality, already half-erect over solid, hair-sprin-kled thighs. Who knew vulnerability could be this sexy?

I put down the glass of oil, and he reached for my breasts. I caught his hands with a smile and kissed his fingers. "Not yet," I whispered. "Not yet."

He groaned but his hands tightened obediently over mine, as if to keep himself from reaching for anything else.

"So are you really willing to do this?" I demanded, with more quiet authority than I'd expected of myself.

Lex swallowed, hard—and nodded. "Are you?"

I took a deep breath, praying that whatever part of me was connected to the force of goddessness, I could draw on that connection to make this work. I squeezed his hands—and let go. "Kneel to the goddess through me."

His chin came up sharply—good. This had to be a sacrifice for him, in order to count; he wasn't some wimp, willing to kneel to just anybody. But, though re-luctant, he did it. He sank to his knees on the richly woven rug that cushioned the polished floor.

His head arched back, so that he could hold my gaze in silent challenge. He'd never looked so regal.

"Alexander Rothschild Stuart III," I murmured, the name sounding strange even from my own throat. "You wish to rule powerful men. You wish the blessings of the goddess in this endeavor. Why should you be chosen as such a leader?"

For a moment he frowned up at me—damned vow of secrecy. Then he made an attempt to answer around it. "Because I was born for such leadership," he said. That wasn't telling me anything I didn't know. Hell, if he meant it metaphorically, it was telling me *less* than I knew.

"And?"

"And because I'll make positive changes with vast repercussions."

"Good. And?"

Even I wasn't sure what I was looking for, until he growled, lower than ever, *"And because I deserve it."*

I shivered at the power of his conviction, the kind of conviction a person would need to do great things. And yet I—or the goddess in me—asked, "Are you sure?"

"Yes. I'm sure."

"And can you do it alone?"

To his credit, his gaze continued to focus on my face, despite both of us being nude. "Nobody can do it alone," he whispered.

Right answer.

I knelt in front of him, one leg tucked under me and the other knee up, like so many statues of Isis herself. We were showing fealty to each other, now. I reached for the glass of oil, dipped my fingers, and smeared its warm richness across his forehead. "Then may the wisdom of the goddess guide your thoughts, Lex, that you may always know what is right."

He closed his eyes as he shuddered, which gave me the perfect chance to brush an oily fingertip gently across each eyelid. "May the vision of the goddess guide your sight, Lex, that you may always see the proper path."

I'm sure this wasn't just coming out of nowhere— but it didn't feel as if I'd been taken over by anybody, by anything, either. It felt more as if I were accessing a part of myself that had been there, dormant, all along. Like Cleopatra—a reincarnation of the goddess? None of it felt normal—my insides were practically vibrating. But neither was it unwelcome.

"May the voice of the goddess guide your words," I continued, sliding oil across his full lower lip with my thumb....

His tongue darted out and tasted me—and I smiled. We really were still us. That was where the true power of this ritual lay, not just in the otherworldliness of it...but in *us*.

The rightness of us.

"That when you *do* speak, Alexander," I half teased, "you may speak the truth."

His dark-gold eyes pleaded with me. "Let me touch you," he whispered hoarsely.

"Not yet," I warned. I put down the glass to rub a generous puddle of oil between both my palms. "May the power of the goddess strengthen you, that whatever responsibilities you shoulder, you can indeed carry through."

And he had such wide, solid shoulders to anoint. My hands then caressed down to the curve of his chest.

"And may the heart of the goddess encourage you," I whispered. "That your courage and conviction never, never fail. Do you accept this charge?"

His voice broke as he said, "I do."

My gaze darted to the ring on my finger, where my hands spread across his now glistening chest, and I felt a brief flare of panic. *I do?* This was more, so much more than I'd initially meant to take on....

Then again, jumping into a void was hardly about control, was it?

"Good can only come from balance," I intoned, breathing quickly to keep my head amid the sensations that surrounded me. The scents, sandalwood and wax and roses and aroused male. The vision of him, always him, so golden and strong and virile in front of me. The beating of our hearts, and of soft drums, drums and the mingling rasp of our breath. The feel of him, so very alive under my hands. All I was missing was taste....

Soon. The word came to me as a reassurance. *Soon.*

"As long as male and female struggle against one another, there can be no unity," I continued. "But as we recognize the strength of each other, the gift of each other, as we join, so can we find balance. You are a warrior. Already you embrace that which is hard. Will you also embrace that which is tender?"

Lex nodded, unable to find his voice, even before I then poured oil onto *his* hands—and drew them gladly to my breasts. He spread his fingers to encompass me, to massage and worship the weight and fullness of my femininity. Again, I had to catch my breath.

But where I slid my oily hands next, down and around, had him catching his own breath with a moan. He *was* hard—hard, and hot, and pulsing. And I'll confess that my fingers, encircling him, stroking him, were greedy. Almost as eager as my own aching need.

"You have the capacity for violence," I warned, then added, before he could protest, "As do we all. Will you choose, whenever possible, to use that power for joy, for…for love?"

Somehow, his hands caressing my breasts, his hips moving within my intimate hold on him, Lex forced his starving eyes open. "I will," he insisted—

Which is when I ducked my head and tasted his chest, sucked on his shoulder, licked straining cords of his neck. The oil was lightly flavored, not at all unpleasant. The taste of Lex, beneath the taste of the oil, was even sexier.

"Then be one with me," I whispered, my words muffled against his skin. Then, just for him, "Please."

It was all the invitation he needed.

In one smooth movement Lex slid his hands down to my hips, cupped my bottom, and lifted me out of my crouch and onto his hard, hot need of me. Between his powerful thrust and gravity, he was suddenly just *there,* filling me, thick and sure and necessary. I cried out my pleasure.

His arms cinched, iron hard around me, as if to keep me from pulling away, but he managed to murmur, "Did I hurt you?"

Hurt? "No. Never."

This joining was as we were meant to be, as close as two human beings could get. It was magical. Spiritual. Everything, everything, everything.

I held out my arms, wide like wings, flying on the sensation. I let his embrace hold me up, and I arched my back. The move curved my belly against his, thrust my bosom upward and pulled my weight backward, so that he had little choice but to lay me down onto the rug, following me with his hard, hot body, taking a breast into his open mouth. Now I was wholly spread out beneath him, an offering, a blessing, a banquet. Like the world before him, should his bid for leadership be granted.

"I can't…" gasped Lex. "I can't…not…"

But he didn't *have* to *not*. I caught the back of his thighs, urged him on. This was part of the ritual, too.

He thrust powerfully, filling me deeper and harder, pressing me into the rug.

"There…" Somehow I managed to gasp ancient words in the midst of our writhing, between moans of pure satisfaction. "There is no dark…without the light…."

"Maggi," whispered Lex into my ear. Then he took my ear into his mouth, searing it with his questing tongue, and whatever he'd meant to say was lost. His body continued to rock against mine, across mine, into mine, owning me….

I turned my head on the rug and, through sated eyes, saw the distant pyramids. Ancient. Permanent as manmade things could ever, ever be. We were a blink to the pyramids…but maybe we encompassed something older, even so.

"There is no beginning…*ah*…without an ending…."

"Mag…*no*…."

Did he just say *no?* I had to have imagined it. And yet— "Don't you want this?" I whispered. Gasped.

It probably didn't hurt that I was stroking one hand down to the small of his flexing, hard-muscled back, then lower, my fingers questing behind his thighs, increasingly intimate.

He whispered, "Yes." Not once, but over and over. "Yes, yes, yes, yes…"

His thrusting, faster and faster, matched his words.

Somehow, with the same instinct that knew how to make love, I knew what had to be said before we could end this.

Assuming we could ever, ever fully end this.

"There is—*oh, Lex!*" His force spread my legs farther, pushed me an inch across the rug.

"Yes," he prayed. "Yes, yes…"

"There is…no man—*please, Lex!*" I wanted to fit every bit of him, his whole being, inside me. When he surged into me yet again, I imagined maybe he could. I wasn't seeing straight. I wasn't breathing anything but his breath and roses and sandalwood. I wasn't tasting anything but him, especially when he covered my mouth with his, drank me, possessed me. But I was feeling everything—the sun, the moon, the stars—and mostly Lex, his strong hands cradling my back and head, his hard body heavy on top of me, and his maleness, rigid and insatiable between my legs, exactly where I wanted him, exactly where I needed him…

"No man without woman!" I insisted, turning my head away from his mouth to do so, desperate to finish—

And at that, with a scream and convulsion of pure rapture, I *did* finish.

Oh heavens, did I finish, sobbing and shuddering and savoring every seismic moment of it.

"And?" grunted Lex, still making love to me, not quite finished himself. Warrior indeed. The man had stamina.

At least now I could speak. My eyes were damp and

my heart was racing and the weave of this rug was probably imprinted in my bare bottom. My body felt as if it were floating, like being weightless, like underwater in the Temple of Isis. But I could speak. And move.

"And there is no woman without man," I agreed with him, getting a little more intimate with my questing fingers—

Now Lex shuddered, groaned, and poured himself, hot and defiant, into me. His weight lowered onto me, heavier than ever, panting and all but helpless.

Which is when I realized why he'd said *no*.

I couldn't fault him for dropping the protest—even as the heir to a powerful bloodline, the bloodline of the grail kings themselves, he was only human. It said a lot that he'd thought of it at all.

I hadn't. Which was unusual, despite the spiritual elements of this particular joining.

Until now, all of our adult lives, we'd used condoms.

The weird thing is, I didn't freak. Not to say that I had any desire to have his baby. Not really. Not just yet.

Did I? Surely not.

But our joining had felt fated, divine. Somehow, I couldn't work up any great reluctance or fear now that it was done. Not from any consequences of me and Lex being together. None at all.

Besides, I felt so damned sated, it would be hard to feel upset about anything. Instead of worrying, I wove my fingers into Lex's thick hair and turned my head to kiss his oil-softened brow. *Mmm.*

With great effort, he wrapped his arms around me and rolled, so that now he was under me, no longer weighing me down. His penis slid, soft and wet, out of me.

Worry about that later.

"Is that…?" He was still having trouble catching his breath. "Is that all?"

"All?" Somehow I found the strength to lever myself up off of him, just high enough to give him the evil eye. "That wasn't enough?"

"I can never get enough of you, Mag."

Sweet talker. "That wasn't just about sex, Lex Stuart. That was a ritual. We were communing with the gods."

"Sex with you is always—"

I kissed him, unsure whether to be amused, flattered…or annoyed. If this meant anything at all—

—well, more than out-of-this-world sex and an end to our current celibacy—

—then he had to take it seriously.

"Don't you dare make fun of this," I warned. And I meant it.

To my immense satisfaction, Lex's eyes widened slightly. "No! Mag, this was more… I never would have asked you if I'd thought…and now…"

Then, clearly lost for words, he turned *his* head to look out the undraped doors at the rapidly darkening pyramids on the horizon. Folding my arms on his chest, and pillowing my head on my arms, I watched them too.

Warm and comfortable and together and…*right*.

Eventually the pyramids lit up with colored lights. Progress marches on.

"Do you think it worked?" asked Lex, after a while.

I propped my chin on my hands to better look at him, and shrugged. "We didn't follow any ancient script. I'm not an official priestess. You're not an official king. We're not brother and sister—"

His eyes widened. *"Excuse me?"*

"An Egyptian royalty thing," I explained, grinning. "The oil wasn't sacred, and we weren't in a temple."

"So why does it feel like it worked?"

"Maybe because none of those other trappings matter. Maybe because what really counted was our joining, the reminder that we're not just individuals but part of…"

Part of a greater whole. But now that we weren't in the middle of a Sacred Marriage, I was scared to say that.

To my relief, Lex said, "So was this a one-shot deal, priestess and prospective king? Or…"

"Oh, no," I assured him. "I'm more than just a vessel for the goddess, buddy. We are definitely on again."

"Then hang on." And with a showy display of strength, he wrapped his arms around me, sat up, then stood and *carried me* into the bedroom.

"I can still walk," I teased, despite being impressed. "You're not *that* good."

"Pull back the covers, please," he said. "My hands are full."

So I reached out and did just that, and he lowered me onto six-hundred-thread-count cotton sheets that felt like silk.

I reached up and drew him down onto me. A few luxurious kisses later…

Was a very inappropriate time to remember to call Rhys.

Chapter 17

It's sad, how quickly things can decline from magic to frustration. The only familiar person the Hotel Athens's front desk could summon was Catrina. She coolly assured me that Rhys had been fine the last time she saw him—an hour previous—and that she would pass on the message that I'd be back in Alex the following day.

I didn't trust her as far as I could overhand a Volkswagen, but I didn't have a choice.

Then Lex, who'd been remarkably cool about me remembering another man while entwined naked with *him,* needed to talk seriously about the forgotten condom. "If you want to be absolutely sure nothing comes of it…"

He meant a morning-after pill. Despite us being in the middle of a hugely conservative country, I had no doubt he could pull it off, too, if I demanded one.

"No," I said firmly. "I don't want to be that sure. Do you?"

His eyes flared. "God, no! Maggi—"

But I kissed him, rather than risk him proposing marriage again.

It had already been a very full week.

We had a glorious night together, this time with the appropriate contraceptives, but that meant I was short on sleep when I woke, stiff and sticky, to an empty bed. Lex had left a note in his too-familiar handwriting on the pillow, gently weighed down by a handful of flowers from one of the suite's many arrangements. It read:

> *My Maggi:*
> *Sorry couldn't stay for breakfast. Gone at least one day on biz can't tell you damned thing about. Will contact you in Alex. Be safe. Love you. L.*
> *PS—Really.*
> *PPS—Thank you for being my goddess.*

Okay, so it wasn't bad, as notes went. I carefully folded and saved it. My first thought at his declaration of love wasn't crap, which showed progress. In fact, I felt kind of melty and happy. But it wasn't cuddles and kisses and breakfast in bed, either. Business he couldn't talk about meant he was doing something involving the Comitatus, right here in Egypt. I didn't like not knowing whether it was minor business or the big takeover, some kind of yearly quorum or a huge who-gets-to-lead-us trial by combat. I didn't like not knowing whether I should be worried.

Which, damn it, would *always* be a problem with Lex, no matter how much good sex was involved.

* * *

"It's not as if you're the only woman to ever have this problem," noted Rhys later that afternoon, once I was back in Alexandria.

To my surprise and suspicion, Catrina had in fact passed on my message, so he hadn't worried overmuch. I was anxious to dive again, to see if I could access that sense of *knowing* which had been interrupted by the other day's boat accident. But diving was canceled for the day, because of high winds and choppy waters—yet another in my series of frustrations. Rhys and I had gone to the roof of the hotel with gyros and cold cans of soft drinks, purchased from a street vendor, to debrief.

I hadn't mentioned the sex, though Rhys may have guessed that part from the fact that I'd spent the night. I sure as hell hadn't mentioned the Sacred Marriage ritual. But no way could I keep quiet about Lex's vanishing act. It weighed far too heavily on my mind.

"You're joking," I said now. "You don't really think that there are other women who are involved with leaders of secret societies which may or may not be working against their own ancestral legacy?"

Rhys crumpled a piece of crinkly paper that had wrapped his sandwich and threw it at me, but it blew away before we could stop it—and we did both try to stop it. "No, I mean to say that there are other women dating men with secrets. Agents who work for MI-6, for example, or your CIA or FBI. Members of military intelligence. Certain politicians."

"And men dating *women* with secrets," I corrected halfheartedly. "Women can be spies and politicians, too."

I hated sounding whiny, but I was tired, and a little achy, and *hot*. Even high winds and an adjacent sea couldn't make much headway against the Egyptian sun. I hated that diving had been canceled.

And I was getting a bit of a sore throat. Was it a side effect from my satisfied vocalizations the night before…or was someone in trouble? Me? Rhys? Lex?

I hadn't seen anything of Hani Rachid since yesterday. Now that I didn't plan to deal with embassies, I'd gone back to wearing my sword under my skirt, just in case. That meant sitting with my legs stretched out in front of me.

It was a good sword. It really did need a name. All the best mythic swords have one.

"Or women," Rhys agreed cheerfully, dragging me back on topic. "Quite."

"Except that spies and politicians can quit their jobs," I pointed out. "They may not ever be able to tell their secrets, but they can at least stop collecting more. I get the feeling Lex is in the Comitatus for life."

Overhead, a bird cried out, hawklike, as it circled by.

"I'm sorry, Maggi," said Rhys, after a long moment's consideration. "I know I'm a trained counselor, but would I be too selfish—would you be all right—if I asked to *not* counsel you about Lex Stuart? I'm afraid I'll be biased."

That caught my attention. "Oh. I'm…sorry."

"Please don't be. So tell me again about the clue that Jane and Tala gave you."

Rather than dwell on where my new intimacy with Lex left Rhys, I recited from memory: "'High in the heavens and under the sea, Isis is everywhere, she cannot be contained. Look for her where she is honored. There, you shall find her cup.'"

Rhys chewed a bite of his gyro thoughtfully, then swallowed and wiped the corner of his mouth with a paper napkin. "Hmm."

The difference between this meal and last night's dinner struck me. Paper-wrapped, street-vendor sandwiches versus smoked duck and quail salad on china. Aluminum cans of soda versus crystal goblets of sparkling water. A shaggy-haired friend in blue jeans and T-shirt, sitting on the roof and leaning against a brick wall, versus a well-groomed, well-dressed lover on an expensive chair of brocade and teak.

The funny thing is, I would have thought that in each case I would have chosen the former....

"What worries me," I continued, forcing myself to focus, "is that it's a different saying than the one Munira told me—you know, the Grailkeeper at the bazaar? When she tried to translate her ancestral rhyme, it had to do with Isis sleeping with no light. And then she said something like, 'She *is,* and always will be such.'"

"Perhaps the part about no light is a vague reference to the heavens and the sea," suggested Rhys. "There's little light under the sea. And Isis being 'always' could translate to her being 'everywhere, uncontained.'"

"It's still not much of a road map for finding her chalice," I grumbled. "You'd think those ancient Grailkeepers could have come up with something a little more specific. 'Thirty paces from the sphinx, toward the sunset' would be nice."

Rhys laughed. "Ah, but which sphinx?"

I nodded and took another long drink of fizzy, canned

juice. I'd chosen against cola because of last night's goof. If there *was* a baby…

Gee, that possibility might also explain some of my moodiness, mightn't it? A baby would be life-changing, for better or worse, and my life was already changing faster than I could keep up.

With a chill, I realized that a baby would also continue my family's Grailkeeper lineage—and Lex's Comitatus bloodline.

Both.

Oh…goddess. Would such a child bring two diverse worlds together, at last? Or would her—or his—diverse roles destroy him—or her—from the inside out?

Assuming Lex got control of the Comitatus at all.

It came down to a battle between hope and fear, didn't it?

"Do you really think you'll be able to sense the chalice again, once we go back down?" asked Rhys, ignorant of my epiphany.

And really, what could I do about the matter right now, except to eat healthy—just in case—and hope the Sacred Marriage had given Lex the edge he needed? Comitatus business was his.

Grail business…

"I hope so," I said, forcing my mind back to business. "Fat lot of good it does right now. Let's focus on Isis herself. Maybe there's a clue there. She's one of the oldest goddesses, if not *the* oldest. She's also one of the wisest, the only goddess ever to have learned the secret name of Ra and gain his powers over life and death."

"By tricking him," Rhys reminded me. "She created

the snake that poisoned him in the first place, knowing Ra would need her, as Goddess of Medicine, to cure him."

"And she wouldn't do it until he told her his secret name," I agreed. "So we know she can be ruthless, too."

"But faithful," Rhys continued to brainstorm. "When Set first kills her husband, she breathes life back into…him…."

"And when Set cuts Osiris up into pieces, Isis uses her magic to find them," I continued—but stopped when I saw Rhys's concerned expression. "What?"

"It's…nothing."

"Uh-huh."

"Well, it's just…you did that."

I raised my eyebrows and shrugged, not comprehending.

"When I was hit by the boat the other day, and you gave me mouth-to-mouth. You breathed life back into me. Not unlike Isis."

That did seem significant, didn't it? I mean, of course it was significant that Rhys had survived! But the parallel…

For just a moment, I had a strangely surreal moment, as if I were submerged in Cleopatra's Palace.

Magic.

"When you went after the Melusine Grail," Rhys continued, "didn't you find similarities between yourself and her? Melusine's husband betrayed her, and Lex Stuart betrayed you."

It was official. I was getting a sore throat. It wasn't that sudden, swallowed-scream feeling that warned me of immediate threat, though. Instead it was a dull ache, like the need to cry, that warned of distant danger.

How distant? Danger to whom?

"I thought… I mean, he…."

Okay—just because we'd worked past that betrayal didn't diminish Rhys's point. But... "How could it not be a coincidence?"

Now he shrugged. "The Lord works in mysterious ways?"

So how about the Lady?

The idea bothered me more than it should have.

"It's not as if my looking for Melusine's Grail would have somehow influenced Lex's behavior."

"It would not."

"Besides, if my helping you was connected to the Isis legends, that would make you my symbolic husband."

Rhys blushed— "It's just a theory" —but I made myself consider him. I mean, when the goddess speaks…

Rhys was a good man, a good friend. I'd kissed him before and, if I weren't currently dating Lex, I wouldn't mind kissing him again. My world would be nowhere near as complicated, if I were with Rhys. With him, I didn't have to worry about vows of secrecy or Comitatus coups or the responsibility of being his goddess. We didn't have the weight of a long and complicated past tugging at us. We could avoid society functions. I could just be me, Maggi, whoever Maggi was or would become.

I considered all that—and suddenly, strangely, felt a lot better about having slept with Lex last night. Rhys was my dear friend, and that was valuable enough. But Lex….

"Besides, Osiris was ambushed by his brother," I said, hunting for contrasts. "Is there any chance that you have a disgruntled brother, or a relative, or even a friend who was driving that car or that speedboat or who works for Hani Rachid?"

"Not likely—" Rhys said with a laugh, and he kept talking, but suddenly I wasn't hearing him, any more than I would have underwater. My throat tightened with nausea, this time. I heard only a rush of fear.

Oh, no. *No!*

Rhys had no relatives to ambush him.

But Lex did.

He'd been preparing for some sort of ritual to remove his cousin Phil from the leadership of the Comitatus. And I already knew Phil rarely played fair. And if there really was something to the parallels between me and my goddesses...

I stumbled on my anonymous sword as I pushed to my feet. Rhys was close behind me, catching my arm, and I heard what he was saying now. "Maggi? Magdalene, what's wrong?"

"I've got to find Lex."

"*Now?* Why?"

I could barely swallow. "I think he's in danger. I think Phil's going to ambush him. Here. In Egypt."

Rhys stared, realizing what I already knew. "You think *he's* in the role of Osiris."

Meaning that he, Rhys, wasn't.

I said, *"Osiris dies!"*

"But they're not the same, Maggi." Still, Rhys was wise enough to grab our trash and open the door to the stairway as he argued. "Think this through before you frighten yourself and Lex, as well. Where would there be room for free will, if the moment you go after a chalice, you're forced into reenacting some ancient legend or another?"

I thought momentarily of the Sacred Marriage. But I was too worried to blush.

"You'd not serve such a goddess," continued Rhys—and he was right. If I'd thought that Isis or Melusine was scripting this, I would be the first to rebel. But I really didn't think that I or Lex or anybody else was being manipulated. Maybe it *was* just a coincidence. Maybe it was a self-fulfilling prophecy. Maybe I was prescient, and the energies leading to Phil's betrayal were what had nudged me subconsciously toward Isis in the first place.

Explanations didn't matter, at the moment.

My throat hurt.

"Let's just find Lex," I insisted.

But we couldn't find out crap. Lex wasn't answering his cell phone or pager, despite my keying in our personal code for emergencies. His office in New York explained that he was scheduled for private meetings all day. When I called the Cairo office of Ahmed Khalef, corporate attorney, he, too, was out. Hell, I even tried calling his Cousin Phil, who "wasn't available."

But when I called Jane Fletcher, still holed up in the British Embassy, she agreed to use her airline access to do a computer search for me. It was through her help that I got my next clue.

Phil Stuart had flown into Cairo that morning.

"And Hani has been giving interviews," she said on the other end of the line, which at least explained one bad guy's absence. "He's trying to convince the Egyptian government to force the embassy to give me up. A BBC reporter is ringing me soon, to get my side of the story."

I couldn't manage anywhere near the concern she deserved, and we soon disconnected.

"It's an ambush," I stated to Rhys as I left the Hotel

Athens, walking fast. "I've got to find them, got to stop Phil."

Rhys spread his hands as he shadowed me. "I understand your concern, Maggi, but this is the Comitatus we're talking about. What else can you do?"

Instead of answering, I broke into a run. I needed to do *something* with this helpless, nervous energy of mine. I didn't stop until blocks later, when we reached the Corniche. Then, as Rhys caught up, I stared out at the dusty, choppy waters of the Alexandrian Harbor.

If I truly loved Lex, certainly if there was even the chance our little fertility ritual had borne fruit, then Comitatus business *was* my business—whether they knew it or not.

Just like that, I demoted the quest that had first brought me here to little more than a means to an end—and I sure as hell made up my mind on that little *in situ* controversy.

"I can ask someone for help," I announced. Lex had admitted *he* couldn't do it alone. Why should I be different?

"Who?" Then Rhys followed my line of sight to the harbor—and his eyes widened. *"Isis?"*

I was going for the grail.

Two hours later, Rhys was still warning me about the foolishness of my plan. But at least he did so while driving the speedboat through choppy, now grimy harbor waters.

At least the gusting sand would help hide what we were doing. It wasn't even midafternoon, but the dust in the air made the sky as dark as twilight.

"Have I mentioned," my friend called over the wind gusts, dropping anchor, "that this is an insane idea?"

I shrugged into the harness that held my rental tanks and adjusted the straps, shifting my hips to keep balance in the pitching boat. "Yes."

Sand blew, gritty against my bare arms and legs. I was wearing just a bathing suit, protected only by mask, tanks and regulator—with fins and dive light, of course. Local dive shops did not carry the expensive dry suits that the archeologists used. None of the divers working in those shops had three heads or glowing eyeballs, so I had to believe short-enough exposure to the water wouldn't be enough to harm me or...

That it would be all right.

I'd just have to stay down as short a time as possible. Considering that we had hazardous diving conditions and worse-than-ever visibility, that wasn't a lousy plan anyway.

"You could drown," Rhys insisted, grasping the edge of the speedboat's windshield as a particularly large wave knocked us violently sideways. "Even if you don't drown, you've no guarantee of finding the chalice. And even if you find the chalice, you'll be no better than an antiquities thief if you take it. *With me as your accomplice!*"

I didn't like that part, either. But... "You didn't have to come," I reminded him, swishing my new mask in the water before pulling it on over my hair.

I sure hoped people like Catrina and d'Alencon, who never wore full dry gear, were right.

"Yes," said Rhys firmly. "I did. You truly may drown."

There was a reason the flag on the so-called beach, which signified the water safety, was flying black. Not that we could even see the concrete blocks at the water's edge.

"Are you absolutely certain this is necessary?" he asked. "There's still time to change your mind."

"Of course I'm not certain. Nothing in life is certain. But if I don't do this, and Lex really is in danger…"

It didn't bear thinking about.

"And if you die, and he isn't?"

But sometimes you have to go on instinct. I kissed his ear—I'd aimed for his cheek, but the boat rolled. Then I stuck the regulator in my mouth and rolled backward, into the harbor.

The last thing I saw was Rhys reaching for me.

Then—chaos.

Had I thought the water that cloaked Cleopatra's Palace was murky before? Between the sand being tossed in from above and stirred up from below, visibility was almost gone. Churning waters pushed me in different directions like a schoolyard bully. I turned on my dive light, but was too busy keeping it from being pulled from my hand to bother following its illumination through the swirling silt. A drag in the water rolled me, then I was caught in a different piece of current and forced downward….

I think it was downward. I was quickly losing track, and I had no dive buddy to keep track for me.

Crap. Rhys was right. I *could* drown!

But not without a fight. And who knew? Maybe I *was* a champion, at that. Given the possible endings, I pretty much had to choose hope over fear.

Despite the tumbling, dragging confusion, I kicked in the direction I prayed was downward, thinking that the farther I got from the wind, the less disturbed the tide would be. Me against Nature.

I could only hope Nature felt like helping.

At least I was managing more of a straight line, the deeper I got. Then suddenly, looming out of nothingness, a huge face appeared before me. I cried out, almost lost the regulator, coughed—

Then stopped and went fetal, drawing my knees to my chest, circling them with my arms. It was the only way I would catch my breath without inhaling water.

Fear would kill me faster than a riptide.

The weight on my belt and ankles dragged me downward—my shoulder scraped lightly across the encrusted shoulder of the stone sphinx that had frightened me. Then I bounced lightly to the harbor floor, landing awkwardly beside a sunken cola bottle.

Only when I was breathing steadily again did I uncurl and shine the light, tethered to my wrist, at the statue beside me. This was a *good* thing. It helped me orient myself to where I was in the underwater palace. If the sphinx was *here,* then I needed to be…

I swam slowly, counting off landmarks in the form of fallen pillars and eroded figurines. More than once, the current swept me off course, but each time I found my way back until I'd reached the place where I'd sensed the call of Isis, only two days before.

It was time for the goddesses to come back.

By now going into the Isis position—one knee down and one up, and arms spread like wings—felt almost practiced.

Isis, I thought as intensely as I could. *Oldest of the Old, Goddess of Ten Thousand Names…*

By the time I reached the end of my invocation, within the pull of the waters, I sensed it. Rather… *Her.*

A ripple of power.

Something in the harbor, beyond the veil of unseeing, beckoned me. And this time, no other diver swept by to distract me from it.

Leaning toward the call, I pushed off the floor and skimmed in that direction, staying mere feet from the bottom so as not to lose my way again. The halogen dive light could cut through at least that much of the murkiness as I paralleled the sweep of sand, the litter of artifacts.

The beckoning strengthened into something almost like a summons, a physical ache. I knew this feeling! I knew it from last night, when I was invoking the goddess for Lex—

—So that really *was* you!—

And I knew it from back when I'd found the Melusine Grail. A sense of belonging. Of strength. Of communion with generations of other women, far into the past, far into the future.

Goddess!

So clearly did I sense Her presence that, as I began to pass Her hiding place, I felt an immediate sense of loss. I reached out to stop myself with one hand on a broken column, then floated backward, shining the light closer. What? *Where?*

I swam across to the other side of the column, leaned closer—

And there She lay, trapped beneath it, half-covered with sand. The remains of Her larger-than-life statue, surely from the temple where Cleopatra herself had once worshipped, was really here. I'd found Her.

Isis.

She had once been seated, though the natural disasters that had sunk this part of Alexandria had thrown her and the throne she sat on to their side. Fish nosed at the algae-spotted folds in her hewn gown, at her roundly carved bare toes. Her sculpted face, beautiful despite the mask of erosion, wasn't quite as flat as those of so many ancient Egyptian statues, probably because of the Greek influence that had taken over Egypt and founded this particular city long before Cleopatra's time. Instead, Isis seemed to wear an expression of eternal calm, of waiting strength.

Hello, she seemed to say, with her unblinking stone eyes. *About damned time.*

I bowed awkwardly, what with being under pushing water. Though I'd come as fast as I could, I felt suddenly guilty that what had finally gotten me to her was the need of her help, not my need to help her.

Then again, if anybody understood having to rescue a…what? Lex wasn't my husband. And yet…

I had to hope Isis would understand, and I began to look for where, in this area that had surely been her temple, her sacred chalice may have been kept. There would have been no reason for anybody to hide it. The Temple of Isis had been swallowed by the harbor long before her worship was forbidden.

Frustratingly, the sense that had drawn me to Isis seemed connected to the statue itself, not the grail. So I began to look more closely at that statue, my nose and dive mask almost rudely close to her figure, and noticed something intriguing. One of her silt-veiled hands, so graceful and delicate despite being larger than my own, was held awkwardly outward, cupped around…what?

The stone fingers curled to just the right size to have held the base of a chalice, but now they held nothing at all.

And the velvety algae that encrusted so many of

these artifacts, especially the column and the rest of the statue, was freshly dislodged from those fingers.

Desperation clenched in my chest as I understood. I knew it, with a knowing that went beyond further proof.

Someone had taken the Isis Grail from the statue's hand.

Recently.

Chapter 18

After an increasingly desperate search of the area around the fallen Isis, sending billows of sand up from my scrabbling hands, I had to give up. *It wasn't here!*

I surfaced in defeat, just in time for a wave to slap me right into the side of the speedboat, knocking me silly. Then Rhys was there, dragging me into the boat, into his arms, helping pull the mask off me as blowing sand began to stick to my wet body.

"It's gone," I gasped, after my first breath of warm, gritty air. "I need it, and it's gone!"

"You mean...you didn't find it?" Rhys wrapped me in a beach towel.

"I mean it was there, but it isn't anymore. I found a statue of Isis—it's beautiful—and she used to be holding something in her hand, but it's gone. You can see where the algae was disturbed. Someone took it!"

"But that's ridiculous, Maggi. Who would steal…?"
Our gazes locked. Then Rhys's eyes widened.
"Surely she would not," he protested.
But she'd stolen a grail from me once before.
Why not this time?

In situ my ass!
"Even if Catrina did take it," argued Rhys, following me as I stalked into the room I shared with my French bitch of a nemesis, "and that's quite a big *if*, surely she'd not hide it in here."

I'd gotten more than a few strange looks in the lobby. My hair hung in wet shanks after the dive and now the blowing wind had coated it with dust. I'd pulled my skirt and blouse back on over my bathing suit before we reached shore, so the dampening material was rubbing grit into my skin.

And I didn't give a damn about any of that.

I just stood in the center of the room and closed my eyes. Outside the window, with a sparking noise and what I assumed was a flash of light, a trolley rumbled through the intersection.

"Any number of explanations—" Rhys continued, but I held up a hand and said, "Shhh."

He shushed, and I took a deep breath…and *sensed*.

I was a Grailkeeper. That meant I had an ancestral connection to these chalices. I'd already found one of them, and it had felt like home. And I might even be a champion. Surely—

Yes. Sensing its call, I went to Catrina's bed and tugged an old, floral-patterned suitcase out from under it. For once, I didn't care why she hadn't bought something better. I unzipped it.

"She'd keep it close," I said.

"Maggi, are you sure you should—"

Then I lifted out a very large jar full of murky sea-water—and inside, like a dingy fish-bowl decoration, an ancient stone goblet.

I'm less than proud of my first reaction.

"Of all the people to have found it. *Catrina?*"

"*Uffach cols,*" swore Rhys.

Me, I just knelt there by the bed and blinked eyes that suddenly burned at the grail's beauty.

Like so much Egyptian pottery, like the stuff I'd seen the other week at the Metropolitan Museum of Art, this cup was blue faience—I could see bits of the color and glints of gold and silver through the algae, especially where it had been separated from Isis's stone hand. Something was carved around it, although until I got the brown gunk off…

Standing, I opened the jar, reached in, and pulled the goblet out barehanded.

Rhys winced. "I'm sure she has it in there to maintain the integrity of the chemical composition that has preserved the piece for this—"

His words seemed to stick in his throat as I left the jar on Catrina's bed—where I kind of hoped it might fall over—and wiped the cup with a towel. Swatches of algae came off it, better revealing patches where the faience had worn smooth and, where bands of gold and silver framed them, a faint pattern of two-dimensional figures, worn to ghostlike indistinction, parading across the outside of the goblet's bowl. Isis, yes. And Osiris. The falcon-headed Horus, their child. The evil Set—I wasn't quite sure what kind of animal that head belonged to, but I recognized him from other illustrations.

Ankhs and stars, both symbols of Isis, filled in negative space.

As if I hadn't already recognized the power thrumming through me from the Isis Grail.

I turned to Rhys and said, with low intensity, "I know that you're an archeologist. I know this is going to seem like blasphemy to you. But I have to go wash this grail now."

His blue eyes widened.

"To find Lex, I have to be able to drink out of it, and I'm not doing that without cleaning it first. I'll be careful, but it's pretty old. If this hurts it, I'll feel guilty forever. But human life is more important than a cup. Even this one."

Rhys just stared.

"Aren't you going to argue with me?" I asked.

"I will not," he said, though clearly pained.

So I hurried down the hall to the bathroom, grail hidden in the towel, while I had the chance.

When I got back, it was with an Isis Cup as clean as I could possibly make it without actually scrubbing the rest of the design off. Patches of it almost glowed its cheerful blue despite the pitting of salt, sand and time. I poured bottled water into it, my hand shaking—and hesitated.

Not from fear, but inadequacy.

The first time I'd ever done this, it had been at a goddess's shrine. The second time had been with the support of other Grailkeepers. For last night's ritual, Lex and I had used candles and scents and music.

Now I had to try this in an aging hotel room? And me, damp and filthy?

No time, my instincts warned.

"Perhaps I should go keep watch," Rhys suggested, either because he was sensing my thoughts or because he wasn't wholly comfortable watching me commune with a goddess. He was still very Catholic, after all.

"Thanks," I murmured, and he slipped out.

And then the grail and I were all alone together. *What if I couldn't do this?*

But I would. I had to.

Closing the room's curtains against the hazy afternoon, I set the grail on the floor, then knelt before it. This time, both my knees stayed on the linoleum in pure, desperate supplication. I'd already taken off my shoes. My feet were still sandy.

"Isis," I whispered into the shadows. I tried to sense the wholeness of Egypt stretching out around me. The sea—a longtime realm of the goddess—above me. The Nile connecting it to the lands of pyramids and tombs below me. Her kingdom. Her world. "Oldest of the Old," I continued, letting the words form in my mouth as they would. "Goddess of Ten Thousand Names. Lady of Compassion and Magic.

"Isis, I invite and welcome Thee into this, my world, which has great need of thy strength. I am a daughter of goddesses, proof that Your glory may have been veiled, but never forgotten. I am a…a champion of women, striving to return Your divine strength to others. I am…"

My bare hand, the one with the ring, clenched, and I blinked back tears.

"I am a bride, the vessel through which you granted your sacred blessings to someone who could be a great leader. If only for him…"

It had to be asked. It would not diminish anybody.

"Help me," I whispered.

Then I lifted the chalice, and I drank.

The last time I'd drunk from a goddess grail, it had been sweet, refreshing. Not this time. Even after its wash, a sharp, briny taste came off the cup. I clenched my teeth against nausea, suddenly dizzy. As if I were again in the harbor, being tossed around by the sea's powerful tides, my world lurched and twisted.

I'd expected a greeting. Instead, I felt a connection that was unsettlingly familiar, and then—memories that were not my own.

Were they?

Flying over the desert, the fertile green of the Nile to the left, the brown barrenness of the desert to the right. We could barely notice the scenery through Our fear and grief as We sought Our murdered lover. Our husband. Osiris…

Lex?

No. I shook my head. *No, no, no…*

With love comes pain, warned a hundred female voices, a thousand female voices, more. They echoed around me and through my head in more languages than I could recognize. Goddess of Ten Thousand Names, for sure! *Embrace it and be a woman, or fear it and live in ignorance as a girl….*

This was no message of welcome. It was nothing less than a challenge.

Along with the voices whirled images, brief glimpses of grieving mothers and lovers and widows. The price of loving. Payment for heaven. Old as time. *We were one.*

Some of the women I saw seemed to glow—goddesses? And yet they, too, grieved. In particular, a flash of bright blues and reds and golds caught my attention, a horned-disk crown, dark skin and darker eyes burning with loss and horror. Then I couldn't see Her because We *were* Her, weeping, pressing Our cheek against the cold, dead cheek of Our husband, Our god...

His own dark cheek lightened; his black hair turned a ginger-brown, then darkened again.

No. No...

But before I went under again, lost in sorrow and anguish, I managed to clutch at what she'd said. If this was already happening, had already happened, then denying it did nothing but keep me ignorant—and helpless.

Choose hope.

I couldn't force myself to say *yes,* to even think it. Not to such a horrible possibility. But I stopped protesting, and sensed harsh satisfaction.

"Show me," I whispered into the tumult of images, into the empty hotel room. *"Show me."*

Some of Isis's voices soothed and comforted me— Goddess of Compassion. Some of Her voices couldn't hear me, lost in Their own grief—the Great Mourner. Some laughed at me, though gently, like the mother of a precocious child—

You wish another *gift?*

Another...? Did she mean a gift beyond the knowledge of Lex's true danger, or a gift beyond the warning instinct that Melusine had given me? Either way, this was why I'd just risked my life for this grail. Isis had a skill that I needed—the magic to find her ambushed lover.

"Yes," I whispered. "I was born to this. I will do good with this. I deserve it. *And so does he.*"

Again, the sense of flying, of the Nile rushing beneath my wings, of pyramids in the distance, coming closer, closer—

My eyes opened to a ringing voice, one powerful utterance made up of many. It was the voice of every woman, ever, who had looked pain and loss right in the eye—and gone to battle.

"Then welcome. Champion. Name it for one who strikes."

And again I sat in the hotel room, a bitter taste in my mouth, a tug at my heart, strength in my veins....

And Catrina's voice, cursing loudly in French for Rhys to let her by, just outside the doorway.

"—scratch your eyes out if you do not let me—" she was threatening, struggling in his firm grip, as I threw open the door.

Her green eyes narrowed. "You..."

"Once a thief, always a thief?" I challenged, turning back into the room to grab a clean towel and the white, fluffy robe I'd taken from the Four Seasons. It wasn't the one I'd worn. It was the one Lex had. It had smelled of him, this morning, and I'd needed it.

If the hotel charged him, I'd just pay him back.

Name it for one who strikes. Was there really a baby, then? I sensed I was missing something.

As I shouldered into the hallway again, Cat saw the grail in my hand. *"You washed it?"*

"Yes." I turned to Rhys. "Can you borrow the car again? We need to head back toward Cairo, as soon as I can clean myself up."

"Certainly." I couldn't blame him for looking confused. "You know where he is, then?"

It was a strange sensation, the gift Isis had given me. I had to concentrate to even recognize it, a tiny tug below my heart, as if there were an invisible cord connecting me to Lex.

That's the direction I pointed, vaguely southward. "Thataway."

"And what about—oof!" That last, because Catrina had elbowed him in the solar plexus.

"Hit her back," I suggested, striding down the hallway to the shared bathroom.

Wouldn't you know the damned thing would be in use?

I knocked on the door, then leaned against the wall to wait while Catrina caught up. Behind her, Rhys shook his head, then went off in search of whoever currently had the car.

"This is why I took the cup before you could," she insisted—in French, of course. "I saw that you had found something, and I knew that if I did not hide it, you would steal it, do something like…*voilà!*"

It was an angry *voilà,* complete with hand gestures. She really hated that I'd interfered with nature's treatment of the cup, didn't she?

"You stole it so that I couldn't?" I challenged. "Interesting ethics."

"You speak of ethics to me?"

"Good point. That would be useless." To my relief, the door behind me opened and a golden-haired gentleman with fogged glasses emerged in a cloud of steam.

"*Guten Tag,*" he said, as he passed.

The Hotel Athens was pretty much full of Westerners.

I went into the bathroom. Cat followed before I could keep her out—since I was hindered by still carrying the grail, still with some bottled water in it—and shut and locked the door behind us.

"You are the thief," she insisted. "I knew as soon as you arrived that you would destroy Cleopatra's Palace as you destroyed Fontevrault."

"I didn't destroy—" But would saying it for the umpteenth time make any difference? In disgust, I turned on the shower.

"You brought the people who destroyed it," she said, so maybe she'd listened—just a bit—after all. "And now you do the same here. We had no trouble until you arrived. Then the pylon falls. Then a boating accident. How is this not your fault?"

"Because I didn't do any of it?" But…what if it *had* been aimed at me? What if it was the work of the Comitatus, led here by me…or Lex?

Without his knowledge, of course.

Guilt made me feel belligerent. Catrina and I glared at each other, like gunslingers deciding who will draw first.

Then I held out the chalice. "Want some?"

Her lip curled. "Do you know where this has been?"

"Yes, and it tastes awful. But it might help explain a few things."

"Do you think I took the same room with you for your companionship? I do not trust you! Why should I trust this? *And how can I put the chalice back now?"*

As if she'd really meant to do that. But…

Who the hell knew? Maybe she had.

With a shrug, I took another swallow of the water— and winced. Goddess, that tasted nasty! But I felt the little tug, between me and Lex strengthen.

Lower.

I hated to pour the rest out.

With a soft curse, Catrina took the chalice—which I still held—and gulped the rest. As if I'd dared her.

Maybe I had.

Her face immediately screwed into a grimace, at the taste. Her eyes widened, watering and accusatory. Then she spun for the toilet.

I stepped into the shower to give her some privacy.

Of course I took the Isis Grail with me.

Name it for one who strikes? Surely, if Isis meant my baby, if there was a baby, she would have known the gender.

When I stepped back out of the shower, now as clean as befitted a champion of the goddess, Catrina sat with her back against the door, a haunted look in her eyes.

I divided my time between drying off, keeping an eye on the chalice, and watching her with growing concern.

And trying not to worry about the tug from Lex, deep in my gut. Or *one who strikes*.

Damn it, I didn't want to feel concern about this woman! I wanted to wrap myself in this thick, soft robe and bury my face in the fuzzy lapel and breathe in Lex, Lex, Lex....

But denial would save neither him nor me. Champions can't be choosy. And there was something freeing in the fact that Isis herself had, at times, been quite the bitch.

"Are you okay?" I asked grudgingly.

"What was that?" she demanded, standing unsteadily.

So the cup hadn't just made her sick, after all. She'd gotten some of Isis's juju.

"Behold the power of the goddess." I smiled dryly.

She didn't. Instead, she just followed me silently back to our room. At least she was no longer eyeing the cup as if she meant to grab it, clobber me over the head with it and run.

But she *was* still eyeing the cup.

It made me nervous as I pulled on clothes, and not because I'm particularly modest. I dressed deliberately for battle—the cargo pants and camisole that I hadn't worn since arriving in this country. Good walking boots.

Sword.

Suddenly I understood the goddess's suggestion. One who *strikes,* indeed! Snakes were an old goddess symbol. And at least one supposed incarnation of Isis had turned into one particular snake in her darkest hour.

"Hello, Asp," I said softly to my Egyptian blade. Then I slid it into its scabbard and strapped it on. Like a warrior.

I transferred what I needed from my fanny pack to my cargo pockets. I rolled the chalice in a towel and tucked it in the fanny pack, with a little six-oz bottle of water. Have goddess, will travel.

My concession to Egyptian conservatism was to then top the whole outfit with a white cotton galabiya, which I'd only bought as a souvenir for a friend back home, and took along a blue-and-gold head scarf, just in case.

The whole time, Cat watched, eyes narrow and cool, like her namesake.

We both jumped when Rhys knocked.

"I've got the car and topped it off with petrol," he panted, holding up the keys. "It took some doing to find Niko, but I've got it."

"Good." I headed out—but when I turned to close the door, Catrina was right behind me.

"Hold it," I protested. "You're not coming."

"You are taking the chalice?" she asked, as if she hadn't seen me strap it around my waist.

"Yes."

"Then you are taking me."

Just what I needed—someone along that I couldn't trust. But from the faint but continual tug below my heart, I sensed I didn't have the time to argue. And I was generally against the idea of clobbering people over the head and leaving them unconscious, even as it applied to Catrina Dauvergne.

"Don't get in my way," I warned, heading down the hallway toward the stairs with a stride that was purely American.

She wisely waited until we were in the car—me driving, despite Rhys's protests—and had headed out past the ornate Greco-Roman gate onto the Desert Road to ask, "So where in God's name are we going?"

"And who," I asked, glancing in the rearview mirror, "are those men who are following us?"

Rhys twisted in the passenger seat to look. So did Catrina, in back.

"Maroon coupe," I said, to direct them to the proper car. "I don't recognize the make—it has a lightning bolt across a circle?"

"Opel," deciphered Catrina.

"*Uffach cols,*" said Rhys.

"No," insisted Catrina. "It's an Opel Vectra."

But Rhys had already turned forward in his seat.

"Not to worry anybody," he said gently, "but I believe that may be the same car that tried to run me down the other week."

Chapter 19

What to do, what to do, what to do?

I had to get to Lex, I *had* to. But I couldn't just ignore the threat to Rhys.

When I changed lanes, the Vectra changed lanes.

The speed limit on the highway was one hundred kilometers per hour, or about sixty miles per hour. When I accelerated to 110, then 120, the Vectra sped up, too.

They were definitely following us.

"Crap," I said—my own version of *uffach cols*.

And I began to slow down—one hundred kilometers per hour.

"Um, Maggi?" That was Rhys. "Far be it from me to encourage another drive like the one we took in France, but…"

"Sooner or later, they either have to pass us, or we'll get pulled over," I said, digging into one of my cargo pockets for…yes. My disposable camera. "Get their license, and a picture or two. We want to be able to identify these bastards once we've rescued Lex."

Ninety kilometers per hour.

"Rescue Lex from whom?" asked Catrina.

Rhys twisted in his seat to watch for a better opportunity. "You think these people will *let* us rescue Lex?"

Eighty kilometers per hour. I'd pulled into the right lane—in Egypt, they drive on the same side of the road as in the States—so that I could exit if necessary.

Thinking.

"I'm not convinced these people care about Lex either way. And I don't plan on giving them the option of not *letting* us do anything. Here they come…"

I half expected to see someone with a gun out the window as the driver of the Vectra, realizing how suspicious they'd become, sped up to pass us. But this was Egypt. There were armored cars on the highway, here and there. They weren't that stupid.

They would just wait for us to get wherever we were going, and then make their move. Considering that I didn't know where we were going—except in the direction where my heart tugged me—or what we'd find there, I didn't want to wait. Rhys snapped several pictures as the coupe flew past. "They looked away, but I think I recognized one of the men who searched your suitcase, outside Tala's villa."

"Hani Rachid's men." I slapped my palm, hard, on the steering wheel. "Remember, back in the cisterns? He said something about you insinuating yourself with Jane. I was afraid he'd kill you right there, but once I realized he hadn't done that much damage…."

"You two have quite the knack for making enemies," mused Catrina. "Who is Jane?"

I would have ignored her, but Rhys said, "Hani Rachid's ex-wife."

"Do you mean the woman who is hiding out with her daughter in the British Embassy?"

I guess Hani really *was* working the publicity.

Now the Vectra was slowing down in an attempt to force us to pass them. I guess the camera had clued them into the fact that they'd been made.

I began slowing down, too. Ninety kilometers per hour.

Rhys asked, "Are you planning to play this game of chicken all the way to Cairo?"

It's not like I've been in enough car chases to have a usual response. But the one time I ran into this, I'd chosen to first outrun them and, when that didn't work, to bash their car into uselessness.

For some reason, I didn't want to do anything that drastic this time.

Eighty kilometers per hour. "What's the worst thing that happens, if we get pulled over for driving too slow?"

"The police find you with a concealed sword and a smuggled artifact?" said Rhys.

Crap! Ninety kilometers per hour. "I'm an idiot," I whispered. Besides, if going slow kept us from getting to Lex on time… "Okay, so what have we got to work with? Anything?"

Catrina began to rummage good-naturedly under the seats. "You could threaten them with a squeegee."

"Real helpful." I passed the Vectra again and so got a decent look myself.

Definitely Hani's thugs. I recognized one of them from more than the morning outside Tala's villa.

And in this game of cat and mouse, they were now back in the role of cat.

"Puncture fixit," continued Catrina. "A paper bag of—*merde!* Do you people never clean out this car?"

I had a sudden hope. "What's puncture fixit?"

"To, how do you say…fix a puncture?" Her tone was condescending.

"A flat tire, right? It's Fix-A-Flat? Pass it here."

"Oh, dear," murmured Rhys, figuring it out as Catrina did. "Maggi…"

"Pull the top off this hosey thing." I began to slow again, unrolling my window. Eighty kilometers per hour. "And roll down your window. I'm not sure which side they'll choose."

Seventy kilometers per hour.

He did. "Are you sure this is wise?"

"Nope."

"Just checking."

Sixty kilometers per hour. We were crawling, by highway standards.

"I think they're…yes. Can either of you see any authorities? Any other cars that could get caught in the cross fire?"

"None," said Catrina. But since I didn't trust her to tell us if we had an entire police escort, I waited for Rhys to say, "It's clear. More or less."

Most of the other traffic was passing us in the far left lane, keeping well clear of the slow crazy people.

"Okay, they're passing on my side," I announced, dividing my attention between the rearview mirror and the road ahead. "Here, Rhys. Take the wheel."

"What?" But after a moment's shock, he snatched it.

Leaning out my driver's window at somewhere around forty miles per hour while keeping my foot on the gas wasn't the easiest thing I've ever done. The wind that whipped past my face was hot as a blow dryer on high. I had to squint against the dust. And yet...

Aiming that can of Fix-A-Flat at the startled faces of Hani's thugs, through their windshield, and pressing the button—

That felt *remarkably* good.

White foam splattered across their windshield. The Vectra swerved blindly, braking too fast for me to finish off the whole can. But I'd done a pretty fair job. As I ducked my head back in the window, dropped my butt back into the driver's seat, and took back the wheel, it was with a sense of true accomplishment.

A glance in the rearview mirror, as I accelerated, confirmed that they'd had to pull over and stop. In moments, they'd vanished from sight.

Neither Rhys nor Catrina said anything.

"And that stuff is made to be really sticky," I noted, in case they hadn't thought of that. "So that it coats the *puncture* from the inside of the tire. Between that and the sand..."

"Their windscreen will need more than a swipe with a towel," agreed Catrina, sounding impressed.

Rhys asked, low, "And what if they had wrecked the car, Maggi? What if they were hurt, or killed?"

"They weren't."

"They could have been." He was staring out the windshield, he was so angry.

"We were barely going forty miles an hour."

"That is no guarantee of their safety."

So I told him. "They're the men who beat you up."

Now he looked at me, surprised.

"You were blindfolded the whole time, but I wasn't. The man riding shotgun is one of the men who kicked you so hard."

After a long moment, he said, "That is no justification."

"You may be a priest," I said, "but I'm—"

Catrina leaned up between us, staring at Rhys. "You are a *priest*? Involved with an Egyptian's ex-wife?"

"He's kind of a rogue priest," I suggested.

Rhys closed his eyes, but I would let him do the explaining. Me, I was marveling at my new, ruthless edge. If I was a priestess—as I'd been the previous night— then it was a completely different role than merely being a female priest. As far as I knew, Rhys was still celibate, even after being laicized. Me, I'd done a sex ritual. Rhys was about peace and fellowship.

But I was currently serving a goddess who had poisoned another god, specifically to take his powers.

Just how far would I go, to ensure the safety of the men in my life?

Still following the inexorable pull in my gut, I suspected I might just find out.

The sun was going down several hours later as I turned off the main highway onto the road to Sakkara. We'd passed Cairo and were in sight of Giza.

When the tug below my heart pulled me west, I turned onto a bumpy track that ran past a small village, glad for my sunglasses against a truly orange sunset.

Even Rhys and Catrina fell silent.

A small mob of peasants—*fellahin,* I think they're called—ran toward the car, waving and shouting. Exchanging concerned glances with Rhys, I slowed and rolled my window partly down.

They were all men, I noticed—men, a couple of goats, and a donkey. The women of the village stood in the background, properly swathed, while the men surrounded us, shaking their heads and insisting...*something.* I was more impatient than frightened—they were all smiling sunny, gap-toothed smiles and, to be honest, I thought we could take them.

But I resented the delay. Lex felt so close....

"Cannot go past," a child stated loudly, weaving through the others to stand near my window. He held out his hand for *baksheesh,* payment for his translation I guess. "The road, it is closed."

Like this even *was* a road.

The pull was definitely coming from beyond here. "Thanks anyway," I said, easing very, very gently onto the accelerator.

The *fellahin* backed quickly away, apparently accustomed to crazy tourists—but they also shouted louder and waved with more determination. *"La'! La'!"*

No, no.

That's when I noticed that the women in the background *weren't* smiling, not even their eyes. I braked again.

Something was up.

I reached into another of my cargo pockets and pulled out a ten-dollar bill, then pressed it against the glass of my window. *Now* I had their attention.

"Who asked you to divert the tourists tonight?" I asked the boy. "Who said to tell us the road is closed?"

He eyed the money. Then he glanced at me, then back to the money—and shook his head.

"Fifty," he challenged. "Fifty American dollar."

The scamp didn't realize that he'd given all the answer I needed—that someone had, in fact, bribed them.

"Shukran," I said as thanks, and passed him out the ten.

He looked decidedly disappointed—but at least the ladies in the background were smiling. Let's hear it for not getting pushed around by the suits.

The boys chased our car for a few yards as I pulled carefully away.

Because of that little encounter I was less than surprised, as the track dead-ended at the edge of the desert, to see no less than a dozen cars already parked there.

Expensive cars.

Not far beyond them stood more *fellahin* with, of all things, camels.

"Comitatus?" guessed Rhys—correctly, I think.

"So much for secrecy," I murmured, braking before we reached them. And yet the belligerence I'd felt toward Hani's men apparently wasn't a one-shot instance. "But I'm not turning back. Not on your…"

Oh. Except it *could* very easily be on his life, and Catrina's, too. I said, "If you'd like to drop me off and head out to a safe distance…"

"'Not on your life,'" echoed Rhys. "Unless Catrina—"

"Oh, we can trust *Catrina* not to strand us."

"Not to strand the chalice, in any case," she said from the back seat. "The priest, he says that these are the men who destroyed the tapestries at Fontevrault, yes?"

"Not the exact same men, probably," I hedged. "But the same organization."

"Then I do not intend to stay behind."

So, feeling unnervingly exposed, I drove us the rest of the way to the end of the track and pulled the Chevy Metro to an incongruous stop beside a silver Aston Martin.

"What is it about you and tapestries?" I asked, under my breath.

"They are one of the few forms of legitimate woman's art from the Middle Ages," she snapped back, with a strong note of *duh* in her voice.

I was confused by a fleeting moment in which I actually approved of her—but I got past it.

Two of the men had begun to lead their camels in our direction, but they stopped to confer with each other when they saw Cat and me get out of the car. Clearly we were not the gender they were expecting this evening. But at least nobody was attacking us. Yet.

I glanced across the desert, past some odd little hills and toward the three distant pyramids of Giza.

The same pyramids I'd gazed at, from a different angle, while Lex was…

I closed my eyes to a rush of sensuous warmth at the memory, and the tug beneath my heart grew more powerful. More desperate.

"It's this way," I said, hurrying toward the camel drivers. "I don't know where we are, but Lex—"

"AbuSir," said Rhys and Catrina, in unison.

"—is definitely this way, and what's Abusir?"

"It's a pyramid complex," said Rhys.

"Fifth Dynasty," added Catrina.

I'd been *sure* those pyramids were the ones at Giza!

Then I realized what was up. They were talking not about the pyramids in the distance, which was Giza, but the odd, rounded hills. *"Those are pyramids?"*

"They are," agreed Rhys, keeping up with his long stride. "Only a few remain out of the original...fourteen, I believe?"

"Fourteen," agreed Catrina. "And several temples."

Camels groaned and gargled as we got closer, and I hailed the nearest driver. "How much for a ride to the, uh...pyramids?" I tried to remember the appropriate phrase from the bazaar for *how much? "Bekam?"*

The man shook his head and motioned for us to go away.

I looked at the second man. *"Bekam?"*

He took a few steps toward us but, before he could coax his camels into following, his fellow drivers stopped him with hands on his shoulders and shaking heads.

Damned Comitatus. "They're scared to anger the men who already paid them."

"Er, Maggi," said Rhys.

"Just throw money at them," suggested Catrina. "Isn't that how Americans solve everything?"

"Bekam?" I called, to the third and last driver. He made a rude gesture and shouted something that sounded both dismissive and familiar. Like from jail.

"That or big guns," Catrina continued.

I closed my eyes and reached for Lex. He was so close!

"Maggi," insisted Rhys. A chill of foreboding shuddered over me at the sympathetic look on his face. "It may mean nothing..."

"What may mean nothing?"

"The name AbuSir once meant 'House of Osiris.' I doubt the Comitatus chose this place for that reason, but…"

But on the chance that Lex and I were following some sort of Osiris-and-Isis script, the coincidence wasn't encouraging.

I felt Lex's presence amid the pyramic complex, as surely as I might have felt sunlight on my face or wind in my hair. Isis had given me this gift—the same gift with which she'd found the ambushed Osiris—but it was up to me how to use it.

"Okay," I murmured, eyeing the men and their camels with narrowing eyes. "Time for Plan B."

This time, when I approached the camel drivers, I was wearing my Isis face: my eyes darkly outlined, and an ankh drawn on my forehead similarly to how Hani Rachid sported a protective Eye of Horus. Then I shadowed the whole effect—for the moment—with the head scarf. Though I've never been a big New Ager, praising ley lines or pyramid power, the energy in this place was significant. If the Comitatus had any sensitivity at all, *that* was why they chose AbuSir for whatever ritual was underway.

Might as well take advantage of it.

Not to mention, *I* felt more powerful this way.

Even the man who tried to leave at my approach wasn't fast enough to avoid me; his camel balked and groaned and shook its head, clearly in a foul mood. That seemed par for the course, with camels. The other two men watched, one wary, the other hopeful.

"*Bekam,*" I demanded, instead of asking, and pointed at the camels. I also held up a twenty-dollar bill.

The older man shook his head, though he seemed pained to have to. The younger hesitated.

"Er, Maggi," said Rhys—a phrase I was starting to dread from him. "Someone's coming."

"More details, please," I murmured, maintaining my look of royal privilege. I drew a second twenty out of my cargo pocket and held it up.

"There's dust coming along the track from the village."

Crap. Probably one of the Comitatus types, late for his ritual. The two *fellahin* still hadn't made up their minds—so it was time to do it for them.

I swept back the head scarf, so that he could get full view of my lined eyes, my protective ankh, my pendant.

"You," I said firmly, pointing at the younger man. Whether he spoke English or not, I meant to make him understand. "Give us rides to where the other men went, *now,* or risk angering forces beyond your comprehension!"

Eyes widening, the younger *fellahin* urged his two camels forward and, barely daring to look at me, took the money. He pointed at himself, still ducking his head.

"Selim," he said. His name.

I pointed to myself without hesitation. *"Isis."*

Maybe he understood, maybe not. Either way, he shouted commands to his beasts and tugged on their lead ropes. Their stubbornly slow response gave me a chance to glance over my shoulder at the track behind the rocky car park.

A wisp of brown floated up from over a ridge. I asked, "Are you sure that's enough dust for a car?"

"They've stopped," noted Rhys. "They are probably being told that the road is closed?"

Normally, I would have protested Selim whacking his camels on the legs as he made them kneel. But the animals, despite their huge eyes and long lashes and split front lips, seemed a lot tougher than the stick he was using. And they did at least kneel. They smelled horrible.

The cloud of dust thickened on the horizon. Damn!

I scrambled up onto the rug-covered saddle like some Middle-Eastern trick rider, though not a very good one. The camel made an awful, groaning noise in protest, half belch and half gag, and its breath smelled even worse than the rest of it.

Catrina climbed on behind me. Rhys and Selim mounted the other camel.

The cloud of dust grew larger. Closer.

Selim shouted some more, whacking his camel with his stick. Both animals stood—

Hind legs first.

"Merde," grunted Catrina, her arms tightening around my waist as we pitched forward, practically over the beast's head.

"Try to take the chalice," I muttered, grasping my fanny pack with the hand that wasn't holding on to the camel's saddle for dear life, "and I'll push you off."

Then the camel straightened its front legs, throwing me back into her.

"You will try," warned Catrina.

As soon as we stopped tipping, I looked over my shoulder. Through the approaching dust, I thought I detected a flash of maroon.

"How can it be the Vectra?" I demanded. "We lost them."

"Unless they used another tracking device," suggested Rhys, from behind Selim, as the camels swayed into motion. Good goddess. Just walking, they pitched worse than the boat had on choppy water this afternoon. "Not on us, perhaps, but the car...?"

"We've got to hurry," I urged Selim. "Fast. *Vite!*"

Since it's what I would have done on a horse, I leaned forward—heavens, but the rocky ground was a long way down—and smacked the camel on its furry hump. No way could I have reached its head.

It turned and gave me a long-lashed look of pure disgust.

Luckily, Selim got the idea. He shouted something in Arabic and began swinging his stick between our camel and his.

Protesting loudly, the camels broke into a heavy, lurching run across the rocky, twilit desert. Ahead of us, the moon was rising.

All I could do was hang on—and sense Lex's nearness increasing.

His nearness and, to judge by the ache in my throat, his danger.

Chapter 20

As we jolted closer, especially after the camels climbed a steep incline, it became more apparent. Those really *were* pyramids—four large, crumbling pyramids, looming up before us. The twilight half hid vast pits in the ground, too, excavations of temples, causeways, tombs. Between those two extremes, rocks and stretches of stone wall crumbled together indiscriminately. A pair of worn columns still stood amid heaps of what otherwise looked like rubble.

Time hadn't been as kind to this place as to nearby Giza. Some things *weren't* immortal.

Oddly, I felt glad for Cat's arms around me, even if she held on only out of necessity on our galloping, bellowing beast. This night suddenly felt too important for just me, too big—too inescapable.

Lex.

Selim raced us down a long dirt grade, stones flying from beneath our camels' padded feet, into an excavated area at the base of one looming, barren pyramid. A final glance toward the distant cars showed me the maroon Vectra drawing nearer.

Then they were out of sight—as were we, into the pit. But had they seen where we'd gone? I certainly wouldn't have guessed that this huge, half-buried complex of ditches and walls was here, not from the road. I sure as hell hadn't seen the signs of activity waiting in the pit. Five saddled camels stood in wait beside two staring drivers. A pair of men who could only be sentries stood to either side of a gated hole into the hillside.

A gate which stood open.

The sentries looked anachronistic in their formal business attire amid the hot twilight, rubble, galabiya-wearing natives and spitting animals. They watched us as we bounded to a welcome stop, the camels gargling yet more complaints.

We were flung forward as our camel knelt with its front legs, then thrown backward as its hind legs went down. I hadn't realized how shaky I felt until I half climbed, half slid from the beast's saddled hump. My legs nearly collapsed beneath me.

The sentries seemed intrigued, concerned even—about us, not for us. But they weren't yet...oh...shooting.

"Any suggestions?" asked Rhys, also eyeing the men as he limped closer to us. I held out Selim's money, which was taken quickly from my hand, and heard the camels being whacked some more, and complaining about it, as he herded them away. But I still watched the sentries.

"Let me think," I murmured, trying to focus past the continual awareness of Lex which called to me from beyond the dark gate—and the continual suspicion of *how*. "Not just anybody has the prestige to meet under a pyramid. Even these crumbly ones."

"These are perfectly good pyramids, and they ought not be put at risk," protested Catrina. "Even the moisture from people's breath—"

I held up a hand to remind her that I'd heard that part of the lecture.

"It would take major connections to arrange it, but that's what the Comitatus is about…power and connections. Still, they wouldn't risk the exposure, or go to the trouble of meeting somewhere this out of the way, unless it was especially important. Like deciding who their new leader will be. That might just require a place with ritual significance."

This could be just what I need, Lex had said of Cairo. He'd been looking for a place, he'd said. *And I'm here because of you.*

One of the sentries headed toward us. "My apologies, ladies," he called with a thick, Spanish accent. "And the gentleman. This site, it is closed to tourists."

"If tonight *is* a ritual—*the* ritual—" I continued quietly, quickly, "there are things they'll have to do. Things they've always done. There would be rules."

"Like 'no women'?" Catrina suggested. She caught on fast.

"And, just maybe, no violence. Or things having to happen at a certain time in order to count. Or—"

"I must be so rude as to insist that you leave," insisted the sentry, drawing closer.

I turned, and let him see me fully.

Ankh. Cleopatra eyes. Chalice-well pendant.

His eyes widened—for, like, a second or two. But as I swept by him, he still grabbed for my arm.

Well, it had been worth a try.

I spun, easily avoiding his grasp, and lowered my center of balance to better prepare for a fight. He reached under his jacket—

And Catrina clobbered him with a rock, from behind. The guard dropped to the rubble at our feet, moaning.

Okay, so she was growing on me.

"That way," she warned simply, glancing past my shoulder. I spun.

Sure enough, here came the second sentry, drawing from his suit not a gun but a long knife. Of course.

I hauled at my galabiya to get at my own sword, pulling the cloth tunic off over my head even as I slid my blade free. I knew how deadly those serrated, cere- monial blades could be.

"You people don't know who you're messing with," he warned, his accent straight American.

"You're not working with full disclosure, either," I warned him, readjusting to the heft of my still-new weapon. *Come on, Asp. Prove your worth.* "We're here for your new leader. He won't appreciate your interference."

I hoped.

He held the blade like an experienced knife fighter. "What makes you think we have one?"

"Because I know Lex Stuart. He'll have a better ar- gument, and he can win any contest your glorified boys' club throws at him." I realized, with some pride, that I actually believed that. Or I would, if they played fair.

It wasn't my imagination. The sentry's expression momentarily flickered.

I lunged, just enough to unnerve him. "You can either let us by," I warned, my feet moving across rubble, "or end up like your friend, there."

"If I let you by, it may not matter *how* I end up."

"Not if Lex is in charge."

He didn't say anything—he had more self-control than that. But something about the self-satisfied humor that flashed across his eyes cinched around my throat like an invisible noose. *Danger.*

And not to me.

I may never know how I did it. Most of my training with swords, beyond college fencing for PE credit, is defensive. But in a flash, with a ring of metal, my sword struck and the sentry's knife spun through the air and landed, blade down, in the sand.

Asp hovered a breath from his Adam's apple. "What do you know?"

He glared down the length of my sword. *"Nothing."*

"Wrong answer. Cat—"

She looked up from where she was binding the first sentry with his own tie.

"Tie him up, too, please." Catrina was proving herself significantly more ruthless than Rhys. Who would have guessed I'd find that a *good* thing?

She sighed—but she did it. The one time he tried to grab her, to use her as leverage I guess, she grabbed two of his fingers and pulled back so hard that he dropped to his knees.

She seemed to enjoy it.

"What do you know about Lex?" I repeated, glaring down at him.

"You won't hurt me," insisted the sentry—even as a particularly enthusiastic tug of Cat's made him wince.

"Not if you're with Lex Stuart. He's weak. His supporters are weak. That's what is defeating him."

Not what *would* defeat him. What *was* defeating him—right now. *Crap!*

"You think?" I asked—and knocked him to the ground. All it took was a well-placed foot between his shoulder blades.

"Maggi," warned Rhys. And true, with his hands tied, the guy couldn't break his fall with anything but his face. Oops.

I guess I could be more ruthless than I'd initially thought.

He grunted, then spat out sand. "I said I'm not worried."

"That's because you're paying attention to the wrong myths," I said, planting a knee on his back. "Catrina, please get the scorpions."

She widened her eyes and spread her hands. But at least she didn't ask, *What scorpions?*

"Thank you," I said, as if she'd handed me a whole jar. Then I deliberately traced a fingernail across the back of the sentry's coat, so lightly he may not have felt it.

To judge from his shiver, I guess he did. "That's one."

"You're crazy, lady."

"Maybe." I skittered two fingers now, closer to his neck, making sure the scrabbling against fabric was audible. "Two. They're pretty big, too—desert scorpions. Is this your first time in Egypt?"

"Not hardly."

"Ever hear of the Sun God, Ra? He was the most powerful of all the gods, but even he spilled his guts to the goddess Isis. He gave her all his magic, told her his sacred name." *Skitter.* I made sure to touch the edge of his hair and—extra aware now, straining for proof or disproof of my ruse—he flinched. "I'm very much into Isis right now—or maybe I should say she's into me— but even I'm not asking for that much."

Was it my imagination, or was his breathing getting faster, more shallow?

"Three," I murmured, adding a third finger to the tracing of imaginary bugs. "Of course, I don't have her power to heal, once you're poisoned. On the other hand, one scorpion probably won't kill a grown man. Which is why I'm using…four."

He definitely flinched.

"So what do you know about Lex Stuart and the ritual?"

"You're bluffing." But his voice shook. He was sweating now.

I tried to sense Lex's nearness, and realized why I was recognizing him with a sensation below my heart. The awareness was, in fact, deep in my gut.

It was, in fact, in my womb.

Logical or not, I now understood my new connection to him. Between that little epiphany, and the constriction of my throat warning me of imminent danger, I guessed I could be ruthless, at that.

"Sic him, pets," I whispered—and caught a piece of his neck between two fingernails, and pinched.

He screamed.

Three months ago, I hadn't known the Comitatus existed.

Now here I was, made up like Isis, an actual goddess

grail in my fanny pack, racing to crash one of their inner circle's rituals.

I wouldn't recommend running in dark, underground passageways. Especially with loose rocks underneath your feet and only two lights—they had been the sentries'—for three people. But I ran like Set himself was after us.

Apparently by Comitatus law, no matter how convincing Lex's argument, the decision would come down to a freaking challenge. *Like trial by combat,* our captive had explained, in exchange for me brushing all but one of the other "scorpions" off of him. *But it doesn't have to be actual combat.*

What does it have to be? I'd demanded.

My light zagged from the floor to the stone walls and back, making random patterns with Catrina's. Rhys's footsteps sounded behind her, which was all I'd heard from him since I'd tortured the sentry into confession.

I refused to feel guilty about that. Not yet, anyway.

Not after what I'd learned.

Any kind of contest, the man had said, grains of sand shifting away from his mouth as he panted. *The injured party gets to choose.*

The injured party being Phil?

As I shortened my steps, to compensate for a particularly severe downslope, I felt a tug to my left—only a moment before we would have flown past an intersecting passageway. I skidded to a stop, catching the crumbling wall and whispering, "This way!"

Cat slapped my hand away—probably to protect the precious rock from the oils in my skin. "And how do you know this?"

But I was already running again. The next time I felt

the tug, I turned on faith alone, even before the light found the passageway.

He's chosen a drinking contest, the sentry had admitted. I'd thought, could Phil be more juvenile? But if that was the procedure, I supposed Lex would go along with it. It wasn't as bad as pistols at ten paces.

Then my informant had added, *Drinking poison.*

Now I could hear something else, and I slowed my footsteps, the need for silence barely—barely!—winning out over the need for speed.

Voices.

I'm not quite sure what I expected from a meeting of the inner circle of the Comitatus. Chanting, I guess. Grandiose titles. They believed in ritual enough to have sought out an ancient, shadowy place of power for their gathering, after all. Enough that most of them were willing to fly to Cairo, just to meet here. Enough that they would resolve their dispute in that most male of traditions—a stupid competition.

But what I heard sounded more like a frat party.

"—three!" The countdown, in a deep and vaguely familiar voice, was followed by a murmur of interested approval. "That is four. So far, neither man appears to feel the valerian. We will move to the fifth round."

They'd already drunk four times?

"We don't have to keep doing this," insisted a voice that resonated through me. *Lex.* I pressed a hand to my mouth to catch back a little cry of relief to hear him still alive, still conscious. "Let me take my rightful place, Phil, and you can be my right-hand man. Together, we can make the Comitatus what it once was."

"I don't have a problem with the way it is now," insisted another familiar voice. Phil's. "Drink."

According to my informant, valerian—which was historically used for this sort of "contest"—was poison only in high doses, and rarely fatal. The point was which combatant's body was weak enough for him to pass out first.

Unfortunately, Phil wasn't playing fair. *And Lex Stuart has no idea,* my captive had gloated. *Weak.*

I knew Lex a hell of a lot better than either Phil or the sentry probably did. Lex might not want to believe his cousin would rig the "combat" in his favor—no poison in Phil's cup, and something far more deadly—"arsenic or something"—in Lex's. But Lex was not so stupid that he would blindly trust Phil, either.

Still, without proof, he *would* drink. It was his only chance to make his point. It had come down to a matter of honor.

After months of me fearing Lex's possible immorality, it was his damned honor that would kill him.

And yet...

"One," counted the deep-voiced referee.

He'd already taken four drinks of arsenic or something. Was I already too late to make a difference?

"Two."

Would I ruin what little he could still gain from this travesty? Isis Herself had told me, *With love comes pain.*

"Maggi?" prompted Rhys. He and Cat were staring. They'd heard the confession, too.

"Three."

A modest cheer followed that. Both men must have downed the contents of their cups. A little piece of me died when I did nothing to stop it. And yet...

"I wouldn't want him to stop me," I whispered. The

Grailkeepers were my business. I'd railed at Lex every time he got in the way of that, even when it was for my supposed safety. *Especially* then! The Comitatus was his business. Would he thank me…?

"That is five," stated the oddly familiar, British-accented voice. Hani Rachid? No! "We will move on to the next round."

Phil's voice asked, "You feeling all right there, Cuz?"

He couldn't hide the edge of gloating. And the clutch of horror in my throat, in my heart, snapped me back to sense.

I *didn't* care about the Comitatus. But I damn well cared about Lex. I cared enough to alienate him from me forever, if that's what it took to keep him alive.

"Again," his steady voice insisted, low and determined.

"One," stated the apparent mediator. I felt sure he *wasn't* Hani Rachid, but it didn't matter anymore. I fumbled at the zipper to my fanny pack, drew out the worn blue Isis Grail and the mini bottle of water, twisted off the cap.

"Two," the apparent mediator continued.

I sloshed water into the grail. One swallow's worth. Two… Presentation would be half the battle. "Stay here—"

"Three," finished the count—

—at the same time that I yelled, "Stop!"

And, grail in both hands, I strode into the middle of the underground chamber where stood thirteen of the most powerful businessmen in the Western world—staring at me.

I kept my step deliberately slow, dignified, as I drew my gaze across each suited figure. A few of them I recognized. An oil CEO. A politician. A media mogul.

And standing in the middle of the rough-hewn chamber, with varying expressions of annoyance, stood Lex, Phil—and Ahmed Khalef, Lex's corporate lawyer.

So this was the innermost circle of the Comitatus.

Nobody wore funny hats or ceremonial robes. The only nod to sacred clothing was that each man had a strip of colored silk draped across his shoulders, like a priest in vestments. And yet the essence of power in here hit me like a wave of Egyptian heat.

Lex broke the silence first, deliberately calm. "Maggi, you shouldn't be here."

"Damn right, she shouldn't!" That, of course, was Phil. He turned to the rest of the circle. "This is the kind of man you're willing to consider as our *leader?* One who leaks our deepest mysteries to any slut—"

"He didn't tell me a thing," I interrupted, before Lex could waste energy in my defense. "This did."

And I held up the Isis Grail.

But I continued to watch Lex.

Despite his mask of indifference, I knew him. I could see intense emotions flicker in his guarded gaze, and only the first was annoyance. Another was pleasure— I'm positive some part of him was glad to see me, maybe had feared never seeing me again. His guilt followed that, guilt for being glad about something that put me in danger.

But mostly he felt despair, a despair the choking sensation in my throat echoed back at him.

He's dying.

The strong stance and steady voice were a ruse. He was already feeling the poison. He knew his cousin, his society, had betrayed him. All he could do now was try to make a statement with the way he died, perhaps send a final, unforgettable message to the rest of the Comitatus—anybody left who might be worth fighting for, worth saving. If such men existed at all.

And here I came, interrupting his dramatic exit.

"How the hell can some stupid cup tell you—?" But despite being slow, Phil must have figured it out. His face stilled into wariness.

Smiling with no humor at all, I crossed the chamber to him. "You know what this is, Phil."

His eyes fixed on the chalice.

"It's a goddess cup. One of the goddess cups you've been determined to—"

He snatched at it, perfect illustration of my charges. Like I hadn't expected that. I drew back fast enough that he lost his balance and had to take a step to catch himself.

"To eliminate," I finished easily. "I've decided it's time to end that foolishness."

"You're interrupting our combat," he warned, but his posturing only betrayed his fear.

The only reason I didn't mock that *combat* was Lex had gone along with it. If he really was dying—

Please let it be reversible. Please don't let that fifth swallow have been the one to kill him.

—the worst thing I could do was to diminish his martyrdom.

Out loud, anyway.

"Your problem, Phil," I said, "is that you try to hurt the things you fear. Like what women can bring to a balance of power. Like the goddess cups.

"Like Lex."

"Maggi," insisted Lex. "No…" It was his battle to fight—but by trying to fight alone, he was already beginning to lose it. I knew him too well. I could see the signs of the poison—a nervousness, a clamminess, a glaze to the eyes.

We were running out of time!

"You're no warrior," I told Phil. "You're a coward."

Which is when Lex swayed, took an uncertain step— and dropped to his knees, looking confused. Not confused about what was happening to him. His golden gaze, on Phil, told me just how poignantly he understood that.

Confused that a body he'd been training since childhood really was failing him. *Dying.*

"I win," gloated Phil, as if I weren't even there.

"You cheated," I said, my voice cutting clearly past his. My day job includes lecturing to halls of up to seventy-five students at once. I know how to project.

Thirteen sets of eyes fixed on me. Only a handful of them seemed unsurprised. Phil's—his expression was the pure, furious rage of the guilty. Ahmed Khalef, the moderator who must have made sure Lex got the poisoned cup. Why hadn't I caught before that he wasn't Lex's attorney, but his *family's* attorney? Two other men whom I did not know but who, I had to assume, were in on Phil's plan the same way the sentry had been.

And Lex, even as he sank forward, tried to catch himself with hands that couldn't hold him.

As Lex slumped to the floor one man, a middle-aged blonde, hurried to his side, felt his pulse, looked concerned.

"I'm no coward," Phil insisted. "And I don't cheat. How dare you interrupt our sacred ritual with your baseless—"

"*Sacred?* If this were sacred, you'd know better than to rig the competition. You don't look sick, Phil. Everyone can see that you haven't even been drinking valerian, much less arsenic."

The blond man, clearly a doctor, swore. "We have to get this man to a hospital. Call in a helicopter, Phil. Now!"

"So that he can challenge me again? We're a warrior society, Ken. Survival of the fittest."

More of the men protested, coming forward, surrounding Lex—but I stopped caring about that. At some point I would care more about bringing down Phil, about escaping from this pyramid with my own life— and all that life entailed. But for now, I had only one concern.

If Lex could be saved, somehow save him.

And if he couldn't…

His supporters, about five of them, parted for me as I went to him, knelt at his side. "Will a helicopter really help?" I asked the doctor named Ken.

He was rummaging in his black bag, drawing out a bottle of black pills. "Probably not."

No. *No no no.* No wonder the goddess's water had tasted so bitter, this time.

Seeing Lex like this felt nothing like last week's fears for an injured Rhys. Seeing Lex felt like *I* was dying.

My soul had made its decision long ago. Him.

I pressed my hand to his clammy cheek, all the more terrified when his gaze took too long to find me. If he was going to die, he deserved to know one thing, anyway. So I leaned close to him, kissed his lips, and whispered, "I seem to be pregnant."

His eyes, holding mine, warmed with gratitude. His lips tried to move, but I couldn't tell what he was trying to say.

Then his eyes went blank.

Chapter 21

Funeral. Tombstone. Widowhood, without ever having married. Single motherhood.

Not if I could help it.

I had to lift Lex's heavy head in order to press the chalice to his lips, to pour a swallow of water between them.

"What are you doing?" protested Ken. "He could choke!"

I stroked his throat. *Swallow, my love. Swallow.*

His Adam's apple moved as he did just that.

The way of the goddess was sometimes unbearably bitter.

So was the water from her chalice.

Lex's body convulsed. Ken and I rolled him quickly onto his side as he threw up not just the briny taste from the Isis Grail, but a great deal of the poison.

"Emetics are chancy with this kind of poison," protested Ken, glaring at me. "If he aspirates it, the damage to his lungs…"

But Lex's lips were moving. I leaned closer.

"Again," he rasped. His hands pushed futilely, trying to sit himself up, so Ken and I and another man helped him, supporting him against the rock wall. Then I lifted the chalice to his mouth.

Please, Lady Isis. You saved Osiris. Please give me the ability…

I didn't sense any response, one way or the other. But after Lex drank again, he was able to weakly turn by himself. Only liquid splashed from his mouth, oily, pearlescent, *evil.*

I didn't have to lean closer to hear him, this time. *"Again."*

"Blessings from the goddess Isis," I said, offering the chalice. "Oldest of the Old. Goddess of Ten Thousand Names."

Lex held my gaze, his eyes losing their dullness by the second. "Thank you, goddess."

And he finished off the goblet's contents. But this time he didn't throw up. This time, I suspected, he wasn't trying to. Water might thin what poison remained in his body…and he *was* still poisoned.

Ken murmured something about Lex taking charcoal pills, if he could keep them down.

"That's cheating," protested Phil, unable to hide his panic. "I challenged him to a simple contest, and you people are *cheating.*"

So I set the Isis Grail carefully beside Lex, then stood. The head scarf had slid from around my hair and now draped my shoulders, like a shawl, like Isis's

brightly colored wings. I went to the table on which
both Phil's cup and Lex's sat forgotten, and picked them
up. I took a sip from the one Phil had been using.
"Mmm," I said. "Good wine."

Then I offered him Lex's.

"Why should I?" he demanded, looking at the cup
like he would a snake. "I've already taken five swallows
of valerian, and unlike Lex, I'm not barfing it up."

"Drink it," said the politician.

"No."

Now several of the inner circle repeated the command. "Drink it." Like a chant. Like an even darker version of a fraternity kegger.

Phil moved to knock the cup from my hand, but I was
faster. I splashed its contents into his face.

He yelled and began wiping his eyes and spitting.
"You bitch!"

The knot of undecided Comitatus, who'd been hanging back from both parties, glanced at each other, then
came to stand beside Lex.

Only Ahmed and the two men I'd noted earlier still
stood with Phil. But they didn't look wholly happy
about it.

"I believe this ritual is over," I announced, and beckoned Catrina and Rhys to come out of the tunnel and
help me with Lex. Then I turned back to my lover. My
king without a country. The father of my baby, if I really was pregnant. The man I meant to marry, whether
I was pregnant or not. *Lex*.

Who was scowling as he realized just how weak he
still was.

"Hang on," I cautioned, getting an arm around him.
Rhys took him from the other side, and Ken caught him

from behind—between us, we managed to lift him to his feet.

"We aren't rescuing you, your highness," I assured him, low in his ear. "We're just *helping*."

His lips quirked, but his gaze, lifting, hardened at whatever he saw. I sensed someone behind me, all size and impatience and body heat. Definitely not in a nice way.

"Maggi," said Phil, from behind me.

Slowly I turned, readjusting my stance for Lex's weight. "You're still here?"

"I need to drink from the Isis cup, too," he said, still wiping at his mouth where that face full of wine must have gotten on his lips. "Just in case."

The grail! I looked down, where I'd left it, and saw nothing but shadowy, bare stone. *No!*

Then I looked at Catrina.

She held up the chalice, smiling her own triumph—then turned it upside down, to show us both that it was empty. *"Quel dommage,"* she murmured. *What a pity.*

"A minute," protested Lex, quietly at first. "Mag…please. I need…"

I caught Rhys's eye, and we stopped while Lex cleared his throat.

"If any of you wish to follow your true leader," he announced, with surprising command for someone half-dead, "we will reconvene outside London. You will know where and when. *Finis.*"

That last, Latin word had the edge of ritual about it. *It is over.*

"You're not the leader of the Comitatus yet," protested Phil. If I hadn't already known what a caricature of a bad loser he was, I wouldn't have believed anybody could be so petty—or so dense.

"Maybe not," said Lex. "But I'm sure as hell the leader of *something* important."

And we left. Him and me, together. Rhys helping us. Catrina protecting the chalice, as she'd wanted to do from the start.

And seven of the Comitatus members.

As soon as we were away from Phil and his followers, into the labyrinthine passageways, Lex's weight sagged harder onto my shoulders.

"What—?" I protested.

"He passed out," said Ken, taking my place under Lex's arm. Okay, so the average man does have an advantage on me where brute strength is concerned. "Throwing up most of the poison bought him time. So will the charcoal. But he wouldn't have been showing symptoms if it weren't already in his system. We've got to get him to a hospital to minimize the damage to his internal organs."

"I'll phone for a helicopter," offered another of the Comitatus, vanishing into the shadowy passageway ahead of us and calling back, "I doubt Phil will do it."

Noises of disgust from Lex's other followers expressed their current opinion of his cousin.

"Maggi." It was Lex, drifting into consciousness again, struggling to lift his head.

"I'm right here," I assured him, catching his chin to help. "I'm not going anywhere."

His brows furrowed. "...can walk..."

"Humor us."

"Did I...dream...?" He shook his head, trying to re-orient himself as our party stumbled up the cramped, rocky incline, flashlights and halogen lanterns criss-crossing our path like a pitiful sound and light show. Without the sound.

"…you said…?"

"Yeah, I really said that. I said I *might* be. Now rest and let us help you, okay?"

His head sank forward—but a smile pulled at his lips. Was he going to be unbearable about this?

No, I thought, a sweet warmth filling me where the beckoning had been. Just amazingly happy. And probably overprotective.

But he'd learn.

We'd reached the last level stretch of tunnel when the man who'd run ahead to call a helicopter appeared in front of us.

"We've got trouble," he said. "Someone's closed the gate out of the tunnels, and he's guarding it with about six men. They look like petty thieves, but they're armed."

Petty…? Oh, *crap!*

The maroon Vectra. Somehow they'd found us without having to follow—tracking device indeed! And they had called for backup.

The man looked at me. "He said nobody comes out until we hand over the witch."

Hani Rachid had come for his revenge.

"They have knives," insisted the lawyer, whose name turned out to be David.

"So…" noted Lex, "…do we."

Like I'd have him trying to protect me just now?

"I'll handle it," I said.

"We…can…fight," he insisted—big words, for someone being supported by two other men. Then again, I'd seen him fight in equally bad circumstances. He seemed to be gaining strength from necessity alone.

"I know," I assured him. *"So can I."*

Hani had reapplied the protective udjat eye design, or Eye of Horus, on his cheek. As we neared the barred gate, he looked delighted to see us. Too delighted. Something about the breadth of his white grin, the roll of his eyes, and his taut posture had an air of madness to it. He wasn't a man used to losing.

He'd lost a great deal, recently.

"You!" he greeted, looking right past me. "You are Mr. Lex Stuart. At last we meet formally."

"Cut the villain crap, Rachid," said Lex, with clear disgust—and no hesitation. It was all I could do not to turn and stare at him. Where did he get these reserves of strength? "How much…will it take to get rid of you?"

I said, *"What?"*

Lower, Lex murmured, "No good…otherwise." Him, or his money?

"A true businessman," Rachid approved dramatically, and pretended to consider it. "Ten million American dollars."

"Done," said Lex.

Right. I wasn't the only person among us to do a double take. He was rich, but nobody was *that* liquid…were they?

"In cash. Right now." Hani laughed at Lex's narrowed, angry eyes. "You Westerners! You think you are better than us because you can buy whatever you wish. But you are not, and you cannot. Clearly you are as weak as I suspected. I will take the woman."

"You can't…*have* her…." As quickly as it had come, Lex's strength was fading. Probably because he was realizing what I'd already known—that he *couldn't* help.

Not this way, at least.

"She took my woman from me, because you cannot control her. I shall take her in replacement. Right here, in front of you all, I shall show her how a true man takes control."

"No…" Lex's words were weak but murderous. "You…"

I whistled sharply, interrupting both of them before this travesty could continue. Lex needed his strength to fight the poison until the helicopter got here, for pity's sake! "Hello? If you two men are through discussing my fate?"

Lex scowled—and I turned on him. "I am not yours to buy off. Even once we're married, I will never be that. If you don't figure that out damned quick, we won't even get that far, and I don't want that. Do you?"

He stared. "Once…?"

"If you can learn when to let me make my own choices, we'll talk about it. I just let you drink poison, didn't I?" I turned to Hani. "If I come out, you let the others go. Right?"

"Of course."

"He's lying," muttered Lex.

"Ya think?" I turned to David. "Does your phone have reception here? Call the helicopter. And you…" Now I turned to Rhys, and pressed the hilt of my sword into his hand. "Cat's a lot better than I thought she'd be, but you I trust. When I say 'now…'"

"Let him take me instead," protested Rhys, low. "I'm the one he thinks seduced his wife."

Lex managed to lift his head enough to stare at my friend.

"He'd eat you for breakfast," I said. Now I turned to the bars and raised my voice. "Deal. Let us out."

Hani said, "You first."

I kissed Lex tenderly and whispered, "Trust me."

His weak, solemn gaze wrung my heart. But he said nothing.

I guess he *did* want to marry me, at that.

Then I turned back to the bars. "I'm coming out."

I could tell from the way Hani's men looked at me that I might as well have worn a merry widow—or nothing—as my cargo pants and camisole top. Their eyes felt like uninvited tongues on my skin, even before they opened the lock.

Yeah, it *was* a gross feeling.

Worse, they grabbed me by both arms as soon as I edged past the iron gate. There in the excavation pit, in the varied illumination of lanterns and flashlights, they dragged me to their supposed leader. Their hands bit into my flesh in a way that would surely leave bruises. One of the sentries we'd left tied up was among them.

I didn't bother to struggle. *Not yet.*

"Now I will show you," warned Hani, "what happens to disobedient women. You are clearly such a slut, you may even enjoy it. But I know your man will not."

He grabbed me by the waist and yanked me against him—his men still gripping my arms, holding me captive just in case. He kissed my neck, squeezed one of my breasts through the thin material of my top. His arousal pushed insistently against me, against my belly where I thought, hoped, *knew* Lex's baby waited.

A child created in love. In every beautiful, sacred thing sex could be.

This creature's violence seemed all the more blasphemous, in contrast. Here stood evil.

I turned my head away from his hungry mouth and

deliberately caught Lex and Rhys's horrified gazes in the barred shadows. Even Catrina looked less than pleased.

It's okay, I mouthed firmly, determined to make that true. Then, with a growl, Hani caught my jaw in his hard grip and twisted my face back to him, possessively covered my lips with his slimy, stinking mouth.

Use his force against him, I thought—an old tai chi basic. Instead of fighting, I parted my lips for him, despite a very strong gag reflex.

He thrust in his sluglike tongue, as I'd known he would.

And I bit it. Not nipped. Not pinched. I sank my teeth in hard and deep, like into a piece of tough steak, and tasted hot blood.

He screamed, flailing to strike me in the head to make me let go, but his two henchmen were in the way. Not that I could stand to be this close to him for much longer. I did let go, allowing him to recoil from me.

Then, using the men who held my arms as a brace, I kicked out with both feet. Hani managed to guard against the first kick—it's not as easy to get men where it hurts as you'd think. But the second booted foot hit him squarely where I wanted it to.

We both went down—me because the men who held me hadn't expected to suddenly have my full weight, and Hani because few men can stand after a direct blow to their privates.

Sandy ground impacted my hip. One of Hani's thugs lost his grip on me as we fell. The other, it was easy to twist free from. In barely a moment, I'd regained my feet and was striding back to the entrance to the pyramid.

Hani's other men stepped quickly back as I passed—maybe due to the violence, maybe due to the Cleopatra eyes and the ankh, or maybe it had something to do with me spitting their leader's blood as I passed them.

I yanked open the gate's grating. "Now," I said to Rhys.

"Yes, ma'am," he said, quickly handing me Asp.

I saw that Lex's hand was under his coat—and I knew what he had. A man who could get a morning-after pill in the Arab Republic of Egypt would have no problem getting hold of a gun.

That he hadn't used it against Phil, that he'd chosen honor over life, was something I'd have to consider when I had more time. For now I stared, just long enough for him to know that I knew, and I mouthed, *Don't.*

His empty hand fell loose to his side. But his glare told me that he wasn't convinced. Well, fine. If Hani killed me, Lex was welcome to shoot him.

"If you gentlemen will take care of the others," I called over my shoulder, as I turned back to Jane Fletcher's ex-husband, "I'm about to give Mr. Rachid a lesson in woman's spirituality."

Particularly the power of the bitch goddess.

Chapter 22

With ten thousand names, Isis must have a few that have nothing to do with healing, mercy or compassion.

It was that aspect of her that I channeled now.

Hani staggered to his feet, hunched but desperate, when he saw me stalking at him with my sword. Blood trailed from the corners of his mouth and down his chin, as if he were some kind of vampire sheikh. Not far from us, a camel gargled its disapproval.

Or maybe it was approval. Who could tell, with camels?

"I want you to understand a couple of things," I said grimly. "I really do. First, women are not property."

He lifted one hand and, with a snick, a switchblade appeared to gleam in the torchlight against the darkness. "Hah!"

"I know you think I'm lying, what with me being a

witch and all," I continued, lifting Asp so that he could get the full effect of his own weapon's inadequacy. The words, I suspected, were an even more effective weapon. "But face reality, Hani. Whether you want it or not, Jane and Kara are safe in the embassy."

"Not forever," he warned, his voice thick and slurred with blood. "They will come out, and I will kill them."

Now he'd *kill* them? He *was* upset, wasn't he? And apparently, he only had one brutal way of handling that upset.

"Tala is doing just fine on her own," I reminded him. "And hey, here I am, about to kick your ass. To believe that women aren't independent beings, in the face of this kind of proof, you can't just be a chauvinist. You'd have to be delusional."

Speaking of delusional, he swung at me with his switchblade.

My sword tip caught it and held it, both of us exerting pressure. But I wasn't having to exert very much, with the leverage I had. Good Asp.

"A second thing you should remember," I said, "is that violence begets violence. You think you can beat the world into submission. But haven't you noticed that everything that's gone wrong in your life is a direct result of your trying to hurt someone else?"

"Shut up," he lisped, clearly not getting rule number one. Delusional it was.

When he lunged at me I spun, letting him stumble by. When he tried again, I simply turned again. Now his back was to…interesting! A particularly long shadow was, in fact, an excavation trench.

I noticed, with the edge of my attention, that the inner circle of the Comitatus did have a few warrior abilities. They seemed to be taking care of Hani's thugs nicely.

"That's the third thing," I continued. "What goes around, comes around. That's why life shouldn't be a competition, but a partnership. You're a textbook example."

He lunged again, not even listening. I spun again.

Now *my* back was to the trench.

The next time he came at me, I let him crowd me backward, nearer to its drop. *Don't stumble on a rock. Do* not *stumble on a rock!*

"If you hadn't mistreated Jane, she may never have divorced you," I said. "You might have had more children, maybe even a son. Instead, you lost your only daughter. Nobody did that but—"

He thrust at me again. I feinted back farther. One of my booted feet slid in the sand—but I regained my balance.

"—you. As far as that goes, if you hadn't bullied me and Rhys, I might have refused to help Jane and Kara escape. If you hadn't…" I was guessing now, but it felt right. "If you hadn't sent that lawyer to me in jail, to get me to sign the false confession… How much did that bribe cost you, anyway?"

He let out a bestial cry as he swung again. My sword tip, resting on his knuckles, swung with him. Again, I sidestepped, still perched there, balanced on the edge of the trench. It was only ten, maybe twelve feet deep. I could jump if I had to.

I had no intention of having to.

"Well, that money's gone forever. If you hadn't tried to run down Rhys, I wouldn't even be here. And if you hadn't stolen my phone, *Lex* might not be here, and he and I might not have gotten past our own differences. So you're partially responsible for my current happiness. How's *that* for irony?"

"Silence!" At least, that's what I think he was saying. His mouth spilled more blood with each attempt at speech; it soaked the front of his shirt like a grisly bib. And his tongue—or what was left of it—must be swelling. *"Shut up!"*

But I kept talking—both because I was figuring some of this out for myself as I spoke, and because I knew that this kind of man found a woman's voice as torturous as anything the Inquisition ever thought up.

A woman's voice saying anything other than what he dictated, anyway.

"One last piece of advice," I continued.

He swung, but my trusty blade followed his, nipping at his knuckles. He swung again, with no better luck.

Eyes increasingly wild, he flipped and then threw the knife—

And somehow, somehow, I dodged it.

Magic. Luck. Both. Neither. It didn't matter. *I dodged it!*

"Next time you decide to protect yourself with a magical symbol," I said, "maybe you should try using one that's not a symbol for the *son of a goddess!*"

He blinked—but even he had to see the connection and the sense there. Even people who aren't big on the Egyptian pantheon have often heard about Isis, Osiris—and their son, the falcon-god Horus.

So—*was* the symbol magic, but a magic that didn't work against Isis? Or had its only power been that Hani believed in it, and now he did not? Was there a difference?

Either way, that's when he rushed me with a bestial bellow. And the udjat eye did not protect him.

I stepped neatly to one side—*first visible, then invisible*—whacking him with the flat of my blade as he stumbled past me. He vanished over the trench's edge, into the excavation ditch, and was silent.

I panted. Could it be that easy?

In that silence, we all heard the faint throb of an approaching helicopter. Its searchlight, as it sought a place to land, illuminated the ancient House of Osiris in stark highlights and shadows. The walls. The causeways. The tombs. The crumbling pyramids, especially the one looming over us.

And the ditch in which Hani Rachid lay, very still, his head at an improbable angle.

I'll admit, I was surprised to see that Sinbad was dead. I really hadn't set out to kill him.

But I sure as hell didn't feel guilty about it.

Three days later found me on a Zodiac in the sunrise-tinted Alexandrian Harbor, adjusting a dive mask over the hood of my dry suit. Overhead a bird cried—perhaps a kite, I thought, sacred to Isis. Rhys was piloting the boat. Catrina would be my diving buddy.

Though the word *buddy* was stretching things considerably. *Guard* was more like it.

"I will not let you take it," she warned, before silencing herself with her regulator.

"Like you could stop me," I countered, before doing the same. Then I glared at Rhys for good measure before Cat and I rolled backward off of opposite sides of the boat, with a splash, into the murky green water of Cleopatra's Palace.

It was early, but we had to move fast before anyone from the project discovered us.

We both made a beeline for the statue of Isis.

Back when the private helicopter landed at AbuSir, kicking up enough sand to infuriate Catrina and annoy the camels, I'd had to make a serious choice.

Go with Lex? Or go with the Isis Grail?

Or, Plan C, fight Catrina there and then to get the chalice back? But that would take time I didn't have. So I'd charged her and Rhys with protecting the cup until I got back, and I climbed into the chopper with Lex and Dr. Ken.

Catrina had already eased some of my worries about the chalice's safety by shutting and locking the barred gate from the tunnels—passageways where Phil, Khalef, and their followers were still hiding. Rhys seemed to have bribed the camel drivers into making sure someone brought the captives water. I had to hope that was enough.

Grailkeeper or not, champion or not, I'd then concentrated on making sure my lover—and, we quickly established, fiancé—survived this latest attempt on his life. Thankfully, he'd recovered faster and more completely than even Dr. Ken had expected. Only once Lex was discharged and on his way to London for more secret meetings, stoically *not* complaining about leaving me behind, did I return to Alexandria to learn…

They'd put the cup back. In situ.

And not just Catrina. Rhys had helped!

They'd secretly returned the Isis Grail to the harbor, back into Isis's hand, then covered both with sand and a chunk of algae-encrusted rock to hide them. Their plan was to then deliberately avoid the area where the statue lay and let someone else discover her. The clean condition of the chalice could then seem to be a mystery to them as surely as to everyone else.

Not a bad plan, except for the minor detail that *I was collecting goddess grails!* That was what had brought me to Egypt in the first place. I'd already learned that a single cup, alone, didn't have the power to protect itself from men like Phil Stuart and his followers. I would need a collection of them before I could risk revealing them to the world and allowing them to work their empowering magic on womankind.

Without the Isis Grail, my collection amounted to *one*.

And yet…

Gliding silently over the sandy harbor floor, past fish and half-veiled statues and columns and sphinxes, I had to admit the bitter truth. My goal of bringing the grails together was, this time at least, in direct opposition to my morals. Damn it, I wasn't just a Grailkeeper—I was an academic.

Further interfering with the integrity of this incredible underwater site went against almost everything I believed in.

We reached the fallen column and, shadowed beneath it, the statue of seated Isis, half-covered in a drift of sand. I reached out a gloved hand to stroke her face, worn smooth over the centuries. How many hundreds—thousands? Tens of thousands?—of women had worshipped at the feet of this ancient, all-encompassing goddess? Empresses like Cleopatra. Priestesses. Everyday women—all seeking that interconnectedness, that sacred sense of womanhood.

My eyes burned, behind the shelter of my mask.

Thank you, I thought. *Thank you for helping me find Lex.* Just because he was no longer in danger didn't mean I hadn't continued to sense where he was—every time the doctors had moved him for tests, I'd known. Even now, I had a vague awareness of him, safe but far, far away. That would be England.

The statue's calm expression seemed amused.

And the baby, I added mentally. Of course I had no absolute proof that I *was* pregnant—the best home pregnancy tests rarely work until two weeks after conception, so I hadn't bothered to find out if kits were even available in Egypt.

But part of me knew, all the same. Sacred rituals were powerful things.

Whatever organization Lex was now leading, be they the true Comitatus or a splinter group, would be damned successful, if his fertility really represented his ability to lead.

Thank you for my strength. For this new...magic.

Isis stared at me, unblinking.

I moved the rock that lay beside her half-hidden torso, then brushed sand away in a brown cloud, until I could see it in the faint green light—the Isis Grail, held in the statue's curled fingers. Worn blue faience. Gold-banded.

So very, very powerful.

And not mine to take. Sometimes, a person does have to make a sacrifice for honor.

Damn it.

So with a heavy heart, I brushed sand back over the hand, over the cup, and replaced the stone. I guessed I'd have to keep looking for goddess grails that I felt I *could* take, or buy, or that needed my immediate protection. But not this one.

This Goddess of Ten Thousand Names, Oldest of the Old, could probably protect her own.

Catrina Dauvergne, to my annoyance, seemed to be smiling. But for once, it wasn't a smile of triumph. She looked...relieved.

With a flip of my swim fins, I rose for the surface, leaving the Temple of Isis behind.

Or so I thought.

Rhys drove me to the Cairo Airport. It was a long, quiet drive—what was left to say? But not far into it, he rested his hand on the open seat between us, palm up. Gratefully, I gave him my hand, the one that still wore Lex's wedding ring.

We entwined fingers in silent acceptance for the rest of the extended drive. I was okay with him helping Catrina put the chalice back. He was okay with my agreeing to marry Lex Stuart. That's what counted.

Being comfortable with each other.

"You know what's interesting?" I mused, breaking the silence only as he pulled into the airport and found a parking space. He slid his blue gaze toward me, waiting. "Over the entrance it says Cairo Airport, first in English and then in Arabic. When I first saw that, I thought it was odd that the English version would be first—as if it had more importance. Then I realized something."

Rhys said, "That Arabic is read right to left?"

"Exactly. So the Arabic version is *also* first. It's a classic case of win-win.

"Don't you wish everything could be win-win?"

Rhys said, "I'm going to miss you, Maggi Sanger."

I unbuckled my seat belt and leaned across to hug him, right there in the too-hot car. His long, lanky arms tightened around me. I think he kissed the top of my head.

"No, you're not," I insisted. "We are friends, and we will stay friends if I have anything to say about it. Let me know if you can come for Christmas."

Then I drew back and grinned at him. "You can bring Catrina."

"Don't even tease about such a thing." But he blushed through his protest. That got my attention....

Except it was no longer any of my business. Damn it.

"Did she ever tell you what she did with the money she got for the Melusine Grail?" I asked, to draw out these last moments.

Rhys replied, "A priest cannot tell."

I was flying to London with Jane Fletcher and Kara Rachid.

Since the discovery and identification of Hani's body—ruled an accidental death—Jane was free to take her daughter home with her at long last. I felt honored that they wanted me along, though I asked them to minimize my role when they told their story. The crush of press was even worse at London Heathrow than it had been in Cairo. Airport officials hustled us through the customs check and to a private room, reserved for VIPs, until our rides arrived.

Asp made it through with my checked luggage, no problem.

It was great to hear announcements in English again, to be able to read the signs. I might still be six hours from New York, but it still felt like home.

As we settled ourselves comfortably, Jane chatting about her plans now that the long ordeal was over, I thought about Lex…and I could sense him, mere miles away, getting closer. Like the way my throat tightened in the presence of danger, this was a goddess gift that might take a while to get used to.

But I felt an almost giddy pleasure at his approach, all the same. _Engaged to be married._ Surely that wasn't in any way contradictory to my Grailkeeper legacy, was it? There couldn't be mothers and daughters without a few fathers along the way.

"Maggi?"

Kara's tentative voice drew me from my reverie, and I smiled at her. She looked as young and innocent as ever, with her dark hair in braids and a fake blue tattoo—an ankh—on her hand. Someday she, too, would grow up and possibly marry. But at least here, without her father's interference, she could do it on her own timetable. This, I decided, was the only victory I needed for this trip. As far as the Isis Grail went…

Well, it had done what needed doing. I couldn't expect more.

"Are you excited to be home, Kara?" I asked.

She nodded solemnly—then handed me a gift-wrapped shape the size of a shoe box. "This is from Grandmother Tala."

I looked at the box. Then I looked at her, confused.

She smiled, pleased with her role as gift giver. "She said to give it to you after we'd gone through customs. She said that it's private property, so she has 'every right to let you have it.'"

Now I looked at Jane, who widened her eyes, equally clueless.

Kara bounced and giggled. "Open it! Open it, open it, open it."

So I did, tearing the tissue paper rather than keeping the child in suspense. And it *was* a shoe box. But inside that, carefully protected with more tissue and quite a bit of bubble wrap, was the wide-mouthed kylix I'd drunk from at Tala's, that first evening.

A cup?

I caught my breath as I lifted it by one of its two ceramic handles and, on closer inspection, recognized its age. It was in pristine condition but, having been passed down within the family, it might easily be from a time before the Temple of Isis was swallowed by the Mediterranean.

Though smaller than most Kylikes, the cup had the shallow bowl and narrow base of a standard Greek offering vessel. But this time, with no wine in it, I could see the image painted inside the concave surface of the bowl.

A Greek-styled rendition of the goddess Isis.

I felt suddenly light-headed—and it had nothing to do with my likely pregnancy! The force with which multiple realizations hit me was dizzying. After its conquest by Alexander the Great in the fourth century BC, Egypt became predominantly Greek. Cleopatra herself had descended from Ptolemaic, aka Greek, ancestors as much as from Pharaonic. This cup was Greek.

"There's more than one Isis Grail," I whispered in amazement. And it made sense. Wouldn't a goddess with ten thousand names and millennia of worship across most of the ancient world have more than one cup?

Just like the rhyme had implied. *Isis is everywhere, she cannot be contained.*

Look for her where she is honored.

I'd drunk from an Isis Grail my first night in Egypt!

Suddenly, so much made sense. The familiarity I'd sensed when I did the ritual in my hotel room. The goddess's indulgent chiding, *You wish* another *gift?*

I'd been given a gift at Tala's house, without even knowing it! And it didn't take long for me to realize what that had been. Tala was a doctor. She'd told me her grandmother had been a midwife. Apparently, medicine ran in her family.

I remembered how sure I'd been that Rhys was badly injured in the cisterns. After I'd inspected his injuries, they seemed less severe. Then there were the accidents in the Alexandrian harbor. Lex's miraculous recovery from the poison.

My limited knowledge of first aid had only helped.

My gift of healing, compliments of the goddess Isis—that was a gift beyond measure. *Magic.*

My eyes burned with gratitude—gratitude toward Isis, gratitude toward Tala, gratitude toward Jane and Kara for giving me the chance to earn this chalice. Now I really did have a collection of goddess grails started. A collection of two.

"Don't you like it?" asked Kara, her little brow furrowing. So I put the kylix back in its padded box and gave her slim frame a hug.

"*Yes,*" I assured her. "Yes, yes, yes. This may be the best gift anybody has ever given me."

Smiling, she poked a finger at my chalice-well pendant. So I gave it to her. Another convert.

Sensing his nearness deep in my womb, I looked up—and saw Lex in the doorway, neatly pressed and watching us as if he took pleasure simply from the sight of me, and I smiled true welcome.

The cup was perhaps the *second* best gift.

* * *

I'd been guarding my emotions with Lex for so long, I'd almost forgotten how blissful just being in love could be. Seeing his smile as our eyes met. Going to him for a welcoming hug…and a long, lingering kiss that seemed to draw us to a place completely outside of time.

Jane cleared her throat. "Children present," she warned us laughingly, as we drew apart.

"My apologies," Lex told her, then asked me, "Are you ready to go?"

We'd already agreed that I'd stay overnight in his hotel before my British cousin, Lilith, came to fetch me. Our nominal excuse was that I could "rest up" from the long flight from Cairo, although how much rest I would actually get…

I felt mildly flushed, from the expectation. If the paparazzi got any pictures of us on the way out of Jane and Kara's press room, I can't imagine anyone would miss the fact that he and I were crazy about each other.

The limousine that pulled up to the curb as we left the terminal shouldn't have surprised me. "If we're getting married," I warned, "you can't keep doing this."

He pretended innocence as the chauffeur opened the back door for us and Lex handed me in. "Doing what?"

"Spending huge amounts of money on everyday things like rides from the airport."

He climbed in on the other side and, as the door shut behind him, frowned. "And why do you say, *if?*"

I kissed his cheek. "Don't be paranoid."

He watched me, looking paranoid. And okay, so I'd broken our engagement twice before—and simply refused his proposals two other times. At least I didn't have to worry that he only wanted to marry me because of the baby.

Then again, he didn't have that certainty about me, did he?

"I think," I said slowly, "my suspicion that you were hiding something is only one reason I hesitated to marry you, before."

"Uh-oh," he said.

"I've also been worried about losing myself," I continued. "We don't live in an age where husbands have legal control over their wives' freedom anymore, thank heavens, and I've never suspected you of being the kind of man who'd take advantage of it if we did. But…"

He waited, listening as if his life depended on it. Beyond him, outside the window, the suburbs of London rolled by.

"It's easier to stay independent when you're not part of a couple," I decided—that wasn't quite it, but it was as close as I could come. "Part of a family. Once we marry, I'll owe you explanations of where I'm going. I'll have to accept that my decisions affect your life, that you have a vote in what I choose to do, as much as I have a vote in your life."

"What…?" He seemed to be searching for the right words himself. "What can I do to help with that?"

"You've already done it," I assured him, brushing his cheek with my fingertips. "You've given me all the time and space I've asked for. Well…*almost* all of it."

Many goddesses *do* marry, without losing any of their sovereignty. For a Grailkeeper, it was the ultimate argument. But that parallel, I still wasn't wholly comfortable with. Isis does save Osiris, and they do have a son. But Osiris becomes King of the Underworld.

What had Lex's coup made him the leader of?

Luckily, Lex distracted me from those particular concerns by drawing a small ring box out of his breast pocket. He opened it, revealing a beautiful diamond, just small enough to avoid being gaudy, set in a platinum band.

It wasn't the ring he'd given me last time.

At first, the design on the band resembled Celtic knotwork. But looking closer, I realized it was a series of overlapping circles—*vesica pisces*. Symbol of the Grailkeepers.

"You had this specially designed?" I breathed, taking it from his expectant hand for a closer look.

"It gave me something to look forward to."

I kissed him, for once refusing to protest the expense or demand assurance that this wasn't a blood diamond. Surely he knew me well enough by now. "It's beautiful, Lex. And you're wonderful. More wonderful than I ever dared to hope."

"I'm not sure anybody could be that wonderful," he warned. "Are you willing to make it official, then? To trade rings with me?"

I almost hated to take off the wedding band—which had to be a good sign. But I did, and let him slide the diamond on in its place. This ring represented one promise I would be glad to keep.

Handing back the original band, I finally remembered to ask. "What does the motto mean?"

Lex blinked at me. "The motto?"

"Your family motto, on the ring. *Virescit vulnere virtus.*"

"Oh. You saw that."

"Yes. And it translates to…?"

"It means courage, or virtue, grows strong at the wound. That only those who have gone through injury can really know what they're made of."

I studied his quietly handsome face, the sweep of his jaw, his nose, his cheekbones. He'd survived leukemia and a knife attack and now a poisoning—not to mention betrayal by one or more close relatives—and he wasn't hesitating to face the future. "Like you," I said softly.

He held my gaze. "Like us, Goddess."

And that, also, was true.

In the dark of the morning, I came awake and stretched, glad for every inch of my well-loved body. I was also glad for every inch of Lex's where he lay, deeply asleep and beautifully naked, beside me in the canopied bed. He had gotten a suite at the Kensington, complete with a marble fireplace and a view of Kensington Palace.

Somehow, it seemed fitting that Lex would take a room so close to a royal residence. If the Stuarts hadn't lost the throne of England, he might be in residence there himself!

Thank the goddess for small favors.

Since I was suddenly wide-awake, I slid from the high-platformed bed, pulling Lex's discarded linen shirt on against a chill that felt all the stranger after more than a week in the heat of Egypt. I went to my luggage. Then I padded to the salon where, beside the tray of canapés the butler had delivered, sat an open bottle of sparkling cider. Lex had wanted expensive champagne to celebrate our engagement, but it was just as well we'd gone with the fruit juice. We'd drunk very little before our thirst for each other overrode any other appetites.

I stretched again, blissfully sated.

Opening the shoe box Kara had given me, I withdrew the Isis Grail—*my* Isis Grail—and set it on the walnut table. Tomorrow I would bring it to my cousin Lilith, who would hide it with the Melusine Grail. But for now...

I poured half an inch of cider, not enough to hide the drawing of Isis in the bowl of the chalice, only enough to give her a golden, glittering glow. Then I went out onto the balcony—chill or not—and looked up at the moon.

You can worship any goddess, and all of them, via the moon.

"Thank you," I whispered, catching its reflection in the sweet juice. Apples are a goddess thing, too. "Thank you for letting me see this man as he truly is. Thank you for this baby. Thank you for the injuries that have strengthened me, tempered me, brought me to this place."

For just a moment, I felt I was there again—underwater in Cleopatra's Palace, amid submerged artifacts and relics.

"And thank you for allowing me the honor of championing you."

Then I drank.

And it tasted sweet.

* * * * *

Author's Note

The problem of international custody disputes is a very real one, by no means limited either to the Middle East or to fathers doing the kidnapping. Although I read extensively about the issue, I tried not to base the situation with Hani Rachid and Jane Fletcher on any one real-life case. Similarly, the issue of children like Samira arrested on the charge of being "vulnerable to delinquency" is a concern that several human rights organizations are currently investigating...but it is important to remember that human rights and children's rights issues exist all over the world. They are not specific to any one country or religion.

Many of the settings in this book are real places, and I tried to be accurate whenever possible, but there were times when I had to take creative license. This happened, in particular, with the pyramids of AbuSir. The likelihood of there being a private entrance into a pyramid's substructure is low...but then again, if anybody knew about it and could get access, wouldn't the Comitatus?

As for the information and scenes concerning Cleopatra's Palace, I owe a great debt of gratitude to the incredible work that real archeologists such as Jean-Yves Empereur and Franck Goddio have been doing in the area. Their discoveries were the inspiration for this book.

And yes, Cleopatra VII (the seduced-by-Julius-Caesar, then-Mark-Antony, heavy-on-the-eye-shadow, death-by-asp Cleopatra) really was an Isis Worshipper! Why not a Grailkeeper, as well?

If you have any questions or comments about this story, or the Grailkeepers in general, I love to hear from readers! Please feel free to check out my Web site at www.evelynvaughn.com, to e-mail me at Yvaughn@aol.com, or to write to me at P.O. Box 6, Euless, TX 76039.

Thank you!

Books by Evelyn Vaughn

ATHENA FORCE

Chosen for their talents.
Trained to be the best.

Expected to change the world.

The women of Athena Academy
share an unforgettable experience
and an unbreakable bond—until
one of their own is murdered.

The adventure begins with these six books:

PROOF by Justine Davis, July 2004

ALIAS by Amy J. Fetzer, August 2004

EXPOSED by Katherine Garbera,
September 2004

DOUBLE-CROSS by Meredith Fletcher,
October 2004

PURSUED by Catherine Mann, November 2004

JUSTICE by Debra Webb, December 2004

**And look for six more Athena Force stories
January to June 2005.**

Available at your favorite retail outlet.

Silhouette®
BOMBSHELL™

COMING NEXT MONTH

#21 SISTER OF FORTUNE—Lindsay McKenna
Sisters of the Ark
An ancient artifact had plagued Vicky Mabrey's dreams
for a year, and now she had to find it—with the help of
an enemy from her past. Vicky couldn't stand the sight of
Griff Hutchinson, but they had to work together to find the precious crystal—before it fell into the wrong hands and destroyed
the people Vicky loved.

#22 JUSTICE—Debra Webb
Athena Force
Her best friend's killer was dead, and so was police lieutenant
Kayla Ryan's best lead to find her friend's missing child. Now
Kayla had to work with a lethally sexy detective to find the per-
son who'd sent the assassin, and to bring him to justice.
But she couldn't shake the feeling that someone was watching
her every move.... Was the enemy closer than she'd ever sus-
pected?

#23 NIGHT LIFE—Katherine Garbera
Sasha Malone Sterling had given up the dark life of a spy to
be a wife and mother. But the agency had called her back
for a mission she couldn't refuse: bringing in a rogue agent.
She was the only one who could catch him—because the
agent was Sasha's own estranged husband, and no one
knew him better than she did.

#24 HOT CASE—Patricia Rosemoor
Detective and confirmed skeptic Shelley Caldwell couldn't have
been more different from her naive twin sister. But when her
twin found a body, drained of blood, that later disappeared,
Shelley was eerily reminded of an old case that still haunted
her. The old trail was heating fast—and to follow it, Shelley
would trade places with her twin and enter the dark world of
Goths, wannabe vampires and maybe even the real deal.

SBCNM1104